Thrill of Love

The Bradens
at Peaceful Harbor

Love in Bloom Series

Melissa Foster

ISBN-10: 1-941480-69-1
ISBN-13: 978-1-941480-69-4

THRILL OF LOVE

Cover Design: Elizabeth Mackey Designs
Cover Photograph: Sara Eirew Photography

WORLD LITERARY PRESS
PRINTED IN THE UNITED STATES OF AMERICA

A Note to Readers

Ty and Aiyla's journey to their happily ever after is a much bigger story than you might be used to. Throughout the series, Ty has been a bit mysterious, but I've known he was extreme since the first time I met—and fell in love with—him. I knew he needed a forever love who could handle his past, and who was just as fierce as he was. Aiyla is most definitely his perfect mate. Their story was not an easy one to write, but every romance is not roses and wine, and theirs is an epic love story that I am proud to have written. I hope you enjoy Ty and Aiyla's story and are looking forward to reading about Beau Braden and Charlotte Sterling in *Anything for Love*, the next Braden novel, and the first of the Bradens at Pleasant Hill.

Sign up for my newsletter to keep up to date with new releases and to receive an exclusive short story.
www.melissafoster.com/News

About the Bradens

The Bradens are just one of the series in the Love in Bloom big-family romance collection. Each Love in Bloom book is written to be enjoyed as a stand-alone novel or as part of the larger series. There are no cliffhangers and no unresolved issues. Characters from each series make appearances in future books, so you never miss an engagement, wedding, or birth. A complete list of all series titles is included at the end of this book, along with previews of upcoming publications.

Visit Melissa's Reader Goodies page for...

- Complete Love in Bloom series list
- FREE Love in Bloom ebooks
- FREE downloadable reading order, series checklists, and more

Love in Bloom Subseries Order
Snow Sisters
The Bradens
The Remingtons
Seaside Summers
The Ryders
Billionaires After Dark
Harborside Nights

Standalone Romance Titles
Tru Blue
Truly, Madly, Whiskey

Chapter One

WHERE THE HECK is my bike helmet? Aiyla Bell had packed and checked her equipment more times than she cared to admit over the past week. Having spent the last decade traveling all over the world taking pictures for her elite line of coffee-table books, while working on the side as a ski instructor or hiking guide, she could pack in her sleep. There was no way she'd dropped the ball in preparation for the craziness that was the Children's Charity Mad Prix and forgotten something as basic as a bike helmet. She'd taken part in similar, though not as lengthy, events when she was a teenager. She had always wanted to compete in the Mad Prix because she'd heard so many great things about it, but her travel schedule had been too crazy until now. The stars had finally aligned, and she'd gotten lucky enough to sign on for her first Mad Prix. Five days in the Colorado Mountains, five different wilderness events, and four nights spent sleeping on the forest floor. *Heaven.*

She opened another equipment bag and began rifling through. A familiar woodsy, earthy scent surrounded her, and her hands stilled. Her pulse quickened. The smell that had haunted her for months thickened, and she sensed him crouching behind her. Her breathing halted, and goose bumps

1

chased up her arms as memories of Saint-Luc, and the five most incredible days of her life, slammed into her.

"Do you believe in fate?"

His warm breath coasted over her cheek, and she swallowed hard, paralyzed by the sound of the deep, seductive voice she'd heard in her dreams so many times she wasn't sure it was real. Her heart thundered against her ribs, and she forced her shaky legs to work. She turned, both of them rising at the same time, bringing all six-plus broad, muscular, feet of Ty Braden into focus. *Oh God. It's really you.* His silky brown hair was in desperate need of a trim, stopping just short of his shoulders and framing his rugged features. The mix of longing and shock in his golden-brown eyes unearthed a storm of memories—her hand in his, his lips on hers, deep conversations as they shared their hopes and dreams, which were as perfectly aligned as the stars in the skies of Saint-Luc.

"Ty" came out ridiculously breathless. She wanted to scale him like a mountain, to kiss his hot, sensuous mouth again and feel him holding her as he once had. But she couldn't do any of those things. She was frozen in place, and that was probably a good thing. He was still *Ty Braden*, the world-renowned mountain climber and photographer, with a reputation as a player that preceded him.

In an effort to regain control, she shifted her gaze away and managed, "What are you doing here?"

"It's fate," he said confidently, as if he believed in it. "Fate has brought us together for another five days."

She forced herself to meet his gaze, her heart thundering at the prospect of more time with him. "You don't believe in fate, remember? You believe people are in charge of their own destiny." Their last night in Switzerland, he'd asked her to leave with him the next day and travel with him "to see where things end up." Oh, how she'd wanted to throw caution to the wind and join him. But she'd worked years to build the life she had always dreamed of, and she couldn't risk it all to be one in a long line of Ty's women. She'd fallen hard for him—fallen in *love* with him—and she hadn't been able to bring herself to confront the rumors about his reputation. Instead, she'd said, *Do you believe in fate?* And though he'd said he didn't, she always had, and she'd said, *if this is meant to be, we'll meet up again.* They'd agreed not to exchange phone numbers or addresses, and not to track each other down by any other means, but to truly leave their future in fate's hands.

"I think that's changed, Aiyla." He said her name like he'd been waiting to say it for all these months. He stepped closer, so close she could smell something minty on his breath. "I can't believe you're *here.* After all this time, you're *really* here."

The longing in his voice confused her even more. She looked into his eyes, and memories swamped her. She remembered the feel of him holding her in his arms as they fell asleep fully clothed and waking to his sweet whispers and gentle kisses. Cuddling under blankets as snow fell around them and they reminisced about their childhoods and families. She felt like she already knew his five siblings, though she'd never met them. A lump rose in her throat, and she shifted her gaze over his shoulder to try to regain control. Two female competitors were whispering and watching them. Her stomach knotted again. Why did the only guy she'd ever fallen for have to come with a womanizing reputation? He hadn't seemed like a player in Saint-Luc. He hadn't even tried to sleep with her until that very last night, when she knew he'd been picking up on all of her sexy signals. Signals she'd then dashed with one sentence. She'd been seconds from going back to his hotel room when he'd stepped away to answer a call. The brief moments it had taken him had given her a chance to clear the lust from her head enough to make a more rational decision. He probably thought she was a cocktease, but it wasn't merely sex she'd been avoiding. She'd thought she was saving her heart. And she'd regretted that decision ever since.

Ty lifted his hand, and her bright red bike helmet swung on its straps from his long fingers—fingers she could still feel running through her hair as they had four months ago, when he'd been on a photography assignment for *National Geographic* in Saint-Luc and she'd been teaching at a ski resort and collecting photos for her latest book. Did he still think about their kisses, which had turned her inside out? And the way they'd held hands and talked into the wee hours of the mornings?

She reached for her helmet and he lifted it higher, his lips quirking up at the edges as he stepped closer and touched her arm. Heat spread through her like liquid fire. She focused on her helmet to keep from looking at *him*, remembering the first day they'd met. She'd been standing on a ridge taking in the snow-covered valley below and he'd come upon her while taking pictures. When she'd asked if she could see what he'd photographed, he'd held the camera up in the same way he was now holding her helmet, with the same coy smile, demanding to know her name before he'd share his pictures.

She wanted to ask so many things: Had he traveled to the places he'd hoped to since the last time they'd seen each other? Were the rumors about his being a player true? But her words got tangled in her befuddled brain and tumbled out too fast. "I live here...in Colorado. I can't believe the race is here. *You're* here." *Oh God! Shut up already.* "Small world, I guess. I need my helmet." *I need my helmet? Jesus, I don't give a damn about my stupid helmet!* She clamped her mouth shut to keep from rambling.

He handed her the helmet, a wolfish grin settling into place. "Surely there's a little reward in it for me, considering I could have let Johnny Jackass keep it."

Oh God, yes. A kiss…or a thousand? She really needed to get a grip. She couldn't afford to get hot and bothered over him, but his sexy brown eyes with flecks of gold and his smart-assery were as addicting as her favorite candy, Tropical Heat Hot Tamales. Maybe his acceptance of fate *had* changed, but had anything else?

She forced herself to focus. "Reward…?"

An announcement sounded with a twenty-minute prerace warning. She zipped up her equipment bags, and as she started to hoist them over her shoulder, Ty took them from her hands.

"I can carry those," she said as he slung them easily over his back.

"Call it a 'thank you' instead of a 'reward' for retrieving your helmet," he said, ignoring what she'd said. "Something simple, like a walk after the race?"

The first leg of the race was a thirty-mile bike ride, the last eight miles were through the mountains, ending at a site where their equipment would be left for them to make camp.

When she didn't answer right away, he said, "Come on, Aiyla. We took lots of walks in Saint-Luc, and I seem to remember your hand fitting perfectly in mine and your lips…" He arched a brow.

A nervous laugh slipped out before she could stop it. Their lips fit together, all right, even more perfectly than their hands, and a walk sounded wonderful. But she needed time to think. As he set her bags by the transportation trucks and they headed for the bikes, she asked, "Who's Johnny Jackass?"

Ty nodded at two guys standing with a group of women. "Johnny Jackson, one of the Jackson brothers. They stop at nothing to bring down their competition. Stealing equipment is tame for those cretins."

"This is a race for charity, not the Olympics. Besides, I'm a woman, not even in their league of competition." There were three groups of winners: men, women, and couples. She knew Ty was a fierce, and honest, competitor. If the articles and online gossip were true, he was a dichotomy of morals when it came to sports competitions versus his personal life, with one similarity—he always achieved his goals. The Mad Prix was probably like just another woman for him to conquer.

What does that make me?

Her stomach sank.

She put on her helmet to give her something to concentrate on just as they reached her bike.

"Chances are they've swiped something key out of everyone's bags. They'll get pulled from the race as soon as the coordinators get wind of it." Ty lowered his broad shoulders, bringing with him the scent of sunshine and rugged virility all wrapped up in one big delicious package.

Great. Now I'm thinking of your package.

Her eyes drifted to the bulge in his bike shorts, which left nothing to the imagination. Who was she kidding? She'd spent so many hours fantasizing about him, there was nothing left *to* imagine.

In a voice that could melt butter, he said, "Now, about our *date.*"

Aiyla looked at him for a long moment, remembering the ease and openness of their conversations and how effortlessly she'd been drawn to him. She couldn't get distracted from the reasons she'd put on the brakes before. But was he really the man rumors made him out to be? What if the rumors were unfounded? If the women standing behind him whispering were just being silly and not talking about him at all?

Another announcement sounded, and Ty's fingertips grazed hers, drawing her eyes to his again.

"Aiyla, I know you felt what I did in Saint-Luc. Give me a reason to win this leg of the race." His lips curved up in a sexy smile, and her insides heated up. "Promise me a walk."

She didn't want to turn him away again, not when fate had truly stepped in. But she needed to know the truth about his personal life, and the only way to find that out was to muster the courage to ask him. More nervous laughter slipped out as she said, "If it means the difference between you winning and losing, then how can I say no?"

His fingers curled around hers, and his expression turned serious. "I don't know how you could say no anyway."

He leaned in close, and she held her breath, readying for a kiss she wasn't sure she should accept—but she wanted nonetheless. She closed her eyes and his lips touched her cheek.

"Good luck out there, baby cakes," he said just above a whisper, and walked away.

The air rushed from her lungs. *Baby cakes.* That's what he'd called her last time they were together, though she'd never known why. Did he call everyone baby cakes? And if so, did those other women feel as special as she did when he said it? She watched him walk away and noticed several other girls also enjoying the view of his fine ass in those tight cycling shorts.

Life would be a whole lot easier if she were more like her much-older sister, Cherise, who had raised her from the time Aiyla was fifteen, when they'd lost their mother. Cherise lived a careful, meticulously orchestrated life, void of any risks, including those that pertained to her heart. She'd married a safe, reliable accountant with no sense of adventure. They had a comfortable home with a white picket fence and two adorable little boys. Just the idea of living such a mundane life made Aiyla's stomach turn. Hadn't their mother's death taught her sister that fate played its hand no matter how many walls one erected? Living a safe, boring life in fear of it all being taken away wasn't *living* at all.

Aiyla had accepted long ago that she'd never be a white-picket-fence type of girl. She loved adventures, thrived on capturing in photographs that would live on forever the faces of people who had lived full, even if torturous, lives. And she felt rejuvenated when surrounded by untamed wilderness. As she forced her gaze away from Ty, her fingers absently brushing over the cheek he'd kissed, she had to admit, she also enjoyed the sheer energy of a man marking his territory.

Now, if only she could focus on the race instead of the man who'd set her heart on fire.

COOL AIR WHIPPED against Ty's cheeks as he pedaled past his competitors cycling up the last big hill before hitting the mountain trail. The sound of tires on pavement was similar to a waterfall, constant and airy, with a wave effect that eased as he cycled farther ahead of the group. He'd been taking part in charity events like this since he was a teenager. Sometimes one of his older brothers, Sam, competed with him, which was always fun. But it was the busy season for Sam's river-rafting adventure company, leaving Ty to blow away the competition on his own.

He gained speed on the incline and rounded a bend, passing a crowd of spectators and volunteers who were cheering them on and offering water. He stayed low over the handlebars, and when the pavement turned to earth, he kicked up his efforts. A cloud of dust erupted in his wake. He sucked down a gel pack and followed a narrow trail into the woods.

Eight miles to go.

He could hear the others gaining on him, then falling farther behind once again. While their lungs and thighs would burn from pedaling over the rough terrain, Ty reveled in the extra exertion. Mountains were to him as oxygen was to others. He'd had a fascination with mountains for as long as he could remember. Their majestic beauty and quiet power fueled a rivaling sense of calm and inspiration within him, the same way spending time with Aiyla had in Switzerland. His mind raced back to the moment he'd first seen her digging through her bag a few hours ago. He'd been checking his equipment with the transportation crew when he'd caught a glimpse of her. Her honey-blond hair had curtained her face, but he'd know her anywhere. She was petite but strong, with lean shoulders, gorgeous legs, and arms that were as delicate as they were defined. And her hair? It was the perfect blend of light brown and dark blond, naturally straight, shining even in the dead of night. His fingers itched with the memory of those silky strands threaded between his fingers as they'd kissed beneath the evening skies.

For four long months he'd looked for her face in every airport, every crowd. They'd promised not to seek each other out, and he'd stayed true to that stupid promise, with the hopes that she knew something about fate that he didn't.

He cranked up his efforts as cyclists encroached from behind, threatening his lead. Memories of that promise, and the frustration he'd felt every time he'd thought about tracking Aiyla down, fired him up, and he kicked up his speed. Her hazel eyes had captured his attention from the second they'd met, and that last night together, the eve of his leaving for his next assignment, they'd held his rapt attention as she'd pleaded her case—*I can't just up and leave my life with the hopes that these five days will lead to forever. If fate brings us back together, then I'll know there's something bigger than lust at play.* He'd tried to argue with her, but she'd been so sure it was the right thing to do, so damn stubborn about not giving up her life. How could he do anything but respect her decision? Ty had never been a one-woman man, but since leaving a piece of his heart in Aiyla's hands, he hadn't been able to so much as think of another woman.

A cyclist blew past him, with others on his tail, pulling him from his thoughts. There was no way he was going to face Aiyla tonight without a first-place win. His body rose off the seat, knees bent, head raised, as he rode the edge of the trail, shredding the competition, pushing himself harder, pedaling faster, until he was neck and neck with the lead racer. Ty focused on the trail ahead, envisioning Aiyla before him, and like a greyhound chasing a rabbit, he surged forward, determined not to let her get away.

Chapter Two

THE CAMPSITE WAS exactly as Aiyla had envisioned it, a plethora of pup tents, collapsible tables and chairs, and equipment bags haphazardly littering the area around the restroom pavilion. The event crew had set up a grilling area with buffet-style tables, offering hamburgers, hot dogs, and other dinner foods. People lay on sleeping bags outside their tents reading or recuperating. Others huddled in groups around the bonfire and picnic tables.

Aiyla set up her tent near the trees, away from most of the commotion, and after waiting in line, she showered and brushed her teeth. She hung her cycling clothes over the ridge of her tent, trying her best to ignore the pain in her left shin. It had been acting up for the past few weeks, but she was used to aches and pains. She'd spent her youth living, breathing, eating, and sleeping sports, and it had paid off, allowing her to work as a hiking guide and ski instructor, which helped pay the bills and fund her trips between publishing advances. She scanned the crowd looking for Ty as she activated one of her chemical ice packs. Her pulse quickened with the realization that this time her searching would not be a futile effort. Ty was there *somewhere*.

She could hardly believe it, but as much as she hated what had happened to her mother, her mother's death had solidified her belief that fate was real. That she could live her life hiding or exploring, and either way, whatever was supposed to happen in the grand scheme of things would still play out. She'd told herself over the past few months that if she ever saw Ty again, she'd let fate take over and would not deny herself the pleasures she wanted to experience with him. But she still needed to know the truth about his reputation.

She sat outside her tent snacking on Tropical Heat Hot Tamales and icing her leg, wishing she and Ty had exchanged numbers so she could call and find him now.

"There's my girl!" Ty's voice boomed from across the clearing, as arrogant and appealing as ever.

Everyone looked up to see who he was talking about—including Aiyla—as he strutted across the dirt in a pair of dark green cargo shorts and open sweatshirt over an impossibly snug shirt. Their eyes met and sparks ignited like a wick, burning up the space between them.

Aiyla set the ice pack on a towel and pushed to her feet, trying desperately not to choke on her candy as her stomach dipped and flipped.

"Your *girl*?" she asked. "Presumptuous, aren't you?"

His eyes took a slow stroll down her body, heating up every inch as his gaze dragged down her breasts, her stomach, all the way to her toes. She wasn't the kind of girl who wore makeup or fussed with fancy hairstyles. And as his eyes took on an appreciative, sinful darkness, she remembered how often in Saint-Luc he'd told her she was beautiful, each time making her blush anew.

"Mm-mm." His smoldering eyes were set off by his cocky

grin. "Shorts and a hoodie have never looked so good." He stepped closer, his tone turning seductive. "You smell *sweet* and *hot*. My favorite combination."

He'd completely ignored her sassy remark. She'd forgotten about how often he did that, and she still found his arrogance as intriguing as ever.

"Ready for our hot date?" he asked.

"Are you?" she countered.

"Am I *ever*." He leaned down and brushed a sweet, feathery kiss on her cheek. "But how's that leg you were icing?"

It would feel a lot better if you kissed it. She waved a hand dismissively, as if she could clear those sexy thoughts from her mind. "Fine."

He arched a brow. "You sure? We can hang out here if you need to rest it."

She loved that he was considerate, but she was eager to talk with him in private and catch up. And maybe, just *maybe*, she'd muster the courage to ask about his reputation—even if she wasn't sure she wanted to know the answer.

He reached for her hand. "Let's go, baby cakes."

Slipping her hand into his was like coming home. He squeezed it gently, smiling as they headed toward a path on the other side of the campsite. "Why do you call me baby cakes?"

His lips curved up, and then his brows knitted. "You don't remember?"

She shook her head, scrambling through memories in search of a reason, but she came up blank. "No."

"We were at the Café de la Poste listening to a band play the second night we were together. They had that heart-shaped metal candleholder on the table, and you were wearing a green sweater that set off your eyes. *Mm.* I loved the way you looked that night. Don't you remember? We shared a bottle of wine, and they set up that little grill right on our table."

"I remember." She'd never forget. It was the single most romantic dinner of her life. "We rearranged the place settings and sat side by side, which irked the waiter." They'd grilled several types of meats and breads and fed each other the most delicious foods. And then they'd danced to a live band that joked with the customers and kept everyone laughing.

"And what did you say when our dessert arrived?"

She remembered the chocolate cake was delicious—and *tiny*! Holy cow, why hadn't she picked up on that? "I said they were baby cakes!"

"And the waiter went back to the kitchen and came out with the chef, remember?"

She laughed. "I was mortified."

"Yes, but when he brought you a cake that was three times the size, we devoured it." He squeezed her hand and said, "From that moment on, you were my baby cakes."

"I love that." She didn't need to ask if he called anyone else that name. She knew in her heart the endearment was all hers, and she reveled in every one of the special feelings it evoked.

"I'm glad, because when I think of you, that's just one of the amazing nights that comes to mind. But that name? That's you, baby cakes, all the way." He was quiet while they passed a man sleeping in a chair outside his tent, and then he said, "You came in eighth today. Congratulations."

"How'd you know?" She was proud of herself, considering it had been ages since she'd ridden a bike.

He gave her a look that said he made it his business to know, and her knees weakened a little at that.

"Hey, Braden!" A brawny blond guy rose to his feet as they

passed a group of people sitting around the bonfire, and he waved Ty over.

"Hey, Speed. How's it going?" Ty released her hand to shake his. "Nice ride today."

"Nice ride? You took my first-place ribbon, you ass. Sit down and shoot the shit for a while." Speed eyed Aiyla curiously and lifted his chin with a flirtatious smile. "How's it going, sweetheart? I'm Jon Butterscotch, but they call me Speed."

"This is Aiyla," Ty said, reaching for her hand again. "Speed and I go way back. He's my brother Cole's business partner." He leaned in closer and said, "You'd better lock your tent tonight. He's a bit of a ladies' man."

Speed scoffed and said, "Damn right I am."

"Ty, take a load off, man. We haven't seen you in forever," a thin, dark-haired guy urged. "Hey, Aiyla, I'm James."

Aiyla waved. "Hi."

"Congrats on number eight," a cheery brunette said to Aiyla. She wore a pair of jeans with a flannel shirt tied above her belly button. Her dark hair fell in long layers, like Daisy Duke from the *Dukes of Hazard*, which was fitting, since she had a slight Southern twang in her speech. "I'm Trixie. I sucked wind today. Came in fifteenth. Guess I need *Braden* genes."

"Thanks. Fifteenth is awesome," Aiyla said. She couldn't help but catch the inquisitive look Trixie was giving Ty, and she wondered just how well they knew each other.

"*Braden* genes my ass." Speed patted the blanket beside him. "Chill, dude. Sit down."

"Yeah, I'd like to get to know Aiyla," Trixie said, and took a sip of her beer.

Ty hiked a thumb over his shoulder. "We were just going to take a walk."

"Oh, come on," Trixie pleaded. "You can't just drag the new girl into the woods like a caveman."

Aiyla's stomach sank. *I guess the rumors aren't so far off.*

Ty shot Trixie a back-off look.

"It's okay," Aiyla said. "We can go on a walk another night."

He made a guttural sound of disappointment.

Trixie pulled two beers from a cooler behind her and handed them each one. "Where are you from, Aiyla?"

Aiyla sat down on the blanket, and Ty opened the beer for her and sat down beside her. His leg brushed against hers, making her acutely aware of how badly she wanted to touch him. She realized Trixie was waiting for an answer and said, "I grew up in Colorado and still call it home, but I travel most of the year for work."

Ty leaned back on his palm, his chest grazing Aiyla's shoulder, making her wish they'd taken that private walk. "She's a photographer, a ski instructor, an EMT, and probably a hundred other things I have yet to discover. We met in Switzerland a few months ago."

Wow. He really did remember everything. She hadn't remembered telling him she was an EMT.

"Wait? This is *her? Saint-Luc?*" Speed asked with wide eyes. "This is *the* girl? I thought Cole was full of shit."

"Cole...?" Ty's brow wrinkled with confusion. "I never told Cole about her."

"Dude," Speed said. "You told your sister Shannon, which is like feeding it directly to the Braden grapevine."

"Christ," Ty said under his breath. He turned to Aiyla and said, "My sister Shannon and I are pretty close."

And you told her about me? Were you pissed that I wouldn't leave Saint-Luc with you, or did you miss me? "You mentioned that to me in Saint-Luc."

"Ah, so she's not the *new girl* to you." Trixie took another drink and winked at Aiyla.

"No." Ty reached for Aiyla's hand, pinning her in place with a serious gaze. "She's the one who got away."

The one who got away? Was that how he thought of her? The *one* as in the *only* one, or the *one* as in, one of many, but the only one who wouldn't sleep with him?

"The one who *got away?*" Trixie's eyes widened, and she took a long, hard look at Aiyla.

Ty brushed his thumb over Aiyla's knuckles, watching her intently. Silent seconds thrummed between them, drenched in sexual tension. When he licked his lips, she heard herself sigh wantonly. She was sure everyone could see desire written all over her face. She withdrew her hand from his in an effort to regain control of her emotions, and guzzled her beer.

He shifted his gaze to Trixie and said, "Jealous?"

"*Please.*" Trixie rolled her eyes. "If I wanted you, I'd have had you by now. You're not cowboy enough for me, mountain boy."

Ty leaned closer to Aiyla and said, "Trixie's a hard-core ranch girl. She lives in Oak Falls, Virginia, with a load of tough-ass brothers. She's a good egg."

Speed draped an arm over Trixie's shoulder. "I'll wear leather chaps if that's what it takes."

Ty eyed them, his body suddenly rigid. Aiyla wondered if he had a thing for Trixie after all.

"Clothes don't make the cowboy." Trixie ducked out from beneath Speed's arm, and Ty glared at him.

"Trix'll need Aiyla's medical skills after she gets a good dose of Speed." James laughed and lifted his beer in a toast. "Here's to another great race."

As Aiyla drank to the toast, Ty whispered, "I'm a man of many talents. Give me a horse and I'll ride her like there's no tomorrow."

"Do you *want* to be a cowboy?" The question slipped out before she thought to stop it, and there was no mistaking the jealousy it rode out on.

He set his beer between his legs and ran his finger down Aiyla's cheek, gazing hungrily into her eyes. "Only if it's you I'm saddling up."

TY DIDN'T KNOW how long he and Aiyla sat with the others around the bonfire, but it was definitely too damn long. They'd shared a second beer, and each time she'd lifted the bottle to her lips, he'd imagined her mouth on *him*. The logs had burned to embers, and most of the other competitors had already turned in for the night. They had a twenty-four-kilometer run tomorrow, fifteen miles that ended with a swim across a lake. They needed to rest. Aiyla and Trixie were sitting side by side now, looking at pictures on their phones. Trixie showed Aiyla pictures of her hotshot brothers, ignoring Ty's disapproving glare.

"Wow, they really are cowboys," Aiyla said, moving closer to get a better look.

She was far too interested for Ty's liking, asking about this one and that. Especially since every time he and Aiyla touched, the temperature spiked fifty degrees. The chemistry between them was just as hot as it had been in Switzerland. Why was she checking out other guys?

He caught Trixie's eye and glared again. They'd been friends for years, and he knew she was well aware of his annoyance. She just laughed under her breath, taunting him like a pain-in-the-ass sister. As much as he wanted to leave, he waited for James to call it a night first. James had a reputation for being overly aggressive with women, and with Trixie around, Ty wasn't about to give him that chance.

Just as he opened his mouth to try to prompt the end of their evening, Speed and James pushed to their feet.

"That's it for me," Speed said as he grabbed his empty bottles. "Good luck tomorrow, Braden. You'll need it."

"Yeah, right." Ty laughed. "Good luck, man. You too, James."

"I'm not even in your league," James said. "I'll be happy if I'm in the top forty-five."

"I'm pulling for you, man." Ty watched them walk away and draped an arm over Aiyla's shoulder. As he leaned in, she tucked her phone into her pocket. "You about ready to call it a night, sweet one?"

"Sure." She smiled at Trixie, who was looking at Ty like she didn't recognize him. "Trixie, it's been fun getting to know you. Good luck tomorrow."

"Thanks. You too."

He gathered the remaining bottles and tossed them in the trash barrel, then reached for Aiyla's hand and said, "Hey, Trix, where's your tent?"

"Right there." She pointed to a green tent by the pavilion. "Good luck tomorrow, you guys."

He nodded and watched her head back to her tent. Aiyla slipped her hand from his, and he turned his attention back to the beautiful woman beside him, wondering why. Considering their date had been lost, he went for levity. "So, my girl's into cowboys?"

"*Your* girl?" Hurt rose in her eyes. "A little overly confident for a guy who looked like he wanted to follow Trixie into her tent."

"Wanted to…?" He hauled her against him, flattening his hand over her back and holding her so tight her chin touched his chest. She had no choice but to look up at him. "Aiyla Lillian Bell, if you think I would hit on another girl while I'm on what was supposed to be a date with you, then you don't know me the way I thought you did. Trixie Jericho has been my friend since college, and James is known for being a bit of a dick. I didn't want her to run into trouble with him."

She put her hands on his chest and pushed, but he didn't loosen his grip. Luckily, she smiled instead of kneeing him in the groin.

"First, I can't believe you remembered my *middle* name. That's kind of sweet." A thoughtful expression appeared on her beautiful face, and her fingers moved absently over his pecs. "And second, I didn't expect that answer. I need a minute to think up a response that doesn't make me sound like a loser."

He ran his hands up her back and into her hair, wondering if she could sense how much he'd missed her. How he'd hoped every airport would bring her to him. How adhering to her sense of fate had frustrated him to the point of nearly giving in and flying back to Switzerland. But his feelings for her had kept him from breaking his promise, and now she was right here in his arms, and it was killing him not to kiss her.

"Of course I remember your middle name. I remember every goddamn word you've ever said to me. But more importantly, what did you expect to hear? And how do you think I felt watching you check out Trixie's brothers?"

"I thought..." Her gaze dropped to his chest, and she shook her head. "I don't know, and I'm sorry about Trixie's brothers. I *was* trying to make you jealous, but only because I was jealous, and I hate that feeling."

Christ. He'd made her jealous? That was as awesome as it was awful, and now he felt guilty. At a loss for words, he touched his forehead to hers, trying to get his arms around his soaring emotions. "Sweet one, making you jealous was not on my agenda."

"You had an agenda? That sounds—"

"Like I used the wrong word." He brushed his lips over her cheek. "Aiyla," came out like a plea. His insides were ablaze, and his heart was beating so hard, it was like he was on his first date *ever.* The voice in his head told him to kiss her good and hard, so she would want more, but a quieter—smarter?—whisper held him back. They needed to get to know each other again, even if it killed him. He didn't want to take a chance of fucking this up. "Tomorrow night, after the event. If you're up for a quiet evening by the water—"

"Yes," flew from her lips.

"Yes," he repeated happily.

"Yes. Definitely *yes.*"

Chapter Three

AIYLA SAT ON a chair, balancing the phone between her shoulder and ear early the next morning and trying to massage a bone-deep ache from her leg while she talked with her sister. She'd already taken down her tent and packed up her gear for the transportation crew to pick up. Her race number was pinned to her running shorts, and she'd written her number across her stomach in permanent marker, something she learned to do as a teenager, when she'd fallen during a race and ripped her bib.

"Eighth is wonderful, Aiy. Heck, crossing the finish line is a feat in and of itself. I'm so proud of you."

"Thanks, sis. Did you guys start painting your living room yet?"

Her sister still lived in their cozy three-bedroom childhood home, which their grandparents had left to their mother, in Rhododendron, Oregon, a town so small, if she sneezed on her way through, she'd miss it. Cherise and her husband, Caleb, could afford a larger home, but her sister wanted to stay in the home where their mother had lived. Their mother had worked as a housekeeper in Mount Hood. She hadn't earned much money, even though it had seemed like she was always working.

She had instilled in her daughters a strong sense of drive, and an even stronger sense of confidence. The combination had served them both well. While Cherise's drive had led her to be the best wife and mother she could, Aiyla's determination had taught her to never give up, no matter what the odds or how difficult the adventure. The confidence had helped them both hold their heads up high even when they'd worn secondhand clothes day in and day out.

As Cherise told her about the painting she was doing and the garden she was planting, Aiyla downed Motrin and Tylenol, hoping to stave off the ache from her overuse injury. It was a career hazard, and lately her leg had been teaching her a lesson.

She went back to massaging her leg, and spotted Ty heading her way, giving high-fives and looking like he'd walked off the cover of *Men's Health* magazine. He wore nothing but a pair of compression shorts and a wide black headband to hold his hair away from his face. His eyes locked on her, filled with wicked intent. She tried to keep up the conversation with her sister, but his eyes taunted her, and his hard, tanned flesh stole the rest of her attention. Some people would say he could bounce a quarter off his abs. She imagined them moving above her, against her, as he gave her all the pleasures she knew he could.

Holy mother of horniness. It had been way too long since she'd scratched that particular itch.

She needed to look away, but as he closed the gap between them, she focused on his scruff, imagining what those sexy whiskers would feel like on her cheeks, her inner thighs…

"Aiyla? Are you there?" Cherise asked.

"Um, yeah. Sorry." She tried again to focus on what Cherise was saying about her nephews, but Ty knelt before her and moved her hand away from where she was rubbing her sore leg.

He ran his hands up either side of her leg, massaging gently. His hands were big and strong and a little rough, giving her more sexy ideas. A needy sound slipped from her lips.

"What happened?" Cherise asked.

Shit. "Nothing," she said breathlessly, eyes on Ty. "Continue, *please.*"

Ty's eyes darkened as Cherise continued telling her story. He lifted Aiyla's leg and pressed his lips to the area just above her ankle, blazing a trail of tender kisses up to her knee. Heat climbed to the juncture of her thighs, and her arm absently fell to her side.

Ty chuckled and guided the phone back up to her ear, reminding her that she was supposed to be talking on it.

"Um, sis? I have to go...get ready for the..." She lost her train of thought as Ty covered her leg with more kisses, working his way from shin to ankle, then up again. Her thoughts scattered as she set the phone aside and said, "Love you. Bye," to the air.

"Leg still giving you trouble?" He went up on his knees and placed his hands on either side of her, trapping her with his magnificent body.

"I think the trouble has moved higher."

He leaned in, brushing his whiskers over her cheek, and said, "Here?" He pressed a kiss beside her ear and lowered his hand to her thigh, squeezing gently. "Or there?"

Her heart was going to explode. The rest of the world faded away, until all that existed was Ty, the heat of his hand branding her leg, and the lust-filled look in his eyes.

"Leg" fell from her lips.

His eyes flamed, and he bent to kiss her thigh. *Oh Lord.* This was too much, too enticing. She'd have noodle legs for the race.

The heck with the race.

Couldn't they just set up her tent again and climb in for the day?

He pressed a kiss just above her knee, and she heard herself whimper. When he did it again, his hands skimming her outer thighs, she felt herself go damp and bolted from her seat, sending him sprawling backward. "Stop, stop, *stop...*"

Ty fell on his ass, laughing.

Aiyla paced, shaking her hands, as if that might cool her body down. Several people were watching them, but Ty met their curious gazes with a threatening one of his own, and they quickly turned away.

"Geez, Ty. What was *that?*"

"Can you blame me? You shouldn't be allowed in public in that skimpy running bra and those painted-on shorts. All these guys are going to have to run with hard-ons. That will *not* be a pretty sight." He reached a hand up with a pleading look in his eyes.

"Oh, *please.*" She huffed out a breath and pulled him up to his feet.

His arms came around her waist, and he grinned down at her, looking all too pleased with himself. "Leg feel better?"

"My leg? How can I even think about my leg after *that?*" She banged her fists on his chest, laughing. "You are—"

"Hot?" he offered.

"No! *Yes,* but—"

"Irresistible?"

"Ohmygod. How had I forgotten this about you?" They both laughed as she tried to squirm out of his arms, but he held her captive. "You're like an invasive plant—with octopus arms and incredible lips."

"My lips *are* pretty incredible."

Yes, they were, and she wanted them a little too badly at the moment. "I don't remember your mouth all over my legs like that in Switzerland."

"And I *lost* you," he said with a shockingly serious tone. "I'm not making that mistake again."

"You didn't *lose* me because of *that*." Her heart thumped harder. "We made a choice," she reminded him.

"*You* made a choice. I agreed because I couldn't convince you to come with me." His gaze softened, but his tone remained firm. "I have spent months looking for you everywhere, while not being allowed to really search. I stuck to the parameters we agreed on. 'No Internet searches, no tracking you down in any other way.' I played by your rules, and thank God, fate stepped in. I've finally got you back in my arms again, Aiyla, and I'm *not* backing off this time."

"I'm not asking you to, but..." She paused as an announcement rang out about checking in for the start of the race. "We need to talk later. I have to wrap my leg before the race."

She tried to step away, and he held tight with a worried expression.

"I saw you taking meds. Are you sure you're okay to run?"

The man didn't miss a thing. Was he that attuned to everyone, or just her?

"Yes!" she assured him. "It's just overuse. I'm going to kick ass today and make my sponsors proud." Aiyla had secured sponsorships and donations from the resorts she'd worked with in and around Colorado over the years to help raise money for the children's charities. All she had to do was finish the race for the companies to donate the funds, but she was too competitive to be content with merely finishing.

He tugged her against him and cradled her face in his hands, breathing hard. Her entire body reached for him, but they needed to talk. She needed answers about his personal life. She bit her lower lip to keep from going up on her toes and taking the kiss she was dying for.

His fingers pressed into her skin, restraint written in the tightness of his jaw. "Just be careful out there, baby cakes. We've got a hot date tonight."

MUCH LATER, AIYLA ran at a strong pace, still trying to push thoughts of Ty, his incredible mouth, and his unconfirmed reputation to the back of her mind and focus on the crisp air as her lungs expanded. The familiar rhythm of her feet pounding the earth and the chill of the air against her sweaty limbs gave her a sense of euphoria. She usually liked to run while listening to music, but not during a race. It was the stampede of the competition that kept her mind centered and her body pushing itself. She'd been competitive all her life. When Aiyla had learned to swim at five, she'd been determined to be a better swimmer than her six-years-older sister. That had been easy, considering Cherise didn't have a competitive bone in her body. And when Cherise had given Aiyla the bicycle she had never had any interest in riding, Aiyla had spent an entire day learning to ride. By nightfall, with skinned knees and bruised elbows, she was driving her mother and sister crazy by riding with no hands.

She smiled as she rounded a bend, remembering how she'd ridden that bike until her legs had grown too long and her knees had hit her chest. Her competitive drive had never wavered, and thanks to Ms. Farrington—*Ms. F*—her mother's wealthiest employer, who had taken Aiyla under her wing when Aiyla was a young girl, she'd had proper skiing lessons and all the right gear for each sport she'd trained in through school—basketball, lacrosse, field hockey, track, cross-country, skiing. Ms. F had been in her seventies at the time, and an avid photographer. She'd never had children of her own, and she'd paid for Aiyla's things in exchange for Aiyla accompanying her on her travels over school breaks and summers from the time Aiyla had turned thirteen. Ms. F had disliked traveling alone, and when they'd traveled, she'd given Aiyla all sorts of duties, from map navigation to ensuring she took her medications on schedule. Ms. F had nurtured Aiyla's curiosity, uncovering a love of traveling, and more importantly, she had opened up the world of photography to her eager-to-learn protégé and companion. As Aiyla matured, she'd realized that the latter was probably Ms. F's goal all along. She'd been so kind to their family, Aiyla thought Ms. F had seen her mother as the daughter she'd never had. And she'd taken on the role of fairy godmother to the girls.

Aiyla slowed to grab a bottle of Gatorade at the nine-mile refueling station, bringing her thoughts back to the race and to the throbbing ache in her leg. She remembered Ty's warm lips pressing against her skin, his big hands rubbing the pain away while his sensuality created a whole new type of ache. She used the promise of more to carry her forward.

BLUE-AND-WHITE banners announcing the competition flapped in the wind at the far end of the shore, where Ty chugged his drink as the late-afternoon sun dipped toward the horizon. He'd taken second place and had crossed the finish line so long ago his shorts were nearly dry. Once the competitors were all accounted for, they'd truck them, and their bags, to the next camping area. He meandered through the crowd gathered along the shoreline, watching swimmers make their way across the lake. Some competitors plowed out of the water at full speed; others were barely able to walk. The race staff was there to help hydrate and tend to the injured.

Ty talked with his friends, but his mind wasn't on how everyone's run had gone or who was partying with whom tonight. He had tunnel vision, scanning the head of every swimmer, waiting for Aiyla to cross that body of water.

"Dude, take a load off your feet and chill for a while." Speed patted him on the back, gazing out at the water. "That was an awesome race. Sorry you didn't take first place."

Sure you are. "Can't knock Theo for being a great athlete."

"We're going to hang out on the rocks until the stragglers make it in." Speed motioned toward a path that led to an outcropping of rocks where others were already gathering. "You coming?"

"Maybe later. I'm going to wait for Aiyla to finish." A few more racers trudged from the water.

Speed crossed his arms, running an assessing eye over Ty. "She's really gotten to you."

"More than you can imagine," Ty said with an unintended edge to his voice as more swimmers approached the shore.

"All righty, then. We'll catch up with you later."

Athletes trickled in over the next hour, and Ty began to worry. He spotted Trixie dragging herself from the water. She was panting and holding her side. He ran over and put an arm

29

around her, bearing her weight.

"You okay, Trix? What do you need?"

She gave him a deadpan look. "A drink, a man who's as good in bed as he is at riding horses, and about eighteen hours of sleep."

Ty laughed. "How about a drink, then? Did you pass Aiyla? I expected her to finish ages ago, and I'm getting worried."

"She's not back?" Her brow furrowed. "She was way ahead of me. I don't remember passing her."

"Shit." He helped her over to a chair. "I'm going to get one of the race staff to help you out. Is that okay? I want to see if Aiyla's at one of the checkpoints."

"Of course. Go."

Ty hollered to one of the staff, and when they came to Trixie's side, he went directly to the race coordinator, Joe Malpas, who was on his way into the food tent.

"Hey, Ty. Great race today."

"Thanks. I need to check on someone, and see if she's injured or resting at one of the checkpoints."

"Something wrong?" Joe pulled a walkie-talkie from his hip.

"I hope not. Aiyla Bell had some trouble with her leg this morning. She's a good runner, Joe, athletic as hell. She should have been in by now. Her race number is 164." He'd seen her number written on her stomach, and it had been etched into his mind ever since.

Joe held up one finger and spoke into the walkie-talkie. "Hey, Rick, can you do a checkpoint rundown of number 164, Aiyla Bell, and get back to me asap? Thanks." He hooked the walkie-talkie to the waist of his shorts. "It shouldn't take too long."

"Great." Ty paced, scanning the water and hoping Aiyla

would appear soon, uninjured. Every minute felt like an hour. Anything could have happened. A snake bite, injury, dehydration. A few minutes later, he was at his wit's end. "I'm going after her. Can I use a boat?"

"Of course, but give me one—"

"Joe?" A voice came over his walkie-talkie.

Ty's heart leapt to his throat.

"Yeah. I'm here," Joe said into the radio.

"Number 164, right?"

"Yes," Ty said, stepping closer, as if that might help Aiyla.

"We've got her passing the first thirteen checkpoints, which puts her about two miles from the lake, but that's it."

"I'm out of here." Ty ran toward the boats. "Joe, can you get volunteers—"

Joe waved him off. "Already on it!"

Ty sped across the water as fast as the boat would carry him, trying to recall the terrain between the lake and checkpoint thirteen. When he hit the beach, he was met by a volunteer, who handed him a walkie-talkie and said Joe had instructed her to give it to him. Clutching it in his hand, he sprinted up the narrow, wooded trail, scanning his surroundings. He moved aside for runners, asking if they'd passed an injured woman along the way, and bolted up the hill and into a clearing. Runners were sparse, and as he covered the distance to the next wooded area, he spotted someone moving slowly up ahead. Adrenaline surged, and he sprinted faster. Aiyla's beautiful face came into view. She was limping, favoring her left leg as she jogged at a turtle's pace. A volunteer appeared behind her in a bright blue-and-white shirt.

"Are you Aiyla Bell?" the female volunteer asked as Ty approached.

"Yes," Aiyla answered. Confusion riddled her brow, but she never missed a step and continued limp-jogging along the trail. "Ty? Why are you going the wrong way?"

"I was worried."

"We got a call that you might be lost or injured," the volunteer explained.

Aiyla glared at Ty. "I'm not lost and I'm *fine*. Thank you, but I don't need any help."

"You're limping. You're clearly not fine," Ty pointed out. "Do you want to get a ride the rest of the way?" The look on her face told him he'd asked the *wrong* question.

"*No*, I do *not* want a ride," Aiyla insisted. "I'm *finishing* this race."

The volunteer smirked, like she'd seen this situation play out too many times to be overly concerned. "All right, then."

"Wait," Ty said to the volunteer. "Aiyla, you've got a mile or more to go, plus the swim. Can your leg take it?"

She turned to the volunteer and said, "Thank you, but you can report me as 'found and finishing the race.'"

She was so damn stubborn it made his blood boil. Ty handed the volunteer the walkie-talkie and said, "Can you please call Joe Malpas, tell him I'm with her?"

"Sure." The volunteer waved and headed back the way she'd come.

As soon as she was out of earshot, Aiyla turned an angry glare on Ty. "Have *you* ever *not* finished a race?"

"No, but your leg—"

"Is *fine!*" she insisted, and picked up her pace—probably just to spite him. "I don't know what the other women in your life are like, but I am not a damsel in distress, and I'm not a quitter. Not now, not ever. So as much as I appreciate your concern, and coming all this way to help me, I do not need or want a knight in shining armor."

"I'm not trying to be your knight in shining armor, and I don't have other women in my life. Jesus, Aiyla. I was worried about you. Is that a fucking crime?"

She narrowed her eyes, as if she were weighing his answer—or possibly her own. "I've been on my own since I was eighteen. That's almost a decade, Ty. I can handle *anything*."

"Obviously," he ground out. "I messed up. Sorry."

"It's okay, and I appreciate your concern. But I don't need anyone making people look for me. Do you even know how embarrassing that is?" She looked away, keeping up her faster pace.

"Better embarrassed than dehydrated and stuck on this fucking mountain." He didn't mean to raise his voice, but his worries had heightened with her uneven gait. "Trixie said she didn't remember passing you. I thought you might have strayed off the trail and gotten injured, or bitten by a snake, or just flat-out exhausted."

Jaw tight, stubborn eyes set on the trail ahead, she said, "Well, I *didn't*."

"Clearly. You don't have to be so bullheaded."

"Ha! Look who's talking."

"What does that mean?" he challenged, trying to slow their pace and give her leg a break, but she didn't follow along, maintaining a moderate pace.

"Listen to yourself," she said, watching him intently now. "You're arguing your point like you did in Switzerland."

"I wanted you to come *with me* when I left Saint-Luc. Of course I argued my point." Where the hell was this coming from? She sounded even angrier than she'd been a moment ago.

"Why? So *Mr. Girl-in-Every-Country* could add one more to his harem? I have a life, Ty. A life I worked really hard to create, and I'm not giving it up to be one of a long line of women making their way through your revolving bedroom door. No matter how good of a kisser you are."

He clenched his jaw, the uneven cadence of their footfalls filling the uncomfortable silence. "Is that what you think?"

"It wasn't when we were together," she said softly, then stronger, "but everyone who follows your career knows about your reputation. Out here, I've had *lots* of time to think about it. And trust me, I've tried not to."

She held his gaze as they jogged, the anger in her eyes replaced with something softer, sadder. "Is it true?"

He'd always known his reputation would catch up with him one day, but he'd never imagined caring about someone enough for it to matter. But that look in her eyes made him wish he could erase every other woman from his past. "Is that why you refused to come with me when I left Saint-Luc?"

"What would you have done if the tables were turned?" she asked confidently. "If I had a rep of sleeping with anyone in my path, would you have given up everything for me?"

"I don't know or care how many men you've slept with," he said, but as too many silent seconds passed between them, he realized that wasn't true. Just the thought of her with another guy made him want to punch something.

She slowed her pace, looking at him like she didn't believe him, either.

"Obviously, I do care," he admitted. "I hate thinking about you and any other guy. But when we were in Saint-Luc, I didn't think about it. Not even once. All I cared about was the person you were when you were with me, the connection we shared, and the way our hopes for the future, and our ideals, aligned. You were *it* for me, Aiyla, and these last few months have totally sucked. I thought about you every second, *willing* fate to step in and fighting the urge to track you down. But I didn't want to break my promise to you."

They entered the wooded trail, and he fell into step behind her, his eyes gravitating naturally to her gorgeous ass. A thread of guilt wound through him for that—he was totally into her for more than her body—but her body was too fricking hot to ignore.

"Then it's true," she said.

"It *was* true. I'm not going to lie to you about who I was before we met. I had no one to answer to, no commitment. It wasn't like I was a cheating bastard. I had no one to cheat *on*."

"Then why did you want me to leave Saint-Luc and travel with you? Why mess up a good thing?" She stopped short, and he plowed into her. They both stumbled, but he planted his legs on the hilly trail, catching her around her waist.

"You okay?" He did a quick visual assessment. "Did I hurt your leg?"

She clung to him, breathing hard. "I'm *fine*. It's *fine*."

"I've got two sisters, and I know damn well *fine* doesn't really mean you're okay, but I get it, as far as the race goes. You're determined to do this on your own, and I respect that." He took her hands in his and said, "I'm not sure what you want to hear about me, but the truth is, I knew you were different the first day we met. What I had before you was *not* a good thing. Maybe I thought it was at the time, or for some of that time, but nothing compares to what we had when we were together. You and I had a *great* thing, Aiyla, and that's what I want. I want *you*."

Chapter Four

AIYLA STOOD BENEATH the stars at the edge of their campsite later that evening, gazing over the inky water, wondering how she was going to make it down the rocks. Her leg had throbbed like fire during the run, but she'd had a minor reprieve while swimming in the cool lake. Now pain settled in again like a toothache. She was beating the hell out of her leg, but she wasn't about to miss her chance at taking part in the Mad Prix—or let the pain stop her from enjoying her date with Ty, who stood beside her looking hotter than hell in cargo shorts, a dark shirt, and an open sweatshirt. She'd wrestled all evening with his honesty—and his confession. *What I had before you was not a good thing... You and I had a great thing, Aiyla, and that's what I want. I want you.* He could have said anything, told her the rumors weren't true, made himself out to be something he wasn't. But he hadn't, and that honesty had sparked even more emotions. It had opened doors for them to communicate in ways she'd been afraid to.

"Race ya," Ty teased.

He'd stayed with her for the duration of the race, including swimming across the lake right beside her. Afterward, he'd insisted on visiting the health tent together, despite the fact that she was a trained EMT and felt she could handle caring for her leg on her own. His response sailed through her mind. *And a carpenter's house is always the worst one on the block.* She smiled with the memory, even though she'd been more than a little annoyed at him for being so overprotective. She couldn't remember the last time anyone had worried so much about her.

"I can totally do this," she lied. She didn't like to admit defeat. She'd taken pain medication, and she was hoping it would kick in soon.

Ty stepped in front of her, a big, bad wall of hotness. "I know you *can*, but I've got a better idea." He turned around and stooped. "Climb on, baby cakes. We're going for a ride."

Laughter bubbled out before she could stop it. "I am not getting on your back like a child."

He rose to his feet and pulled her closer, rubbing against her as he gazed into her eyes. Every press of his delicious muscles chipped away at her resolve. His hand slid down her hip as his whiskers scratched sensually against her cheek, sending shivers along her spine.

"How about you climb on like the sexy woman you are," he said in a seductive voice, "so I can feel all your sweetness pressed against my back?"

The combination of his hands clutching her hips, the scratchy taunt of his scruff against her skin, and his gravelly voice was about the sexiest thing she'd ever experienced. "When you say it like that, how can I refuse?"

She climbed onto his back and wrapped her arms around his neck. He moaned lecherously, then chuckled at his tease. She couldn't resist running her hands over his chest. His shirt was soft, his muscles hard and defined. She stretched her fingers lower, trying to touch his abs, and earning another guttural sound of desire. She'd thought of touching him for so long, she allowed herself this time on her *Ty playground*, even knowing it might not go any further. She still needed to understand what *wanting her* meant to him in the long run. She wasn't about to get tied into some sort of open relationship.

His hand slid up her calves as he navigated the rocky terrain with ease. "Oh yeah, baby. This is *nice*."

She put her mouth beside his ear as he neared the bottom of the hill and said, "So nice you might have to carry me everywhere."

He turned as he lowered her to her feet, keeping her close. She felt his hardness against her belly, and he began to sway, singing just above a whisper about how they should take this back to his place. His hands were on a mission, running up her hips, across her back, into her hair, and *boy, oh boy*, did she *love* it. She knew she should slow him down and figure out where they really stood, but he was singing about wanting to take his time, and doing this all night long, and she realized he was singing along with Niall Horan's "Slow Hands," one of her favorite songs, as it played nearby.

He turned to his side, motioning in the direction of the music, where a blanket was spread out on the ground, another folded beneath his backpack. The music was coming from his phone. He'd remembered her favorite song, too?

"You set all this up for us?" When they were in Saint-Luc he'd played his guitar and sang to her every night. It was so romantic, his voice so compelling, that he'd mesmerized her with every lyric. And when he sang, he'd looked at her like he was right at that very second, like she was the only thing that existed, opening up her heart even more.

"For you, baby cakes. Always for you."

He danced seductively and slowly as he sang, and memories of the longing she'd felt after he'd left Saint-Luc swamped her. The pain of knowing neither of them could call or text had been almost too much to bear. She'd wanted to hear his voice, *needed* it like she'd needed oxygen to survive. But her mother had taught her from a young age that wanting and needing were two very different things. True needs, like food, clothing, and a roof over her head in winter were things she should never leave up to chance. Those were things that, as an adult, she needed to work to achieve. But *wants?* Wants were taunts and teases, with the power to undermine everything she'd worked so hard for. Wants could only be handled by fate. If fate intervened, then nothing could stop what was meant to be.

As she danced in Ty's arms, she was lulled into his sultry seduction. His warm body pressed against her as he sang, and she wanted to believe *they* were meant to be. She'd spent years being careful. If her mother's early death had taught her anything, it was that opening her heart and relying on someone else was dangerous. But she *could* count on Ty. Hadn't he proven that by coming after her this afternoon, even if she hadn't wanted him to? And by not breaking his promise for all this time? The days they'd spent together in Switzerland had been full of opportunities for him to let her down, but he hadn't. Not once.

"I still can't believe you're really here with me," he said softly, and ran his finger along her jaw, no longer looking *at* her.

He was looking *through* her, into her very heart and soul, the way he had their last night together. The night she'd wanted desperately to feel his strong arms around her, his rough hands caressing her naked body as he made love to her. She'd held back then, and the rational part of her knew she needed to hold back now, but every glide of his hands heightened her desires, her *greed* for him.

"I have missed you so much," he confessed. "I ache with it."

The longing in his voice, in *her* heart, broke the last of her fraying resolve. There beneath the stars, on this gorgeous summer night, she threw caution to the wind and gave herself over to the music and the incredible man she was dancing with, allowing the pain in her leg, and the rest of the world, to take a backseat to the heat thrumming between them.

"Kiss me," she pleaded, and went up on her toes.

His full lips came down over hers, soft and demanding at once, sending her senses reeling. One of his hands dove into her hair, the other pressed to her back, bringing their bodies so close she could feel his heart beating against her own. He deepened the kiss, a hungry sound escaping his lips, vibrating through her, awakening desires that had lain dormant for far too long. He tasted like sins and blessings all tangled up and impossible to separate. And she wanted *him*, wanted *this*—more kisses, longer touches. The anticipation was killing her. He eased his efforts to a slow, lingering slide of their tongues, ending in a series of featherlight kisses along her mouth and jaw. Heat spread down her limbs, and she tried to catch her breath as he placed openmouthed kisses around her neck, tasting her all the way up to her ear. Her entire body electrified, every nerve ending flaming on the surface of her skin.

"Just as sweet and special as I remember. *My* Aiyla," he whispered, and caught her earlobe between his teeth, sending electrifying pinpricks beneath her skin.

She inhaled sharply, and he captured her mouth again, easing the sting with more delicious kisses. She clung to his neck, pushed her fingers into his hair, holding on for dear life as his hips pressed forward. His arousal was hard and tempting. His tongue moved over her teeth, along the roof of her mouth, possessing every inch of her. She was trembling, and her thoughts scrambled away. And then she was in his arms as he carried her to the blanket, reclaiming her mouth as he lay down beside her. His thigh moved over hers and her whole body arched toward him. She couldn't keep a moan from escaping into their kiss.

"Love that sound," he ground out, and dove in for more, kissing her in the same way he did everything: smooth as butter and hot as fire.

His hands moved up her torso, grazing the undersides of her breasts, and she held her breath. They hadn't gone further than kissing in Saint-Luc, and she felt his hesitation—and her own— warring with the heat pulsing between them. But she wanted his touch, *craved* it. She covered his hand with hers, and he held them together.

He drew back from the kiss, and she lifted her head, trying to recapture it.

"Your kisses *wreck* me" slipped from his lips, and then he was kissing her again, long and deep, his body sinking deliciously into hers.

Their joined hands remained still, his fingers clinging to hers, as if he needed that anchor to keep himself in check. His hot, hungry mouth moved along her jaw and down her neck, every touch of his lips sending darts of lust to her core. She didn't want him to keep himself in check. She wanted *more*.

RAW, UNBRIDLED PASSION radiated from every fiber of

Aiyla's being. Ty was as sure of it as he had ever been of anything in his life. But he'd been here before, so lost in her she was all he could see, and she'd sent him away. He'd spent the last several months picking apart what had gone wrong, and now that he knew, he wasn't leaving anything else up to fate or chance or the goddamn tooth fairy. He forced himself to pull away.

Air rushed from her lungs, and his gut clenched tight. He couldn't do it, couldn't go cold turkey after he'd just found her again.

Lowering his mouth to hers, he said, "We need to talk," between kisses. His hips rocked, his fingers clung to hers, and his cock twitched painfully beneath his shorts. But he knew he had to put on the brakes. When he forced himself to back off again, she made a mewling sound that nearly did him in. How the hell was he supposed to resist her?

He brushed his lips over hers in a series of painstakingly light kisses, easing himself away. "Aiyla, I can't do this again."

The sweetest smile he'd ever seen spread across her face. "You were doing pretty well. I'm already drunk on you."

He laughed and brought their joined hands to his lips, pressing a kiss to her fingers. "I can't get so lost in you again that I can't see straight. It messed me up last time. I'm not sure I'd survive it again."

She trapped her lower lip between her teeth, looking adorable and sexy and so fucking desirable the voice in his head called him a fool for stopping. He gazed into her eyes, willing himself not to lose control, but a tidal wave of emotions bowled him over, and he couldn't stop the truth from coming out.

"I want to make love to you until the sun comes up, and then I want to do it again and again, until the next day passes and we've used every ounce of energy, and we fall asleep in each other's arms from sheer exhaustion. And right now, with the moonlight reflecting in your eyes, you look like a dreamer, making me want to be in those dreams with you. But I know you're not. You're too grounded for that, and I feel too much for you to pretend we're something we aren't."

Her brows knitted. "What are you saying?"

"You sent me away before, and now that I understand why, I think we need to clear the air before we go any further."

She tried to pull her hand away, but he held on tight. "*Don't,*" he said too harshly, and paused, tempering his tone before saying, "Please don't pull away. This isn't going to be easy for either of us, but walking away from you is not an option, and I'm hoping that after we talk, it won't be an option for you, either."

She pushed up to a sitting position, confusion written all over her face. "I have a feeling I'm going to wish you'd just kept kissing me."

"No, you won't. You had a chance to keep kissing me forever, to travel with me and explore the world. You chose not to and for a good reason."

She looked down at her lap and he lifted her chin, gazing into her sad eyes. "You wanted to know about my past. I'm not sure what you've heard about me, but chances are it's probably true."

She shifted her eyes away again.

"Aiyla, please look at me. I want you to hear what I have to say and to know that I mean it."

"It's not exactly easy to digest what you've already said."

"I know, but nothing worth anything is easy. Remember when you told me about losing your mother? And about the first time you went white-water rafting and you fell out of the raft? You said those were the scariest times in your life. That you almost drowned in sorrow, and three years later, you almost drowned in a river, and it took everything you had to make it to the surface of both situations. That's what I feel like right now. Like everything I'm going to tell you is another wave dragging me under, but the way I see it, I can sink or I can swim. And I want to swim, Aiyla. I want to swim my fucking heart out. All I need you to do is sit in the boat and decide if you want to toss me a line or not."

She blew out a breath, fidgeting absently with the edge of her shorts. "I know I asked for this, but maybe I should have kept my mouth shut. I already hate the answer."

He expected her to get up and leave, and when she took his hand and said, "You walked away when I needed you to. I guess it's my turn to do what you need me to do," he felt like he'd been given a gift—and had to walk through a firing line to claim it.

"Thank you." He hoped he didn't appear as nervous as he felt. "The most important thing you should know is that my past is just that. My *past*."

"That has to be someone's last words somewhere. Like the thief who swears he'll never steal again?"

"I probably deserve that," he said evenly. "But I want you to know the truth. Before we met, I *was* the kind of guy who had one-night stands. I'd hook up with a beautiful woman, or two. It was a way to pass a few hours. I'm clean. I always used protection and got tested once a year—"

"Okay, first of all," she interrupted. "Two women at once? I can't even…" She turned away, and then quickly turned back and shot him a disgusted look. "Just so you know, being safe does *not* make it any better."

"I know, babe."

"And don't call me *babe*. I don't want to be one of many, Ty. I'm willing to listen, but I shouldn't have let my emotions run away like I did. It was stupid."

"Aiyla, please hear me out. I'm being blatantly honest because I care about you, and I don't want to lie to you. Not today, not ever. *Yes*, I was *that* guy, and it wasn't because I was screwed up by bad parenting or a sucky life. I have amazing parents, a supportive family, and a freaking awesome life. The truth is, I never questioned *why* I did it until I met you. And ever since I left you in Saint-Luc, I have been dissecting my relationships, if you can even call them that."

"Okay, I get it." She pushed to her feet and winced, sinking right back down to the blanket, and rubbed her leg.

"Are you okay?" He moved to touch her leg, and she shifted out of reach.

"*Fine*," she said stubbornly, though she looked like she was in even more pain than earlier. "Please don't tell me any more about you and other girls. I'm sure you don't want to picture me with other guys."

"I wasn't going to say anything else about that. And trust me, I've already tortured myself explicitly about you and other guys."

She was rubbing her leg, her face pinched in pain. Pain that was probably caused by him as much as her leg.

"Please let me help you."

"Stop, Ty. It's too hard for me to hear you say the things you're telling me *while* you're touching me like that." She bent her knees and wound her arms around her legs. "Go on. I obviously can't walk away, so I'm stuck listening."

"Maybe we should get you to an urgent care center."

She glared at him. "It's fine. You heard what the guy in the health tent told me. It's probably overuse. You're an athlete. You know how overuse injuries wax and wane. I'll be even better tomorrow. Just finish whatever it is you wanted to say."

"Okay. I'm sorry," he relented. She was as stubborn as he was, and arguing over her leg would get them nowhere. He focused on clearing the air instead. "When we were together before, I never made a move on you."

"I sure hope this is going somewhere different from where I think it's headed, because you're not doing my ego any favors now that I know your history."

"It is going somewhere. That's how I knew what we had was real, Aiyla, and different, and not something I could just put out of my mind. Don't you see? We spent five incredible days together. We went on hikes and took pictures, and stayed up until all hours of the night talking about our lives. Remember the Saint-Luc winter carnival?" It was a day he'd never forget, tobogganing down the mountain together, his hips cradling hers, his body cocooning her from behind. He could still hear her melodic laughter sailing through the air.

A reluctant smile appeared on her beautiful face, but it didn't reach her eyes, and that slayed him.

"The point is, we were never naked. Our feelings weren't built on lust. *You* were enough, Aiyla. Being with you was like nothing else I've ever experienced. Better than conquering the highest mountains or capturing the best picture. Your laughter filled me up, and your smiles, which I've envisioned every day since our last night together, made me want to do everything within my power to see more of them. We didn't just talk to each other. We shared more in those five days than some people share in a year, and not one second of it had to do with sex."

He took her hand in his and gazed openly into her eyes, knowing she'd see his hopes, as well as his fears, and wanting that honesty between them. "I haven't so much as checked out another woman since the very first day we met. If nothing else tells you how what I feel for you and what we have together is different and special, then maybe that will."

"You want me to believe you went from being a manwhore to being celibate for *me*?"

"'Manwhore' is a little harsh…"

She narrowed her eyes, and he held up his hands in surrender.

"Okay. Call me whatever you want. But yes, I expect you to believe it because it's the truth."

"You changed that much for someone you knew for only five days?" The disbelief in her eyes was taken down a notch by the trust in her voice.

"For *you*, yes. But don't you see? I didn't get up one morning and say to myself that I was going to change. It happened seamlessly, like you woke me up from a life in which I thought I was living, but really, I was searching. Or maybe *hiding*. I don't know. All I know is that the man I was before I met you and the man I became over those days we spent together are two very different people. Didn't you feel changed? Or different?"

Her expression grew serious, and his heart sank.

"If you didn't, then—"

"I did," she said quickly. "I do. Our time together changed me, too. I thought the most terrifying thing I ever did was survive my mother's death, and then that rafting incident nearly did me in. But then I met you, and I had to let you go. I was sure life couldn't get any more difficult than telling you I couldn't leave Saint-Luc with you. Maybe part of me thought I could send you away and still be okay. Or that even though I told you to stay away, you'd come running back and we could talk all of this out then. I don't know what I thought, but I believed leaving it up to fate was the right thing to do. Then, every day without you was harder than the last. I looked for you everywhere. In every crowd, every sports magazine, every online article, which I guess might sound like I broke my promise. But I didn't try to find out where you were. I just wanted to see your face and know you were okay."

A pained expression came over her, and she said, "That's not true. I wanted to see your *eyes*. I wanted to see if what I saw when we were together, what I see *right now*, was still there."

"It's still here, Aiyla, and it's not going anywhere." He reached into the backpack that was lying by his feet and set two books in her hands.

She realized they were copies of her coffee-table books, *Faces of Nature* and *Reflections*.

"I've got copies of all five of your books, and I've pored through the pages so many times, trying to see them through your eyes and trying to feel you through your pictures, that I have each of them memorized."

She leafed through a few pages. The edges were no longer crisp, but dirty with his fingerprints and soft from being touched.

"You told me that you take pictures of the elderly because of your fairy godmother, Ms. Farrington, who taught you that nothing was more beautiful than the history written in the faces of people who had lived long enough to experience all facets of love and loss. I have studied the faces in these books, and, Aiyla, I *see* what you *see*. They're exquisite in their own right. But as an artist, I have my own photographic eye, and I have seen something even more complex and beautiful."

He withdrew another book from the backpack and set it on the others. Her fingers played over the image on the cover, the hillside where they'd first met, and her eyes misted over. She traced the letters of the title and whispered, "Aeonian."

"It means ageless," he explained. "Perpetual, everlasting, permanent." All the words that reminded him of Aiyla, in one succinct adjective.

She inhaled a ragged breath as she lifted the cover and read the dedication. *For Aiyla, wherever you are.* "Oh, Ty..."

Blinking against damp eyes, she turned the page, revealing the first picture he'd ever taken of her, standing with her back to him as she gazed out at the valley below. The sun hovered over the trees in the distance, and ribbons of orange and red burned like fire in the sky, illuminating Aiyla like a vision. Heat and ice spread through his chest, the same way it had when he'd first come upon her and had taken the picture.

She turned the page, and a soft laugh escaped her lips. "Lefty Lucy."

The first evening they'd spent together in Saint-Luc, they'd walked through town and he'd asked her where a certain café was. She'd said they needed to turn right, but she'd pointed left, something she'd told him she'd done all her life. He'd made an L shape with his finger and thumb on his left hand and crossed his first two fingers on his right, teasing her about Lefty Lucy and Right Tighty. She'd made the same symbols and he'd taken the picture, capturing her laughing, her eyes dancing with amusement.

They went through all fifty pages, reliving each stolen moment—Aiyla in profile, her hair catching the morning light, her chin resting on her hand, a small smile on her lips as she watched the sunrise from the window of his hotel room after they'd stayed up all night talking. And a picture of her asleep in the passenger seat of his rental car the next afternoon, when she'd insisted they go to a particular museum. She'd fallen asleep fifteen minutes into the trip, and he'd driven around for two hours just so she wouldn't wake up. There were pictures from the winter carnival, and silly selfies of the two of them. More than an hour later, she turned to the last page, looking at his favorite picture. He'd taken it the morning after she'd told him to leave their future in fate's hands. She was sitting in the café window where they'd had breakfast every morning, at *their* table, with a faraway look in her eyes.

She lifted her gaze to his, a lone tear sliding down her cheek. "I thought you left before dawn that day."

"I was supposed to. I delayed my flight to try to talk you into coming with me. And then I chickened out. I thought it would push you further away." He wiped her tear with the pad of his thumb. "When I look at that picture, I like to think you were envisioning the day we'd meet again."

"I was thinking about buying a plane ticket and following you." A sweet, soulful smile appeared on her lips, and she reached for his hand. "I wonder what it says about me that I fell for a player when I've only been with thirty-five men in my entire life."

He felt his eyes widen and tried to school his expression, but *holy hell. Thirty-five men?* Who was he to judge? He couldn't even imagine her sitting in a bar picking up guys. Maybe she met them on the slopes. *Or on hillsides in Switzerland.* He ground his teeth together, wanting to ask if she'd been with anyone since she'd met him, but that would make him even more of a jerk, wouldn't it? Would it matter if she had?

Is this what went through your head when I told you the truth? Man, I hate this.

"Relax, macho man." She scooted closer. "However many it's really been, it's surely a better number than yours."

He cradled her beautiful face between his hands, his insides aching with adoration and jealousy. "I never thought my past could hurt anyone, but now I know I was wrong. I will do everything within my power to prove to you how much I've changed."

She leaned forward and pressed her lips to his. "You just did."

His mouth descended upon hers, sealing his vow and reveling in her sweetness. The din of the campers on the ridge above faded, replaced with the gentle sounds of the water, the chirping of crickets, and other nightly nature sounds. They kissed and talked, and eventually they fell silent, their fully clothed bodies intertwined as they gazed up at the stars. Ty pulled the extra blanket around them and wrapped her in his arms, listening to the even cadence of her breathing as she drifted in and out of sleep. Tonight ranked right up there with the most difficult— and most beautiful—moments of his life. His fingers itched for his camera, but he knew not even the best photographer in the world could capture the immensity of his emotions.

"Three," she whispered.

He figured she was in the gray space between sleep and wakefulness. Dreaming with her eyes open. "Three?"

"That's my number." She snuggled closer.

He kissed the top of her head and closed his eyes, eager to prove himself worthy of being number four—her best, and *final*, partner.

Chapter Five

AIYLA STARTLED AWAKE at the sound of Ty's phone alarm, their bodies still intertwined. He tightened his hold around her, the colorful sunrise reflecting in his eyes.

"Just one more minute," he said in a groggy voice.

The alarm continued beeping from somewhere behind him. "Shouldn't you at least turn it off?"

He nuzzled against her. "Not if it means letting go of you."

"Finally y'all are awake." Trixie's voice startled them.

Ty groaned and pressed his hand to the back of Aiyla's head, holding her still. "Don't move," he whispered conspiratorially. "She might mistake us for part of the landscape."

A shadow fell over them as Trixie turned off Ty's alarm and tossed his phone beside them. Her dark hair was pinned up in a high ponytail. She set her hands on her hips, flashing a playful smile. "That whole landscape thing isn't really happening. Please tell me you've got pants on under there, because you've got an audience."

She pointed up at the top of the ridge, where Speed and James and a handful of other people cheered and whistled and hollered.

"Thank God we're *not* naked," Aiyla said.

"There are worse things in life than getting caught in the arms of Ty Braden," Trixie said. "Like skinny-dipping in a neighbor's pool and realizing too late that they have motion sensor lights pointed directly at you."

Aiyla winced. "*That* would be embarrassing."

"Especially if you weren't alone," Trixie said on her way up the hill.

"I don't want to know this about you." Ty covered his ears.

Aiyla crawled out from under the blanket, and as Ty sat up, he grabbed her around the waist, hauling her onto his lap. Drawn to him like a bee to honey, she wrapped her arms around his neck. He pressed his lips to hers, causing more cheers to ring out from the peanut gallery.

"Thank you for hearing me out last night," he said.

"Thank you for being honest with me."

He eyed the gawkers at the top of the hill. "Shall we give them something to talk about?"

"Who gives a crap about them? Give *me* something to talk about."

He kissed her deeply, earning a round of applause. She felt a momentary pang of embarrassment, but as quickly as the applause had sounded, it faded away, taking her embarrassment with it, until all she heard were the hungry sounds of her and Ty's kisses and all she felt was the desire for more. His hands moved into her hair, something she'd already come to expect. When he wound her hair around his fingers, her insides flamed, and she felt him get hard beneath her.

He smiled against her lips. "If we didn't have an audience, you might be in big trouble." The devilish intent in his eyes left no room for misinterpretation.

"I wish we could stay right here all day." *Kissing and touch-*

ing and making up for lost time.

"Ride with me today. Be my partner in the rafting race."

Her heart screamed, *Yes!* But she was determined to complete this race on her own. "We signed up as singles, not a couple."

"Hurry up, guys!" Trixie called. "You need to take down your tents!"

They pushed to their feet, and pain shot down her leg. She dug a few pain pills from her pocket, and Ty handed her a bottle of water from his backpack. "Thanks."

He watched her take the pills as he gathered the blankets. "You're basically living on those things."

She grabbed his backpack and he took it from her and swung it over his shoulder.

"It's just Motrin and Tylenol, to take the edge off. Today's the rafting race, so there'll be no strain on my leg, and by tomorrow I'll be as good as new."

He carried the blankets in one arm and put his other around her. "You know that's not true. You'll use your legs to anchor you in the boat in rough water."

"I'll be fine." She didn't want to argue about her capabilities, not after the beautiful night they'd had.

"Listen, Speed—*Jon*—is a doctor. Why don't you let him check you out?"

"The ladies' man? No thanks. I'm fine. It's just overuse." He was loaded down like a packrat with the backpack and blankets. "Do you want me to take one of those blankets?"

He draped one blanket around his neck, carrying the other under his arm. "Not a chance, my stubborn girl. I'm not putting any more weight on your leg than necessary. And I'm going up the hill behind you in case you have trouble."

"What am I, five?" She cringed at her knee-jerk reaction and began climbing the rocky hill, stifling the urge to curse at the dull ache in her leg.

"You're stubborn enough to be," he teased.

"So I've been told." *Too many times to count.* At the top of the hill, she pushed off with her foot. "Ow, *shit.*"

He put his hand on her ass, boosting her up to flat ground. "Babe, what have you got to prove? You'll still finish the race for your sponsors."

"I told you," she ground out, limping toward her tent. She didn't *want* to fight with him, but between the ache in her leg and not wanting to appear weak, she was stuck in some confusing middle ground. "I don't need a knight in shining armor. I've got this."

"Goddamn it, woman," he said sharply. "I'm not trying to do the race *for* you. We just got past a major hurdle last night, and I want to spend time with you. Is that a fucking crime?"

She spun around, her heart squashing her pride one beat at a time. "You just want to spend *time* with me?"

"Yes! Is that so hard to believe?"

"*Not* because I'm limping?" she challenged. "Or because you think I'm scared to do it alone because of almost drowning? Because I'm not. That incident just made me more determined to kick every river's butt every chance I get."

"Jesus." His tone softened, and her resolve followed. "How did I fall for the one woman who doesn't want help?" A sexy smile lifted his lips. "I worry for the rivers you take on. I want you with me, Aiyla. Stubbornness and all."

"Why didn't you just say that?" she snapped. A whirlwind of emotions burgeoned inside her, and the frustration over the unrelenting pain in her leg made it difficult to control her emotions.

He dropped the blankets and closed the distance between them. "Either you need a hearing aid or I need English lessons."

"I'm sorry," she relented. "It's my fault. My leg *does* hurt, and I hate to admit it, much less accept help to get past it. I thought you were just trying to…"

"Do the right thing?" he offered. "Be your *boyfriend*? Because that's what I am now. We spent the night together under the stars. In some cultures, that means we're married."

She laughed and touched her forehead to the center of his chest, wishing she hadn't reacted so poorly. "For a world traveler, you know very little about other cultures."

"Are you saying I'm wrong? Because I'm pretty sure it's the Bradonian way."

"Ah, *that* culture. By that standard, we were married back in Saint-Luc."

"Which explains my fidelity. Now kiss me before I drag you by your hair back to my tent and show you what happens to women who argue with Bradonian men."

"Promises, promises."

TY HAD TO do some fast talking and shell out a few bucks on the ride over to the river to get his buddies to give up their two-person raft and take his and Aiyla's singles. As they geared up for the race, stealing kisses every chance they got, Trixie teased them about getting a room. He was all in, wanting privacy as badly as Trixie wanted them to find it. And from the heat in Aiyla's touch, he knew she was on the same page. They were right back where they'd been his last night in Saint-Luc—only this time she knew the truth about his past, and she *wasn't* holding back. By the time they started the race, Aiyla was favoring her leg even more than she had that morning, and they were closer than they'd been just hours earlier.

Aiyla sat in the front of the raft, paddling like her arms were made for it, keeping up a demanding pace to remain near the front of the competition. By midafternoon, her skin glistened with the sheen of a golden tan. The unforgiving sun beat down on them like a competitor all its own, oppressive and constant. The splash of the icy water was a welcome reprieve.

"My girlfriend is a fierce competitor in her own right," he called out to her. "But together we're unstoppable."

"Double trouble," they said in unison.

Ty had traveled all over the world, but as far as rivers went, none compared to the wild Colorado, which had carved its path over time, creating epic scenery of jagged cliffs, mountainous terrain, and flowering prairies. Ty had taken one of his favorite nature photographs on this very river—a rainbow in the mist by a waterfall. It was a heart-stopping picture. But when they hit calmer water and Aiyla glanced over her shoulder, locking her bright hazel eyes on him, *nothing* compared to the beauty sitting an arm's length away.

"How are you holding up back there, Bradonian?" Before he could answer, she said, "Are your fingers itching to climb those rocks?"

"My fingers are itching, and there's something I want to climb, but it's not rocks." He wanted to guide the boat to the shore and show her just how much he'd missed her. He'd start with massaging her leg, kissing away the pain, and work his way up her body, until he'd tasted and memorized every inch. He gripped the paddle tighter, trying to fight the onslaught of dirty thoughts.

Her laughter sailed around them, and she tipped her head up toward the sky and sighed. He imagined her gazing up at him when he was buried deep inside her, and just like that he was hard as stone. He dipped his hand into the cool water and splashed it on his face, but the image of her lying beneath him was too strong and the desire to make it real was even stronger. He doused his chest and groin with water, mentally trying to calculate the time it would take him to hike the final leg of the race tomorrow. Anything to distract himself from more cock-hardening thoughts.

When he was able to breathe a little easier, he said, "How's your leg holding up?"

"Fine." A second later she said, "Not exactly fine, but it's okay. I could have done it alone, but I'm glad you asked me to ride with you. I've missed you."

How could three words make his heart feel so full? "I've missed *us*."

Damn, had he ever missed her. Her voice, that smile, those lips. Staying on safer topics than exploring the dips and curves of her body, he said, "Did you get to that little village outside Saint-Luc to take pictures?"

"You really do remember everything." She glanced at him again, and in the few seconds their eyes connected, sparks ignited.

She faced front again and thrust her paddle in the water. He doused himself with more cold water, but short of diving in, he held no hope of his erection deflating.

"I never got there," she said. "But I hope to someday. What about you? Did you get the assignment in South Africa you were vying for? In that Xhosa village?"

"It looks like it. We're hoping to schedule time early next year."

She *whoop*ed just as they hit the rapids. "I'm so happy for you! You're going to get amazing pictures."

When he'd first told her about the potential assignment, they'd talked for hours about the remote South African villages she'd visited with Ms. F as a teenager, and the ones she still wanted to visit. He'd imagined taking those trips together, spending days exploring, climbing, taking pictures and learning about the cultures, and spending long steamy nights wrapped in each other's arms.

Come with me was on the tip of his tongue, but he forced himself to hold back, afraid of rushing her and wanting to push her in equal measure. Instead he said, "Remember when we made that list of the places we wanted to show each other?"

The nose of the raft lifted and fell over the rapids, dousing them with water, earning a shriek of delight from Aiyla. Music to his ears.

"How could I forget?" she hollered. "Your list included three of the world's tallest mountains, and mine were mostly desolate little villages."

They fell silent as they navigated rougher water, struggling to keep pace with the others as the raft careened at angles that could toss them out at any second. Ty's entire focus shifted from winning the race to keeping Aiyla safe. But she was shrieking and laughing, taking it all in stride, as fearless as ever.

When the river widened and the rapids tamed, she glanced over her shoulder and he leaned in, stealing a slippery, rocky kiss, as the competition paddled by.

"We make a great team, baby." He pulled her into another kiss, hearing more rafts approaching and Speed's voice hollering something about taking their time.

He and Aiyla came away laughing. Her eyes were as bright as her smile. Her hair clung to her shoulders, drenched, like her clothing. Her arms were red from their efforts, and if she was fatigued, it didn't show. He was falling head over heels for her all over again, with no desire to put on the brakes.

He leaned in for another kiss, and she said, "We'll fall behind."

He felt a smile tugging at his lips. "Never again, baby cakes. Don't you feel it? We're an invincible force. No one can touch us."

Chapter Six

THE RIVER RACE had stopping points along the shore with volunteers waiting with food and first aid. Aiyla and Ty chose not to stop and ate energy bars on the raft to make up for their impromptu make-out sessions, of which they'd had many over the course of the day. Ty had been making sexy innuendos all afternoon, flashing his killer smile, and touching her every chance he got. Aiyla wasn't sure she'd be able to keep her hands to herself once they were on dry land, especially knowing that his feelings for her had driven him to introspection, and in turn, to becoming an even better man.

As they neared the finish line, spectators cheered from the shore. Aiyla and Ty were neck and neck with Speed and two other competitors. Even though they'd reregistered as a couple for this leg of the race and weren't technically in competition with Speed or the other two solo rafters, with the *win* in sight, adrenaline surged inside Aiyla, and the drive for first place took over. Crossing the finish line together with Ty would be even more meaningful. All of her senses were heightened as they paddled down the final stretch. They moved wordlessly onto the sides of the raft, their arms pumping harder with every downward strike.

"Hell no!" Speed yelled when they plowed past him. He kicked up his efforts, the nose of his raft sailing ahead, then falling behind as they plowed past.

"Faster!" Aiyla hollered, rising onto one knee to deepen her strides.

Ty's laughter was swallowed by the cheers of the crowd. "We've got this, baby!"

They flew past the other competitors, putting them in first place. Aiyla cheered, but just as the high-pitched sound left her lungs, Speed flew past again. In the next stroke, she and Ty nosed past him by a handful of inches, crossing the finish line first, with a trail of competitors in their wake. They held up their paddles, screaming and cheering, and fell into each other's arms—and out of the boat—laughing and kissing as their entangled bodies crashed into the cold, dark water.

Ty clung to her with one arm, using his other to help propel them upward. They breached the surface, bobbing beside their raft, panting, and kicking their feet to stay afloat. All around them rafts sailed past, collecting in groups near the shore. Aiyla had won races before, but never had she felt so fulfilled, so completely and utterly elated, as she did right then in the cold water, clinging to her man. She pressed her mouth to his, and as always, she quickly got lost in him. Her legs failed to function, and they began to sink below the surface. Someone grabbed her from behind, lifting her a few inches out of the water. She blinked away the heat of the moment and followed Ty's annoyed gaze to Speed, who was holding her up by the shoulder of her life vest.

"Christ, Braden," he said with a smirk. "You trying to drown the poor woman?"

Ty's gaze shifted to her. As if he'd read her thoughts, all that annoyance turned to something much deeper, causing her heart to tumble out. "I could drown in you and I'd still be more alive than ever."

"Aw, baby." His words were full of emotion, and as his mouth came down over hers, Speed uttered a curse and released her life jacket, sending them sinking once again.

A few hours later, they were taken to their campsite, where they showered and changed into warm, dry clothes. Aiyla took another round of painkillers, wondering how she was going to get through tomorrow's hike but unwilling to give up. She was gathering her toiletries when Trixie came into the bathroom.

"There's the girl who's got Ty's heart all aflutter." Trixie opened one of the shower stalls and hung up her towel.

"Hi," Aiyla said, doing a silent happy dance over her comment. "We had fun today."

"Clearly. He's out there setting up your tent beside his, *far* away from everyone else." She stepped inside the stall and turned on the shower, speaking loudly from behind the door. "I've never seen him like this."

He's setting up my tent? "Like what?" Aiyla ran a brush through her hair.

"I've known Ty for years, and he's always been an every-man-for-himself type of competitor. But with you, everything's different."

"I hope you mean different in a good way."

"Yes, in a good way."

"Do you guys see each other a lot?" Aiyla asked.

"A few times a year at charity events, and when I'm in Maryland working with his cousin Nick, who's a freestyle horse trainer. We get together for drinks or dinner. You know, hang out and give each other a hard time." A few minutes later the water shut off, and she said, "He's like an overprotective brother to me. Wait. When did you last see him?"

"Over the winter. About four months ago."

"That explains a lot." Her towel flopped over the top of the stall, and Aiyla heard her getting dressed. She stepped out of the stall in a pair of jeans and a hoodie, finger-combing her hair. "Don't take this wrong. I love Ty. He'll give a stranger the shirt off his own back. But I'm used to seeing him check out anything in a skirt, and when we had drinks a couple months ago, he wouldn't give anyone the time of day, and I mean *anyone*."

Aiyla couldn't help but smile. "He sort of mentioned that to me."

"He did? That's different, too. Ty's a master at keeping women at arm's length. I guess when you hooked up in Switzerland, you two really hit it off. I mean, it's obvious how hot you are together. Y'all practically combust every time you look at each other." She flipped her head over and began drying her hair.

"We didn't *hook up*," Aiyla corrected her.

Trixie gave her an incredulous look. "Come on. Y'all never..."

She shook her head. "I can't believe I'm telling you this, but no." She pushed herself up and sat on the counter. "We were together twenty-four seven for five days, but we never..." Her confession hung in the air between them.

"No freaking way. Holy shit, Aiyla. Why not? I mean, *look* at him."

"It wasn't like we didn't want to, but you know, he's *Ty Braden*, and I'd heard about his reputation, so I wasn't in a hurry to jump into bed with him. But we hiked, and went to museums, and were busy every second. We stayed up most nights talking, and we didn't leave each other's side for five whole days. The few hours we did sleep, we were in each other's arms, but fully dressed, and we usually fell asleep wherever we were talking. On the balcony, on a couch, on the floor. It was like we were instantly so connected, we didn't need *that* to make it real. I fell *hard* for him, but I honestly wasn't even sure we'd ever see each other again." She explained what happened on their last night together and how they'd left their relationship up to fate. "And now here we are, and it's like no time—*and a lifetime*—has passed. Everything feels more intense. Even better than I ever imagined it could be."

"Wow. That's what my mama calls 'the real thing.' My parents met when they were teenagers. My mother said no matter how many times they broke up, life kept leading them back to each other." She went back to drying her hair and said, "I need to get myself a dose of whatever you and Ty found in Switzerland."

They talked for a few more minutes, and then Aiyla went in search of Ty. She followed the dimly lit lanterns illuminating the tents to the far reaches of the camp, wondering if magic like her and Ty's ever struck twice.

She saw Ty pacing on the far side of a line of shrubs, his phone pressed to his ear. Their tents were set up a few feet away. He hadn't spotted her, and she took a moment to really look at him. He stopped pacing and raked a hand through his hair, staring into the darkness, his back to her. Worn denim hugged his powerful thighs and slim waist, making his shoulders appear even broader beneath his long-sleeved black shirt. She wanted to wrap her arms around him, press her cheek against that soft shirt, and feel his hard muscles. Her insides went ten types of crazy at the thought of being close.

How did that happen from just looking at him?

There was something magnetic about him. He seemed to always be in motion, even when he was still. Like his mind was whirring and it created an energy around him, calling out to her and drawing her in.

She went to put her clothes away, and a few minutes later Ty's handsome face appeared through the flaps of the tent.

"Hey, sweet girl. Want some company?"

She sat on her sleeping bag and motioned for him to come closer. He crawled to her like a lion on the prowl, moving over her, one hand on either side, nipping at her lips as he caged her in beneath him. She lowered herself down to the sleeping bag, her heart racing at the predatory look in his eyes. He smelled fresh and manly, his hair still damp from the shower. She tried to lift her hand to touch him, but he laced their fingers together beside her head. His hard body pressed down on her, and *boy,* did he feel incredible.

"Thank you for setting up my tent," she said as he kissed the edges of her mouth, working his way down her neck, making all her best parts buzz with desire.

"I couldn't let my girl do it all by herself."

"That was really sweet of you," she said as he tugged the neckline of her shirt down with his teeth and kissed her breastbone. *Lord, that's hot.* He dragged his tongue along her collarbone, his warm breath sending shivers of heat racing down her chest as she gathered her courage and said, "I was kind of hoping we would share *one* tent tonight."

Their eyes connected, and for a beat everything stilled. She could barely see past the desire burning within her as his mouth claimed hers, hard and demanding, kissing her like he was never going to let her go. *Yes! Please!* He intensified the kiss. His hands slipped from hers, and he cradled her face as if he wouldn't take a chance of her breaking their connection—or he couldn't get enough of her. Lord knew she couldn't get enough of him.

Her hips rose beneath him and he gyrated his hard length against her, obliterating her ability to think. His fingers tangled in her hair, angling her mouth so he could take the kiss even deeper. She'd dreamed of this moment, fantasized about *how* and *when* and *if*—but nothing could ever have prepared her for the way the rest of the world failed to exist, or the incredible heightening of her senses. She heard his every breath, felt each powerful stroke of his tongue as if it were in slow motion, dragging her under, dangerously intoxicating. Their hearts slammed out a frantic rhythm, and their bodies rocked and arched. She clawed at his back, her knees opening wider, wanting every plane of him touching her. Wanton sounds streamed from her lungs, and he made an utterly *male* noise that sped through her, revving her up, making her needier, *greedier* for more.

She tugged at the back of his shirt. "Off," she said into their kiss.

He reached over his back with one hand and yanked his shirt over his head as she grabbed the hem of hers.

"Mine too." She rose beneath him, and he helped her take off her shirt.

She pushed at her bra straps, and he made quick work of ridding her of that, too. She fell back to the sleeping bag, and he lowered his chest to hers. His skin was warm and soft, his muscles hard, a heady combination made even more enticing by the hunger and emotions in his eyes. She ran her hands up his arms, reveling in his strength, anxiously awaiting another kiss.

He held her gaze and brushed his lips teasingly over hers before moving lower, kissing her chin, her neck, and placing open-mouthed, mind-numbing kisses across each shoulder. He took his time, each kiss chased by goose bumps, every touch making her tremble and shake. She closed her eyes. Every kiss was slow and tender, as if he were savoring every second of his journey from her shoulder to the swell of her breasts.

He teased her nipples between his finger and thumb, kissing the valley between her breasts. The tantalizing sensations were almost too much to bear. She felt like she might burst. The air rushed from her lungs as he ran his tongue around her nipple, circling one, then the other, in a maddening rhythm, making her body hum with anticipation. His hot breath coasted over the wet trails, sending ice and heat crashing through her.

"Ty, *please.*" She grabbed his head, arching up as he lowered his mouth over one taut peak. "Oh God, *yes—*"

TY WAS IN heaven, finally able to love Aiyla the way he craved. Every stroke of his tongue brought another tremor, more sinful sounds from her beautiful mouth. He wanted to stay right there, earning more wanton noises, feeling the need in her building beneath him. But it wasn't nearly enough. His cock throbbed, his heart ached, and every taste brought more dark, lascivious thoughts. He slicked his tongue along the center of her body, down her belly, but had to return to her gorgeous breasts again and again, loving the way she writhed beneath him, moaning and pleading for more. Her breasts were warm and full, and he filled his palms with them as he kissed his way down the center of her body again, and she made more greedy sounds. Thrills bolted through him. *Fuck*. He wanted to hear that sound in his sleep. He wanted to *be* that sound, heating her up inside until she couldn't hold back.

He dragged his tongue around her belly button and sank his teeth into the surrounding tender skin, sucking hard enough to cause a sting that he knew she'd feel between her legs. She bowed up beneath him, her fingers digging into his scalp, sending spikes of pleasure and pain straight to his cock.

"Oh my *God*—"

"Too much?" he asked quickly, kissing the tender spot he'd caused.

"*No, no, no*. Don't stop."

"I'm not stopping, baby. Not now, not ever."

He loved her belly, sucking and biting, kissing and caressing, as her nails dragged across his shoulders, digging into his skin. He drank in every sexy moan. His heart hammered against his ribs as he unbuttoned her jeans. She pushed at the waist, shoving them down her hips, and he was quick to comply, tossing them, and her pretty panties, aside. He slipped off her socks, and was momentarily overwhelmed at his beautiful, trusting girlfriend laying bare before him. Her hair fanned out around her, her hands fisted in the sleeping bag, her skin flushed and gorgeous. Emotions bubbled up inside him, his heart swelling to painful proportions. He went a little wild, carefully kissing his way up her legs, around her knees, and lavished her thighs with wet, heated kisses, until she was moaning, her sex glistening temptingly, luring him in. There was no holding back, no slowing down, as he lowered his mouth between her legs and her essence spread over his tongue. He couldn't suppress a groan at his first taste of her sweetness.

Her hips rose, and he grabbed hold of them, his forearms

trapping her thighs against the sleeping bag as he devoured her sex. His tongue thrust in deep, then slicked along the length of her swollen lips. He teased over her most sensitive nerves with his fingers. Her thighs flexed, and when he sealed his mouth over her sex again, she cried out.

Her hand flew over her mouth, silencing her magnificent sounds. Her hips bucked in fast, jerking movements, but he didn't relent. He filled his hands with her sweet ass, lifting her to a better angle, and took her right up to the edge again, holding her there, teasing her with his tongue and earning a series of muffled gasps and pleas.

"Ty!" came out as a whispered demand. "*Please!*"

He thrust two fingers into her velvety heat and sucked her clit between his teeth.

"*Oooooooh!*" Her body quaked and quivered, rising beneath him. Her heels dug into the ground as she came, crying, "Ty!" so loud he was sure it echoed in the forest.

He was okay with that. He wanted the entire world to know she was his—and he was hers. *So damn hers.* She fucking owned him.

When she came down from the peak, panting and trembling, he kissed her inner thighs, her sex, her belly, and went back again for another taste between her legs, before stripping off his jeans and sheathing his cock. She clung to his biceps as he came down over her, aligning their bodies and gazing into her eyes.

"I always thought I was living the life I wanted, but from the moment I met you, I knew I was wrong." The words came unbidden, but he wanted her to feel their powerful truth. "I was living the best life I could without the only person who could complete me. *You're* the life I want, Aiyla. *You* by my side, in my bed, sharing adventures, every moment of every day."

"Love me, Ty. Let me feel everything you've been holding back."

As their bodies came together, adrenaline and love *whooshed* through him, sending him higher as he cradled her body against him and they found their rhythm. They made love slowly and tenderly, then fast and demanding. Her fingers pressed into his shoulders as he clutched her hips, lifting and angling, loving her deeper, harder.

"There, *there!*" she cried out. "*Don't stop!*"

Stop? Nothing could stop him now. Heat coursed through his veins, down his spine, burning hotter with every thrust. She felt so tight, so good. When she cried out his name again, his mouth descended upon hers, swallowing every erotic sound, pulling him deeper into her, until he succumbed to his own powerful release.

Chapter Seven

AIYLA AWOKE THE next morning to the feel of Ty's lips tickling her waist and trailing up her ribs. She closed her eyes, running her fingers through his soft hair and enjoying every titillating sensation as he rolled her onto her back. His rough hands moved down to her hips as he kissed her neck and jaw the way he knew drove her crazy. They'd fallen asleep in each other's arms last night and had awoken a few hours later, enraptured once more. Not exactly the best night's sleep before a twelve-mile hike, but she didn't care if she was tired. She didn't care if she came in last in the race. All that mattered was that fate had stepped in and brought her back to the man who had captured her heart from their first encounter.

Ty settled his hips between her legs, his hard length nestled against her sex, his eyes dark and alluring as he smiled down at her. "How's my favorite girl this morning?"

"Wishing we didn't have to race today, so we could stay like this all day long."

"Mm. I like the sound of that." He lowered his mouth to hers and dragged his hard length along her entrance until she was wet, her sex pulsing with desire.

He lowered his mouth to her breast and she arched up,

holding him there. "*God*," came out in one long breath.

"You can call me *Ty*, baby cakes." He chuckled, and she guided his mouth to her other breast.

"You make my whole body come alive when you do that."

He grazed his teeth over the taut peak, sending electrical pulses between her legs.

"Ty," she panted out. "You said you got tested. You're clean?"

He lifted his head with a serious expression. "I wouldn't be with you if I weren't. I'd never risk your health. Not for anything."

She wound her arms around him and lifted her hips, burying the head of his cock inside her. He groaned, his eyes dark and hungry. She had a burning desire, an aching *need* to feel every inch of him inside her.

"Careful, baby. I've got no control when it comes to you."

"Good. I want you to lose control. I'm on birth control, and I want to feel *all* of you with nothing between us."

"Baby" flew from his lips.

His mouth came down over hers at the same moment he thrust his hips, burying himself to the hilt. They both stilled, and in the next breath they were grasping and groping, their bodies thrusting to an urgent beat.

"Aiyla, baby," he said against her neck. "Jesus, our bodies were made for each other."

His hands pushed beneath her ass, lifting as her legs circled his waist. He took her harder, groaning low in his throat. His tongue plundered as he pounded into her. *Yes! Yes!* She reached low on his back, feeling the power of his hips with each magnificent movement as he filled her so completely, stroking over the magical spot that made her thighs lock. Her nails dug into his skin, and she knew it had to hurt, but she couldn't stop, didn't want to miss a second of the fiery pleasures burning between them.

He released her ass, and she met every thrust with a rock of her hips as he buried his fingers in her hair, holding on so tight she felt the sting rippling through her, unleashing waves of ecstasy.

"Ty! Oh God, *Ty*—"

Her climax was pure and explosive, and he kept her at the peak so long her legs shook, her belly burned, and her sex pulsed relentlessly. She felt transported, carried away by dizzying sensations. When he finally slowed his pace, allowing her to come down from the clouds, he took her in a tender, loving kiss. Her body flooded with emotions too big to deny. They'd been there from the very start all those months ago and had grown more powerful with every passing day. Memories of his laughter, his kisses, and his strong hands in hers had nourished those emotions, turning them into invisible cables, binding them together even while they were worlds apart. It was no surprise that now, as he lavished her with his love, they were soaring to a new level.

He pressed his cheek to hers, dragging his hard length in and out of her at an excruciatingly slow pace. "You anchor me, baby. Heart, mind, and soul. I'm yours, every blessed inch of me."

Fire spread through her as his lips came coaxingly down over hers, quickly overridden by the turbulence of their passion. Tingles began in her legs and engulfed her core, until her body shuddered in ecstasy, and it was all she could do to remember how to breathe. Ty was right there with her, cradling her beneath him as he followed her into oblivion.

They lay together for a long while afterward, their bodies tangled and damp from their lovemaking. Ty nuzzled against her neck, his hands moving soothingly over her back. He made her feel safe and special, and they'd lost so many months that could have been spent together. She wished she'd never asked him to leave Switzerland without her.

"How's your leg?"

"Okay, but I need some Motrin."

As he handed her the bottle, he said, "Let's watch the sunrise."

"Okay, but I want to get cleaned up first." She took the meds and set the bottle aside.

A spark of mischief rose in his eyes. "Good idea. Shower with me."

"Where? It isn't like they set up coed showers just for us." She laughed.

He handed her the sweatshirt she'd worn last night and peeked out of the tent as he put on his own. "It's quiet, too early for anyone else to be awake. We'll be done before anyone else wakes up."

"What if someone catches us?" She pulled on her underwear and shorts.

He tackled her beneath him. "I'll say I kidnapped you. Come on. It'll be fun, and I'm not done putting my hands all over you."

That thought, and a few steamy kisses, not only convinced her it was a good idea, but as they tiptoed through the camp, she was excited at the prospect of their secret shared shower.

"You go in first," he said at the entrance to the ladies' room. "Make sure it's empty so I don't freak anyone out."

She took a step away and he tugged her back. She landed

against his chest with an *oomph* and a smile as he planted a hard kiss on her lips.

"Can't go too long without one of those." He smacked her ass, chuckling as she headed into the bathroom.

She caught sight of herself in the mirror. A ridiculous grin was plastered on her face, her hair was a knotted mess, and her cheeks were pink from her arousal and the brisk mountain air. She looked *happy*. Truly, deeply joyful. The last time she was this happy, they were tossing a coin to decide which way to turn on their first adventure together in Switzerland. She was sure they were the luckiest people on earth to have found each other again, and as she checked the stalls, she wondered where they'd go from here. There was no way in hell she was making the same mistake again, but she didn't want to give up traveling, or her dreams of going to the villages Ms. Farrington had told her about. And she didn't want Ty to miss out on the places he wanted to go either.

With the coast clear, she opened the door and motioned for Ty to come in. He put their towels and toiletries in the stall while she pinned up her hair so she wouldn't have to take the time to dry it before watching the sunrise. They stripped quickly, shivering as the shower heated up. He ran his hands from her thighs to her shoulders, warming her as he guided her beneath the shower spray. Careful not to get her hair wet, he lowered his lips to hers. Their bodies slid against each other. He groped her bottom, caressing each cheek, and she felt him get hard.

"I love your body, baby," he said as he soaped up his hands and began washing her.

He washed along her shoulders, down her arms, all the way to her fingertips as he kissed her. His cock slid against her belly as he bathed her breasts, under her arms, and down her waist, taking his time and caressing every bit of her, until all her nerves were heightened and she was damp between her legs. When he sank down, washing her legs, all the way down to her ankles, the rest of her body missed him, and her hands moved over her breasts, soaking them with bubbles.

Ty looked up from where he was crouched before her, water falling like rain down his back, sliding along his pecs. Her gaze followed the water sliding down his abs to his eager erection. God, she wanted him again—badly.

"You keep touching yourself like that and you're going to get dirty again." He pressed his lips to her leg as he washed her inner thighs.

"Do you think that helps?" She shifted her leg, brushing against his hard length, and let her hand drop to the apex of her thighs. "You took away my play toy. What do you *want* me to do?"

"Exactly what you're doing." He guided her beneath the spray, washing away the soap and watching her every move as she teased over her swollen sex. "Fuck, baby. I could come just watching you touch yourself."

Now, there's an idea.

He kissed her thighs, his gaze boring into her, making her feel sexy and spurring her on.

"Lick me," she said a little nervously, and he brought his mouth to her sex, licking and kissing until she was trembling. "I'll come if you keep doing that."

He rose, and she pushed him back down by his shoulder. "Don't stop what you're doing. I want to watch you touch me *and* yourself."

His eyes darkened, but she saw a second of hesitation. "You want me to...?"

She nodded. She was dying to drop to her knees and taste him, but he made her feel adventurous and safe, and she'd never felt that way with a man before. She'd spent months conjuring all sorts of erotic fantasies with Ty featured front and center. She didn't want to put off *any* of their desires, and it made her feel bold and willing to push her boundaries. "I want to watch you, you know…"

"*Fuck*, baby. You've got a naughty side."

"I've had lots of time to think about you doing all sorts of things."

She dipped her fingers into her sex. He grabbed her wrist and sucked her fingers clean; then he guided them between her legs. "There is nothing I won't do for you."

As he brought his mouth to her sex, he fisted his cock, and her insides flamed. The sight of his big hand wrapped around his shaft, watching him stroke himself as he pleasured her, nearly made her lose her mind. Her fingers moved faster, chasing the orgasm stacking up inside her. She wanted to feel what he did—his cock swelling within her hand. Wanted to be the reason his breathing stilted and his eyes darkened. She was so focused on watching him that when he did something with his tongue that sent waves of pleasure crashing over her, she reached for the wall to stabilize her numbing legs. She pulled up on Ty's arms, bringing him to his feet, while she sank down to her knees and took him in her mouth.

"*Christ*, baby."

Her love for him swelled, filling up all her empty spaces. And when he stumbled back, leaning against the wall, and watching, she loved him with all she had—hands and mouth, heart and soul.

AFTER AIYLA BLEW Ty's mind, he took a few minutes to recover, because *damn*…she did things with her tongue that held him at the edge so long, he came harder than he ever had. They washed up amid more kisses and sweet words, and Ty helped her dry her hair, which had gotten wet despite their initial efforts to the contrary. It was such a simple thing, running his fingers through her hair as she blew it dry, but it felt intimate and special, like she was allowing him to do more than what guys typically did for their girlfriends. He never imagined himself helping a woman dry her hair, but there was nothing he didn't want to experience with Aiyla. He finally understood how his siblings had all fallen so hard and so fast for their significant others. He'd thought they were nuts, giving up their freedom. What he'd never realized was that living a life free of commitments, without that special someone who made every minute feel more powerful, brighter, and made him feel even more alive than ever, wasn't freedom at all. It was like playing Hot Potato, jumping from one wrong situation to the next.

They dropped their things off at the tent and headed out to a ridge Ty had spotted the day before. They draped a blanket around their shoulders to ward off the brisk morning chill, and Aiyla rested her head against the crook of his shoulder as they watched rivers of orange, red, yellow, and gray leak across the sky.

Ty took a few pictures with his phone, wishing he had his real camera, and then he and Aiyla took selfies, smiling and kissing and making goofy faces.

"I'm so happy right now," he said, unable to contain his burgeoning emotions.

"Me too."

"I feel like I'm living that song 'Love Someone' by Brett

Eldredge."

"Oh my gosh! I love that song!" She hummed the tune to the song, wiggling her shoulders to the beat, and he joined right in.

"I don't want to screw it up again, Aiyla."

"You didn't screw it up before," she assured him. "It was *my* issue. I was afraid of getting lost in a line of women. I should have said something in Saint-Luc. I should have believed that you really wanted *me* and that you could be faithful. I mean, I did believe you wanted me. But I was scared to open myself up to being hurt." She laced her fingers with his and said, "I'm not scared anymore. I trust you, and I'm happy. I don't think I've ever been happier."

"Thank you for trusting me, babe. We only have two more race days—the hike today and then the climb tomorrow. How's your leg holding up?"

"It's painful," she said casually. "But I'll get through it."

"I'm going to hike with you, but will you please let Jon check it out before we go?" He ran his hand along her sore leg.

"You can't hike with me. You'll have no chance of winning, not even as a couple."

"This is a charity event, remember? Not the Olympics. You're the only prize, the only *win*, I want to accomplish."

"But—"

He silenced her with a kiss. "Baby cakes, I know you're stubborn, but you're not going to win this one. Not when your well-being is on the line. There's no campsite tonight. If you're not signed on for a couples hike, then it's every man and woman for themselves. Except for you. You've got me."

She inhaled a long breath and blew it out slowly, shaking her head. "I don't need to win this one. Thank you for giving up the win to be with me. I'll let Jon check out my leg. I don't want you to worry any more than you already are."

"Jesus." He exhaled a sigh of relief. "I thought you were going to say no." He hugged her tight, his heart racing. "Can I push my luck?"

She laughed. "That depends."

"What are you doing after the race? Remember when I mentioned that Tempest had gotten engaged?"

"Mm-hm. In Saint-Luc you said her fiancé...*Nash*? The artist? Had a little boy named *Flip*, right?" she asked. "I remember. She's the one who had started teaching children's music classes."

Phillip had just turned four. Nash had raised him on his own, and when Tempe had met them, Phillip had called himself "Flip" because Nash had always said his name so fast, that's how it had sounded to the little guy.

"They're getting married on Saturday back home in Peaceful Harbor. I want you to come with me to the wedding and meet my family."

"This sounds serious," she whispered playfully.

"We are serious," he whispered back. "What do you say? Be my wedding date?"

Her smile reached all the way up to her eyes. "I just happen to have three weeks free before I go to New Zealand for another ski instructing job. I think I can manage a few days in Maryland with my hot boyfriend."

He stole another kiss, feeling like he'd won the lottery. "Awesome. *Perfect.* I'm so happy. I'm going to make the arrangements right this second, before you have time to rethink your answer."

"I have to stop by my apartment, which is about two hours

from here, and pack, and we have the awards ceremony Thursday morning."

"That's not a problem. Just be sure to pack a skimpy bathing suit." He gave her a lusty look. "I've ordered a rental car, so we'll go straight to your place, then catch a flight late Thursday afternoon." Using his phone, he arranged their flights, getting more excited by the minute.

She settled against his chest again. "You're an easy boyfriend. A little sex, visit your family…"

"I've been called a lot of things, but 'easy' and 'boyfriend' have never been two of them. Damn, baby. I love the sound of 'boyfriend' when it's tied to you, but I'm pretty sure you're going to take back 'easy' in a second because I'm going to push my luck even more."

She looked at him with a curious expression.

"I'm supposed to go on a cross-country climbing trip with my cousin Graham and a few buddies two weeks after I get back home. Come with me on the trip?"

"I just told you that I have a job waiting for me in New Zealand, and I'd probably slow you down with my leg anyway."

"Then I'll go with you to New Zealand," he said quickly. "You could slow me to a stop and I'd still want to be with you. I don't care what we do or where we go. I'm not going months without seeing you again."

"I don't want to go without seeing you, either, but if I hold you back or slow you down, you will start to resent me. I don't want either of us to miss out on the things we love."

"Then we're in agreement about being together one way or another."

She smiled and nodded. "Yes. I want that. But *how*? I'm worried about slowing you down if my leg doesn't heal in time for your trip. But I actually wouldn't mind skipping New Zealand because I've been there before and the manager of the resort was just doing me a favor, letting me earn some extra cash while I'm taking pictures in a few of the nearby towns. One of the pictures I took a few years ago while I was working there was featured in *World Life* magazine after the editor saw it in the second book I ever published, *Through Their Eyes*. Now I pretty much have a job waiting for me there whenever I want."

He was thrilled for her to have been featured by such a prominent magazine. *World Life* was second only to *National Geographic*. "I had no idea you were featured. That's amazing, but not surprising. Your work is phenomenal. I'd like to get a copy of that issue."

"Thank you. It was published in May." She shrugged like it was no big deal, but he saw the light in her eyes and knew how proud she was, as she should be. "As I said, I don't mind missing New Zealand, but there are other places I *really* want to go to photograph the elderly, like to the remote villages Ms. F told me about in South Africa. And at some point I want to get back to see her, too. She moved to Algarve, Portugal, and I was hoping to get there later this year."

"South Africa has majestic mountains. Table Mountain, Signal Hill, Lion's Head…And Portugal? There's a coastline of climbs just waiting for us."

A relieved laugh slipped from her lips.

"I know how important photography is to you, and as a fellow photographer, I understand how finding the right subjects makes it all worthwhile. I'd never want to stand in your way of that."

"But it can't be at the expense of you missing your climbing trips or your photography assignments. Or with my bum leg, of me slowing you down. I won't let that happen." She climbed over him, straddling his lap with a sexy smile, a hint of worry in her eyes. "How do two people who are constantly traveling find a way to be together without losing pieces of themselves?"

Ty wasn't locked down to a schedule, and money had never been an issue since he had more endorsement offers than he could ever accept and he earned a pretty penny with his nature photography. The truth was, money meant very little to him, but being with Aiyla was priceless. "We *plan*, and *schedule*, and *compromise*." He pressed his lips to hers. "And if we're lucky, fate will always be on our side."

Her brows knitted. "And if we're not lucky? Because I'm not sure fate strikes more than once."

"It's already struck twice for us—Saint-Luc and here. And if it's not on our side, then we'll rely on my initial belief—that we're in charge of our own destiny—and we'll make it work."

"Make our own fate? I like the sound of that." She put her arms around him and rested her head on his shoulder.

He pulled the blanket around her, feeling whole for the first time in so long, he thought it might have been the first time *ever*. "You can't see the sunrise from there."

"I've seen dozens of sunrises, but I've never felt the dawn of a new day from my new favorite place on earth." She kissed his neck and said, "Everything is better when I'm in your arms."

The sun greeted them slowly, and they remained in each other's arms until Ty's alarm went off. Then they packed up their things and headed back to camp.

"Since we're hiking together, we'll only need one tent." Ty wasn't about to let her carry unnecessary equipment, though he knew she'd argue about him carrying everything. He planned to pack one light backpack for her and bear most of the burden himself.

"And two sleeping bags," she said. When he gave her a questioning look, she added, "We'll zip them together so we have more room to roll around."

He chuckled and pulled her in for a kiss. "I like the way you think."

When they arrived at the campsite, they hit the coffee station first, and found Trixie filling her mug.

"I thought for sure I'd have to drag your butts out of your tents this morning after you disappeared and never came back last night," Trixie said. "But when I went looking for you, both tents were empty. Did the mountain man make you sleep under the stars again?"

"No. We got up early to watch the sunrise." Aiyla wrapped her hands around the warm coffee cup and looked at Ty with an expression so full of emotions he was sure Trixie would give them shit about it.

Trixie touched his forehead, and he shrugged out of her reach. "What are you doing?"

"Checking to see if you're sick." She smiled and said, "Not hanging out with everyone at night, waking up to watch the sunrise. Sounds like Cupid has left his mark on you."

"Damn right," he said proudly. "Where's Speed? I want him to check out Aiyla's leg."

"Speak of the cockiest devil in the land." Trixie pointed over Ty's shoulder.

Ty followed her gaze and saw Speed carrying his bags to one of the trucks. He took Aiyla's hand and headed over. "Spee—*Jon*. Hold up." He wanted to speak with Jon Butterscotch, the physician, and he hoped by using Jon's given name, he would convey how worried he was about Aiyla's leg without him having to say it in front of her.

Jon flashed a bright smile. "What's up, man?" He was a big dude who didn't fit the stereotypical image of a doctor. His hair was a bit shaggy, he was built like he was made for a fight, and when he wasn't working, he collected phone numbers like coins. He was the exact opposite of Ty's brother Cole, who was the epitome of professional even in his time off. Cole had always been careful with his body and his heart, and would never think of a one-night stand as something to strive for. But the two of them complemented each other, and their thriving orthopedic practice was proof of that.

"Do you have a minute to check out Aiyla's leg?"

"It's just overuse," she chimed in.

Jon tossed his bags in the truck and wiped his hands on his shorts. "Sure. Let's take a look."

They sat at one of the tables, and Jon knelt in front of Aiyla. As if a curtain had fallen, his face went from joking competitor to serious physician.

"Tell me what's been going on," he said to Aiyla.

She rolled up her sweatpants. "I'm sure it's overuse. It started hurting a few weeks ago when I was skiing, right here." She ran her finger along the area from just above her ankle to her shin. "Like a deep, dull ache most of the time."

Jon rolled up the other pants leg and visually examined both. "Did you have any falls? Were you skiing more than usual?"

"No," she said.

"Did it come on suddenly, or was it bothering you for a while but not enough to really pay attention?"

Aiyla's brow wrinkled. "I guess it's sort of been on and off for a while. But it's usually not this painful."

Jon examined her hurt leg, checking range of motion, her joints, her foot, and asking if it hurt when he did this or that. He pressed on different areas, checking for tender spots, and then examined the leg that didn't hurt in the same way. He asked a number of questions about her family, and Ty knew enough to realize he was assessing her risk factors.

"Does it ever swell up?" Jon asked.

"After the races it has been a little swollen."

"So have mine," Jon said with a reassuring smile. "Any abnormal weight loss or fatigue?"

"No weight loss." Her cheeks blushed, and she looked at Ty. "And the reason I'm tired has nothing to do with my leg."

Jon didn't even smile at that, which told Ty he was deeply entrenched in physician mode. "Do you ever wake up from the pain?" he asked.

"Well, sure," she said casually. "Doesn't every athlete?"

Ty reached for her hand, not liking her last answer. "Have you been waking up in pain while you've been with me?"

She shrugged. "Sometimes, but I take Motrin and Tylenol and it usually calms down again. Get that worried look off your face. I'm *fine*."

He wasn't so sure. "What do you think, Doc?"

"I think we're out in the middle of the mountains without the ability to do any medical tests or make a proper diagnosis." Jon ran an assessing eye over Aiyla. "As a doctor, I'd say you should stay off it and go in for further testing to cover all your bases."

"I'm not missing the rest of this race," Aiyla insisted.

"I assumed you'd say that." He slid a concerned look to Ty and then returned his attention to Aiyla. "If you're determined to do the hike and the climb, then keep up the anti-inflammatories and Tylenol. I'm sure you know the drill. Rest. Ice. Compress. Elevate."

"I've got a few chemical cold packs," Ty said. "But, Aiyla, maybe you should—"

She narrowed her eyes. "Don't even suggest that I sit this out."

Jon pushed to his feet. "You're competitive, and that's admirable. But use your head and listen to your body. If it gets to be too bad, *stop*. No race is worth permanent damage. I've got some instant cold packs I can give you."

Ty shook his hand. "Thanks a lot, man."

"Thank you," she said. "I really appreciate your time and your advice."

"Listen, sweetie, you doing this race is against my better judgment," Jon advised. "I get it. I really do. But we don't know what's going on with your leg. It could be as simple as shin splints from the constant pounding, or there could be something bigger going on. Whatever the cause, the race is sure to exacerbate your pain."

"I know, and I'm okay with that." She drew in a deep breath. "No pain, no gain, right?"

Jon shifted a knowing look to Ty. "I guess, but you should have your doctor set up X-rays, just to be sure. An MRI would be even better."

"If it still hurts when the race is over, I'll go see my doctor and get a referral for an MRI," she said, then quickly added, "Actually, I'll do it after I get back from Ty's sister's wedding."

"You're going to Tempe's wedding?" Jon asked. "Why don't you let me do a full workup while you're in Peaceful Harbor?"

She said, "You don't have to do that," at the same time Ty said, "That's perfect. Thank you."

"I'd feel better if you got it done sooner rather than later," Jon said to Aiyla in a physician-like tone that left no room for negotiation.

"Are you sure? You must have a million patients waiting to see you after being gone for the race."

"I'm Superman," Jon said with a smirk. "A million and one seems like the perfect number. We'll need to get some insurance information, but we can take care of that after the race. Until then, Ty has my cell number. If you need anything at all, use it."

Ty breathed a little easier. "Great. Thanks, man. And just for that, I won't try to beat you out there today."

Jon laughed. "Dude, the way you're sticking to Aiyla like glue, I doubt you even have this race on your mind."

Chapter Eight

TY AND AIYLA kept up a brisk pace during the first few hours of the GPS-driven hike. There were people ahead of them and behind, but while they'd started out as a group, everyone had found their own pace. Aiyla was surprised at how spread out the group had become. She didn't want to slow Ty down. She knew if he'd been racing on his own, he'd have remained at the front of the pack. She felt as grateful as she did guilty about his sticking with her, but selfishly, she was thrilled to have more time with him. Today they were hiking as far as they could in the direction of the finish line, and then they'd make camp for the night. Tomorrow they'd trek to the top of the mountain and cross the finish line, which was on the grounds of the Sterling House, an old rustic inn. They'd spend the last night of the event at the inn, where the awards ceremony would take place the following day. Aiyla was excited about having creature comforts at their fingertips, but she preferred sleeping outdoors. Besides, all the luxuries in the world wouldn't be better than simply being in Ty's arms, no matter where they were.

The blazing late-afternoon sun slowed them down as they headed up a steep, rocky incline absent of trees or shade. Ty and Aiyla passed a water bottle between them and noshed on protein bars, talking about the places they'd visited over the years and the places they hoped to go together. Their lifestyles and dreams were so in sync, it might be scary if it weren't so beautiful. Clouds hovered over the crest of the mountains like puffs of unruly hair, constantly moving and shifting. Birds of prey circled and dove for their next meal, and as they reached the top of the hill, they came upon a forest of conifers. Towering lodgepole and ponderosa pines brought a mix of earthy and sweet vanilla scents. Hiking with Ty made the experience even more enjoyable. They'd been playing I Spy on and off all day, and Ty caught her up on each of his siblings. When he talked about them, he got this calm look in his eyes. She recognized that look from when he'd first told her about his family back in Saint-Luc. She had a feeling they centered him in a way that other people couldn't. She understood that, because she felt the same way about her sister and Ms. Farrington.

As they trudged up the hill, it struck her that most people would think there was nothing glamorous about hiking from sunup to sundown. But as the afternoon sun dipped below the horizon, bringing rise to cooler temperatures, Aiyla couldn't think of anyplace she'd rather be or anyone she'd rather be with—despite the throbbing ache in her leg.

When they reached the ridge of the mountain, they walked single file, the land falling away on either side, giving them a spectacular view of flowering meadows, and forests, as far as the eye could see.

"How's your leg holding up?" he asked for the millionth time.

"Pretty well." She'd taken another dose of medicine about an hour ago. "I don't even think about it unless you ask." That was pretty much true, except when the pain flared up. "Let's go back to playing I Spy."

"I spy something roundish," Ty said from behind her.

"That's your big clue? *Roundish?*" She looked over her shoulder, and he blew her a kiss. Her stomach fluttered, and she wondered if she'd ever get used to that feeling.

"It's edible," he said with a coy smile.

She looked around, perplexed by his clues. "A flower?"

"More beautiful than a flower."

"*Roundish...*" She pointed across the meadow to a patch of trees. "The woods over there?"

"Nope. Actually, it's a little heart shaped."

She looked up and inspected the clouds, but they weren't even close to heart shaped. "You've got to give me more than that."

His hand covered her ass and he gave it a squeeze. She spun around, smiling despite trying her best to scowl. "Seriously? My *ass?* That's not part of nature."

He hauled her against him and kissed her *hard.* "Baby, you're all I see out here."

"How do you do it?" she asked, though she knew he had no idea what she meant. How could he, when she was still getting used to how different he was with her than with everyone else? He continued to show her a side of himself that she had a feeling not many people got to see. Sure, he said things off-the-cuff, but it was the way he looked when he said them that was different. Like he meant every single word.

He reached around her and squeezed her butt again. "It's a hand action. You curl your fingers and press with your thumb."

She laughed, but her insides melted a little more with every playful thing he did and said. "Not that! You're the perfect combination of *sweet* and *hot.*" She gasped, her eyes widening with sudden realization. "Oh my God. You're *tropical heat!* You're my favorite candy!"

"Hell, yeah, I am, baby. Are you hungry?" He waggled his brows. "Let's find out how many licks it takes to get to my creamy center."

She unzipped the pack around her waist and pulled out a baggie of Tropical Heat Hot Tamales. "This is *you.* I'm going to have to start calling you Hot Tom. No, just *Tom.*"

"First, I can't believe you *still* love those. And second, baby, if you call me some other guy's name, we're going to have *big* problems."

"Really?" She was going to have fun with this. "Then *Tom* it is. Or maybe *Tommy.* Or—"

He grabbed her ribs, and she squealed with delight as he tugged her in close, kissing her smiling lips. "Gonna call me Tom?"

"No. But I kind of like *Hottie.*"

He nipped at her lower lip. "How about you call me *Ty?*"

She stepped closer, grabbed his shirt, and pulled him down so they were eye to eye. "How about I call you *mine?*"

"There's nothing I'd like more."

He sealed his mouth over hers, taking her in a series of slow, drugging kisses so intense, her knees weakened.

His arms swept around her waist, keeping her close as he gazed into her eyes and said, "I'm falling so hard for you all over again, I can barely see straight."

"Me too. It's like nothing has changed and everything has changed at once."

"For the better."

He kissed her again and they fell into step side by side, holding hands and stealing kisses. Time passed in a blur of happiness, and before Aiyla knew it, the ground leveled out and the sun gave way to a cool early evening. They hiked for a short while longer before choosing a place to stop for the night. They didn't talk much as they set up camp, but the emotions billowing between them were as loud and expressive as words could ever be. Everything felt so right and *real*, she had a hard time remembering what her days were like before she'd spent them with Ty.

In the distance, other hikers set up tents, as if she and Ty had been the ringleaders. Maybe she should feel guiltier for not thinking of the race, but there was no denying that it had taken a back seat to the handsome, rugged man currently spreading a blanket out over the ground. Was she really going to meet his family? That was a huge step, as was revealing how she felt about the future. Shouldn't she be scared? Nervous, at least?

She took stock of her emotions and realized she wasn't either of those things. Talking about what they wanted felt like a natural next step for them, even if she had no idea how they would figure out schedules and compromises. Just knowing he felt the same way calmed her concerns and gave her confidence that they'd figure it out.

"Come over here, babe. Let's take the pressure off your leg."

Ty slipped his arm around her waist, bearing most of her weight. He helped her down to the blanket and knelt to untie her shoes. She couldn't remember anyone helping her take off her shoes, *ever*, not even her mother, although she was sure she had at some point when she was a little girl. But she was no longer a little girl, and she hadn't allowed anyone to help her with anything in so long that a small part of her still wanted to resist. That part quickly faded, and she began to see Ty's efforts not as someone helping her because she couldn't do something herself but rather as a boyfriend doing something utterly romantic just because he wanted to. She was surprised at how that realization helped her to let go of the chip she'd carried since she'd lost her mother. At least where her relationship with Ty was concerned.

He set her shoes aside and began gently massaging her sore leg. She closed her eyes for a moment, overcome with gratitude. She hadn't realized how fatigued she felt, or how much her leg ached until that very moment, like the emotional crash after taking final exams.

"That feels incredible, but you don't have to rub my leg." She reached for him. "You've got to be tired, too."

He took her hand and pressed a kiss to it. "I'm good, baby. Just relax. Let me do this for another minute. Then we'll put a few cold packs on it and eat some dinner."

She mouthed, *Thank you*, as he caressed her leg, his biceps flexing even with his tender touch. He pressed kisses along her leg, in the exact places she'd shown Jon that it hurt. The shadow of worry in his eyes made her heart ache and fill up in equal measure.

He was so careful with her in everything he did. When he retrieved the cold packs, no matter how many times she assured him she could handle wrapping her own leg, he insisted on doing it.

When he finally came to her side, it was with a plethora of food, one of his sweatshirts—which he helped her put on—and a slew of steamy kisses.

He turned on an app on his phone of a candle burning and set it beside her. "Dinner by candlelight for my one and only."

Thank goodness for solar phone chargers. "Who knew you were so romantic?"

He brushed his lips over hers and said, "No one. Before you, this part of me didn't exist."

"WHERE DID YOU go after Saint-Luc?" Aiyla asked later that night as they lay stargazing. "Did you stick to your plan and go to Germany?"

She sounded so sleepy, Ty almost hated to answer. "Yes, for a little while, but honestly, all I could think about was going back to Saint-Luc. It was a rough time. I cut my trip short and went home to hang with my family and to try to figure out how to move forward after falling for a woman who'd sent me away." He kissed her cheek with a pained expression.

"I'm sorry. It was hard for me, too. I took some of the worst pictures of my life after you left." She cuddled closer. "We can never break up again, or my career will tank and I'll start to resent the resort jobs because they'll be fillers for the photography I *really* want to do. It would be ugly, so let's not do that again."

He leaned over her and gazed into her smiling eyes. "Never again. I think we should plan a trip that will be new for both of us, to someplace remarkable. We can take pictures together, of the elderly *and* the regions that shaped their lives. A joint project."

"We can publish a coffee-table book of our travels. Can you imagine how fun that would be? We can plan the trips around climbing adventures, so you don't miss out."

"And every year we'll choose eight weeks to stay put in a cold climate so you can ski and teach." He lay down beside her, holding her hand. "See, baby? *Plan. Compromise.* We can do this."

"I think you might be right, but what if your family doesn't approve of us as a couple?"

"Are you kidding? Babe, you're not seriously worried about that, are you?"

She shrugged. "You grew up with an amazing family. You have supportive parents who are still married, lots of siblings, each of whom have done pretty fantastic things. I grew up very differently, and—"

He leaned on one arm so he could see her face more clearly. "I'm proud of my family, but the only *amazing* thing about any of us is that we are still sane. The pressure of growing up a Braden is huge. My parents expected us to work hard, get top grades, learn to play an instrument, take part in sports."

"Except for the instrument thing, isn't that what most parents expect?"

"Yes, but most childhoods are filled with...I don't know what. Frolicking around? Playing in the dirt? Being a *kid*. My childhood was built on lessons about taking responsibility, and not just for ourselves, but for each other. We volunteered *all* the time, went to every community event, stood up for anyone who was being bullied. They taught us well, but man, the pressure to do the right thing was *always* there. We couldn't just go out and do something asinine like other teenagers could."

"Those aren't hardships, Ty. Think about how different we grew up and where we are today. You're a world-renowned mountain climber and nature photographer. You've done great things. I barely earn enough to do the things I *want* to do, and I can only do them because I'm careful with money. I always buy refundable airline tickets just in case I get sick or can't make a trip. I could never just decide to fly somewhere and buy tickets like you did for our trip to Maryland. I'm not complaining. I adore my life and wouldn't change any of it. But make no mistake, we were raised very differently. I come from nothing, Ty. *Nothing.* I worked from the time I was old enough to convince someone to pay me to rake their yard, mow their lawn, or babysit their children. By middle school my mom was gone when I got up most mornings, cleaning houses, and she never got to attend my sporting events, because she had to work. Her *employer* paid for my ski lessons, sports clubs, and all of my gear when I was a kid in exchange for my being her traveling companion."

"I know. You told me all of this in Saint-Luc. Why is it suddenly worrying you now?"

She looked at him like she couldn't believe he was missing the point. "Because now I'm going to *meet* your family and we're making plans to stay together. I'm not ashamed of my family, or feel unworthy of you, or anything like that. But what will your family think about a girl whose mother cleaned houses for a living and whose sister is a housewife? I don't want them to think I'm after your money or fame or *anything* other than your heart."

"They'll think your mother was a hardworking woman who taught her children the meaning of love and responsibility and who loved you both enough to make sure you knew how to set goals and do the things in life that would allow you to be happy. You told me that your sister loves being a housewife. That she was *made* to be a wife and mother. How can *anyone* think that's not a life to be admired?"

"Do you really think so? I mean, *I* see my family that way, but…"

"I *know* so, baby. You see your family as being so different from mine, but we were brought up with the same beliefs you were. We might have had more money and more siblings, but we worked for the things we wanted, and we were raised to see people for who they are inside and how they treat others. Not for the things they have."

"That's easy to say," she said. "But is it really true, or just something you want me to believe?"

"Babe, I know what our family looks like from the outside. People think Cole and his wife, Leesa, live a charmed life because he's a doctor and they have a beautiful baby girl. But what people don't know is that when they met, Leesa had been accused of inappropriately touching a student in her hometown. Cole *believed* in her, and he didn't let that accusation hold him back—and neither did we. And my brother Nate? I told you that he followed in my father's footsteps in the military and now owns a bar. How can you top being the son your father has always dreamed of having? Right?" When they were in Saint-Luc, he'd told her that his father had experienced a horrible landing-gone-wrong during an air-jump training mission and he'd lost his left leg from the knee down, which had resulted in a medical discharge. It was no secret that his father had always hoped one of his sons would follow in his military footsteps.

"Well, the side of the story you don't hear about is that Nate struggled with years of survivor's guilt for making it out of the war alive, when his best friend—the older brother of his now wife, Jewel—was killed due to an order Nate gave. He damn near disappeared from the family for a number of years, but we didn't give up on him. And we were there for Jewel and her family years before Nate and Rick joined the military. Jewel's family didn't have much. Her mother didn't have a fancy career. None of that has *ever* mattered. And if Nate had decided that what he'd gone through was too much and had decided to deliver pizza for a living, we wouldn't love him any less."

"Those things must have been horrible to go through," she said.

"They were, but we were all there for them. And if you think for a minute that my family cares about what you do or don't have, just look at my sister Shannon. She runs a land trust, and her fiancé, Steve, is a ranger and wildlife consultant who is about as reclusive as a guy can get. They don't earn much, or have much. Their cabin is freaking tiny. But they love each other to the ends of the earth, and that's *all* that matters."

"They're the ones who live here in Colorado, right?"

"You remembered. Yes. The point is, if you take away what we do for a living and consider how we live, you'll see what I mean. I live in tents most of the year. That's not the sign of a guy who grew up with judgmental parents. You see my life as something remarkable, but, babe, I *climb mountains* for a living. It's no great shakes." He shrugged. "The truth is, I don't have what it takes to be a doctor. I'm too restless to settle down and run a business and too rebellious to take orders. Something inside me *demands* new adventures. I'm the guy they all shake their head at. The one they can't control *or* understand. But they love me anyway, and they'll love you for a million reasons, just like I do. My family is wonderful, but none of us are perfect, baby. Not by a long shot."

He took her hand in his and said, "You don't need to worry about anyone judging your family unfairly, or judging your feelings for me incorrectly. What my parents will see is the person you are. They'll see how you treat me, how you look at me, and the way you touch me."

She wrinkled her nose and said, "I'm pretty sure we can skip that last part. I don't want them to think I'm like all the other women they know you've been with."

He closed his eyes for a second, wishing he could have known long ago that he would eventually meet Aiyla. Maybe then his past wouldn't be so checkered.

When he opened his eyes, she wore a serious expression.

"I didn't mean that like it came out," she said.

"I know you didn't. Baby, you're different from any woman I've ever been with, which is what makes you special. My parents haven't met a girlfriend of mine since I was a teenager. That alone will send the loudest message of all. But when they hear you talk about life, or your family, when they experience *you*—your adventurous spirit, your humor, your innate ability to see beauty in the things and people others might overlook— they'll know we are a perfect match, just like I do."

Chapter Nine

THE FINAL DAY of the race was the most grueling challenge. Ty and Aiyla hiked several miles to the base of another steep mountain, the last major obstacle before the finish line. Once they reached the peak, they would have to cover almost a mile of rocky, though mostly flat, terrain to reach the finish line. It was a bittersweet goal. Aiyla didn't want their adventure to end. Like their time in Saint-Luc, she and Ty had become so close it was as though all those months in between didn't exist. And out here in the wilderness, it felt like they were living in a world of their own, despite being among dozens of competitors and volunteers.

Selfishly, she wanted more time alone with him. But she wasn't a selfish person, and she hated holding Ty back. People were passing them at a quicker pace now, fueled by the scent of the finish line, but Aiyla's leg was beyond fatigued. They'd been walking for hours, and her leg throbbed like a son of a bitch. She couldn't take another step.

She jammed the walking stick Ty had made for her from a tree branch into the ground, leaning on it to take the pressure off her injury, and dropped her backpack to the dirt. "Ty, you should go ahead. I need to rest my leg."

"Here, baby, sit down." He guided her to a boulder and knelt before her, placing her backpack beneath her foot to elevate her leg.

"Ty, really. I can get up the mountain, but this is going to take me some time, and I don't want to hold you up. You've been great. You've stuck with me and done more than any boyfriend ever would. But we're not needy people. You know I won't be upset if you go ahead, and I know you realize I can handle the rest on my own."

He scrubbed a hand down his face with an irritated expression. He was so very worried and caring.

She reached out and took his hand. "Go. I'm fine."

"I think the heat is messing with your head, babe." He set his gear beside him and fished out a chemical pack and some Motrin and Tylenol, handing it and a bottle of water to her. As she took it, he activated the ice pack and secured it to her leg with a bandage. "If you think for a minute that I give one shit about what place I come in, you're wrong."

"But, Ty, I didn't know you were going to be at this race. If you hadn't been here, I'd be doing it on my own. I can get through this and you don't have to lose out by hanging around with me."

"*Lose out?*" He sat on the boulder beside her and leaned his forearms on his thighs, rubbing his hands together. "Maybe I'm the dense one. Are you *trying* to get rid of me?"

She laughed and shook her head. "Not in the sense you're asking."

"Then don't take this wrong, but *shut up.*" He placed his hands on her shoulders and stared deeply into her eyes. "I'm making the rules this time. We're chasing our destiny together, so put all those silly thoughts about winning or anything else to the side. Got it?"

"Yeah, I get it." She wound her arms around his neck. "I've got it *bad*, but I still hate slowing you down."

"I can think of many ways you can make it up to me tonight when we're in our nice, comfortable bed at the resort." He touched his lips to hers, as light as a whisper. "And in the lake." He buried his face in her neck and kissed her there. "And on the grass."

She closed her eyes, reveling in the feel of his warm lips teasing over the hollow of her neck, stirring the embers he'd been stoking all day with intimate touches and furtive glances. He kissed the edge of her mouth, her chin, and finally, his lips met hers, as insistent as a hurricane, sending shock waves through her entire body.

His hands moved to her shoulders and down her arms. She was aware of the roughness of his fingers, the firmness of his palms, as they slid all the way to her fingertips, interlacing with her hands. He smiled against her lips. Boy, she loved when he did that. It was so... *Ty*. Such a positive, happy sensation, sprinkling light over the cloud of her injury. She wanted to lie with him right there on the ground among the rocks and tufts of grass and kiss into the night. But she refused to be the cause of Ty Braden's worst race in history.

Forcing herself to pull away, her heart fluttering like the wings of a thousand butterflies, she said, "We have to climb."

"Even after that kiss you're still thinking about the race?" Laughter slipped from his lips. "I adore you, Aiyla Bell. You fricking blow me away."

"Good. Then get your lazy ass up and let's conquer this mountain." She gritted her teeth through the pain as they put away the ice pack and rewrapped her leg. After too many *Are you sure you can make its*, they finally began their upward journey. Every step came with a spear of pain as Aiyla navigated around jagged rocks and ruts in the land.

"Want help, babe?"

She shook her head.

"Thank God you're as strong as you are stubborn," he said with a disapproving shake of his head, which warred with the glimmer of respect in his eyes. "You've got this, babe. And when you need me, I'm right here."

She knew it was killing him not to be able to help her, but she needed to do this on her own. She bulldozed her way with every step, leaning on the walking stick and fueled by Ty's support. The incline was too steep, the sun too hot. All around her, climbers were bent over, as if they were pulling weeds, their packs rising off their backs like humps of a camel. People shouted encouraging words to each other. But it was all Aiyla could manage to grit her teeth, willing herself to make it up the mountain.

"Come on, baby," Ty urged. "One more step." His tone was purely supportive, and it helped her focus. "That's it. Use the stick, Aiyla. You've got this."

She used that stick every step of the way. *One more step. I've got this*, played in her head like a mantra. She wasn't going to let herself, or Ty, down. Using mental bribes of finish-line kisses and two solid weeks of babying her leg, she plowed forward.

With the peak in sight, she felt a rush of adrenaline, but the pain was excruciating, and despite her best efforts, painful sounds of hurt and frustration escaped.

Ty begged her to give him her pack, but she refused. He put his arm around her waist, trying to take the burden off her leg, but it made her feel weak and ridiculous. She was an athlete, and a damn good one. Maybe not on Ty's level, or the level of many other competitors here, but she could—*would*—make it up this frigging mountain even if it was the last thing she did.

After what seemed like hours, but in reality was probably more like one, they crested the hill and she set her feet on flatter ground. Relief swept in, but it wasn't enough to alleviate the bone-deep treachery going on in her leg. All around them spectators cheered, lining the final leg of the race to the finish line. The magnificent resort loomed in the distance. But the pain was too great, and as Ty threw his arms around her and lifted her off her feet, she managed a smile.

"You did it, baby cakes." He kissed her hard. "You're a beast! We're on the homestretch."

When he set her on the ground, a tortured cry flew from her lungs. The fear in Ty's face was as palpable as the tears of frustration she struggled to hold back. "I'm okay. I'm fine. I'm okay."

With one strong arm around her waist, he lifted her off her legs again. "Fine my ass."

TY WAS DONE messing around. He couldn't stand by and pretend Aiyla was okay any longer, or let her do any more damage to her leg.

"You can put me down, Ty," Aiyla complained. "I can finish the race."

"Yeah, I *can* put you down. And I can also throw you to the fucking wolves. But neither of those things are going to happen. If you want to finish this race, you're doing it attached to me."

"Aiyla! Ty!"

They turned at the sound of Trixie's voice and found her sitting on the ground a short distance away. Jon knelt before her, wrapping her ankle. Ty tightened his grip on Aiyla's waist and lifted her higher. Using his hip as leverage against her belly, he carried her like an extra appendage, her feet dangling above the ground.

"I can walk," she insisted.

"No."

"*Ty*—"

"Don't waste your breath," he said, weaving around competitors as he made his way toward Trixie and Jon.

Trixie motioned toward Jon. "I twisted my ankle. It's a good thing there's a doc in the house, but the freak insists I call him 'Dr. Jon' or 'Dr. Butterscotch' instead of 'Speed.'"

"Now, sugar, you know that's not true. I told you you could call me 'Fifty Shades of Sweetness.'" Jon flashed a cocky grin and winked.

"He also said I could *lick* him if I was into butterscotch." Trixie rolled her eyes. "Why are you holding Aiyla like she's a rag doll?"

"She's injured."

"I'm fine," Aiyla insisted. "Sort of," she admitted. "I can walk, but he won't let me."

"That makes two of us," Jon said. "This pretty little gal isn't walking either." He shot a challenging look at Ty. "You up for a little manly competition?"

Ty scoffed. "Up for it? Always."

Jon pushed to his feet. "Set your packs down with ours."

He offered a hand to Trixie, helping her up as Ty shrugged off his pack and gently lowered Aiyla to her feet. "Do *not* try to put weight on that foot." He placed her hand on his shoulder.

"Lean on me."

"When did you get so bossy?" She held on to him as he helped her off with her pack and set it with the others.

"When you refused to honor your body's need for rest."

"What type of caveman idea do you have now?" Trixie asked Jon.

"Piggyback race. Best man wins." Jon turned his back to Trixie. "Hop on, sweet thing."

"Seriously?" Trixie looked at Aiyla.

"It's better than the way he's been carrying me," Aiyla said. "But I warn you, my man will blow your ride away."

"As much as I'm all for *love is love*," Jon said with a wolfish grin, "if there's any blowing to be done, it's by this hot mama, not that scruffy dude."

"In your frigging dreams," Trixie said. "I'll limp to the finish line."

"No limping, no blowing." Ty glared at Jon. "Think you can behave long enough to get her to the finish line, or do I need to put you to shame and carry both of them?"

Jon scoffed and crouched before Trixie. "I've got this. Climb on *Dr. Jon*, sweetheart."

"If you so much as put a hand on my thigh," Trixie warned, "I will personally see to it that you cannot use your favorite male body part for at least a month."

Jon cringed. Ty and Aiyla laughed.

As Aiyla climbed onto Ty's back, she said, "I fully expect you to do as much groping as possible, got it?"

"Man, do I like you, sweet girl." He turned as far as his neck would allow and kissed her. Jon sprinted off. "Fuck—"

Ty was on his heels in seconds, and then they were neck and neck, the girls cheering them on.

"You've got this!" Aiyla yelled. "Go, baby, go!"

"Faster, *Speed!* Show him who's boss!" Trixie hollered.

Ty leapt over a rock, holding tight to Aiyla, and stole a glance at Jon, who was ducking under a limb to avoid running into a group of competitors.

"Hang on, baby!" Ty pushed faster.

"You've got nothin' on me, Braden!" Jon hollered from a few feet away.

Aiyla's hands roved over Ty's chest, distracting him.

"If you win, I'll do *everything* you want tonight," she said in his ear.

Adrenaline and lust coalesced, rushing through his veins, and he surged ahead, out of breath and pushing himself harder than he had all day. He heard Jon's fast footfalls beside him and knew better than to look. Looking would slow him down.

He focused on the flags up ahead, the cheering crowd, and the promise of the woman hanging on to him for dear life as he bolted toward the finish line, crossing it two steps before Jon.

Aiyla squealed, her lips covering Ty's cheek as he slowed to a walk. Trixie and the crowd cheered. Jon mumbled a curse.

The smile on Ty's face hurt his cheeks, but it was his heart that wouldn't let him lower Aiyla to the ground. He shifted her along his side, her legs winding around his waist as they came face to face and their mouths collided in a fiery kiss. *This* was the most magnificent *win* of his life. The most rewarding, the one he'd remember long after he'd forgotten the feel of the air on the highest mountain peaks.

"I love you, baby," he said between kisses as hikers breezed by, and the crowd hooted and hollered. "I fucking love you so hard I can't even—"

"Then *don't*," she said quickly. "Whatever it is you can't do, I don't care. Just love me, Ty, because I love you. I've loved you since Saint-Luc."

Chapter Ten

THE THREE-STORY stone, cedar, and glass resort had several elegant terraces overlooking gorgeous meadows peppered with trees and blankets of wildflowers. Aiyla and Trixie sat waiting in the grass beside the heart-shaped lake while Ty and Jon ran back to retrieve their bags. With picturesque mountains in every direction, it was the perfect recuperation spot after their grueling competition.

"Can you believe we're done? Several days of wilderness, hundreds of thousands of dollars raised for children's charities, and even gimping along, we *did* it." Aiyla inhaled deeply, feeling good about the challenge and the money raised and elated about her relationship with Ty. "How'd you do that to your ankle anyway? The last trek up the mountain?"

Trixie tucked her dark hair behind her ear and said, "You aren't going to believe it. I made it all the way up to the top, took one step and my foot slipped off a rock. I twisted my ankle, and Speed—*Dr. Jon*," she said in a mockingly deep voice, "was right there to catch me before I hit the ground. I thought he'd be at the finish line way before me, but it turned out he hadn't even crossed yet. Instead of going for the win, he'd been helping people all along."

"Really? I guess all that bravado was for show? He seems like a good guy."

"It wasn't for show. He's really that much of a flirt and that competitive, but he's also a good guy. He even made it all the way to the finish line without copping a feel." She laughed, and her hazel eyes brightened, then sparked with curiosity. "So...You and Ty? I *love* seeing you two together. I can't imagine what it must be like being with a guy who enjoys the same things you do."

"I never imagined myself with any guy, to be honest. My life is all over the place. I spend more time traveling than I do at home. Luckily, Ty is the same way."

"I envy all that travel sometimes." Trixie plucked a few blades of grass and began shredding them. "I live in a small rural town, where we grow cowboys from dirt. I love it there, but sometimes I wonder what it would be like to live like you and Ty do, moving from one place to the next based on the next adventure you want to conquer."

"Or *photograph*," Aiyla said. "I love taking pictures of older people. I think for me, that's as exciting as scaling a mountain is for Ty."

"Really? So you both do photography, too?" Trixie sighed. "Now, that's fated to be. I rarely go anywhere."

Aiyla's heart skipped at her use of *fated to be*.

"Then you must have dozens of cowboys to choose from back home."

"Not really," Trixie said. "I help my brothers run our family ranch, and I train horses and whatnot, and sometimes I help my friend Morgyn in her clothing boutique. But I've known the guys in my hometown for so long, we have *too* much in common, if you know what I mean. Do you ever get lonely moving around so much?"

Aiyla saw Ty and Jon heading their way without their bags and waved. She'd never been lonely for a man, except after Ty left Saint-Luc, but she didn't need to share that piece of intel. "I'm usually so busy, I don't have time for loneliness. And I grew up with only one sister, who is six years older than me, so I spent a lot of time entertaining myself. I guess I'm used to it."

"I've got a slew of brothers, and everyone knows *everyone* in my town, so it's like having a huge extended family around all the time. I think I'd get lonely without it. But maybe one day I'll get up the courage to try it for a few weeks."

"Look, Ty," Jon said as they approached. "It's the two most beautiful girls in Colorado."

Trixie ran her fingers through her hair, fluttering her eyelashes. "That's us, all right. Did you lose our bags along the way?"

"We had them brought up to our rooms. Hey, babe." Ty leaned in for a kiss.

"Hey, babe." Jon crouched beside Trixie and went for a kiss.

Trixie ducked out of reach. "Sorry, but I don't make out with my doctors."

"Then just call me 'Speed,' darlin'." Jon winked.

"I told Jon we'd have dinner with him and Trixie tonight. Do you mind?" Ty asked.

"Wait," Trixie interrupted, turning an annoyed look on Jon. "You just *assume* I have nothing better to do?"

Jon patted his chest with both hands, flashing a cocky grin. "Something better to do than Jon *Sweetness* Butterscotch? Are you kidding? That's not even a possibility."

"Did I mention he's aggressive?" Ty teased.

"Seriously, Trixie," Jon said, "it's just dinner. Unless, of course, you *want* it to be more."

"I'll tell you what. How about you help me get to my room so I can take a nice, warm shower, leave me *at the door*, and I'll meet you guys for dinner." Trixie went up on her knees and Jon helped her to her feet.

"Leave you at the door, huh?" Jon grumbled, and put an arm around her waist.

"I made that clear for a reason." Trixie leaned on him and said to Ty and Aiyla, "Sevenish?"

"Sounds good." Ty helped Aiyla to her feet and turned around. "Climb on, baby cakes. Let Prince Charming carry you to our room."

"I want to go with *him*," Trixie said. "The man knows how to give a woman fairy tales."

Jon scoffed. "Come back to my room, baby, and I'll show you the biggest *wood* in the Enchanted Forest."

Trixie swatted his arm. "*Pig*. My room. *Now*."

"Now we're talking." Jon chuckled as they walked away.

"He's so funny," Aiyla said as she climbed onto Ty's back, knowing arguing with her man was a futile effort. "I could get used to this."

"I hope you will." He carried her toward the resort. "What do you think of the resort?"

"It's gorgeous. I can't wait to explore the inside." Aiyla loved antique furniture and buildings. Her sister often teased her about liking anything *aged* and told her she'd probably fall in love with a gray-haired old man one day.

"I've known Charlotte Sterling, the owner of the resort, for a few years from doing this event. The resort is no longer open to the public, but her parents were the original coordinators of the Mad Prix, and she opens the inn to host the awards ceremony and honor her parents." He pulled open a heavy wooden door and navigated through a beautiful room with a stone fireplace and antique furniture, where a number of people she recognized from the event were mingling. "I found out last year that she knows my uncle Hal and my cousins from Weston, Colorado. Hal was married here, and his son, Josh, got married here last year."

"I guess it really is a small world. You can put me down now." She wiggled down his back until her right foot touched the hardwood floor.

He put an arm around her, bearing her weight. "You sure you're okay?"

"I think so. It's not as bad as it was. It feels like a really bad toothache. A deep pain that flares up and then just hangs on."

"When we get to our room, you can rest it. That will help."

"*Our* room?" Her pulse quickened. She'd assumed they'd stay together, but hearing him say it made it even more real.

"I had Charlotte move us to one of the suites with a Jacuzzi tub so you could really relax. I probably should have run that by you first, huh?"

She shrugged a shoulder, loving that he had taken care of it.

He gathered her in his arms, and it felt so good to be there, she never wanted to move. "I thought I'd pamper my girl for a while."

"Pamper me? You do remember who I am, right? The girl who is used to doing everything herself?"

He touched his lips to hers and said, "Yes, and I'm the guy who isn't used to doing things for a special woman. This is new territory for both of us. Let's go see how we make out with our new roles."

"*Oh*, role-playing and making out. Sounds like the perfect

night." They headed for the stairs and she said, "You can be a cabana boy. Preferably a *naked* one."

"And you can be *mine*." He swept her off her feet and into his arms. "Oh, wait, that's not role-playing, is it?" He kissed her as he carried her up the stairs. "How about I'm a lucky bastard and you're the adoring girlfriend I get to spoil?"

"While naked," she said, and proceeded to kiss him all the way to their suite.

THEY FOUND THEIR bags waiting for them in the large, elegant suite. A king-size bed was tucked in a nook on the left side of the room, and just beyond, double doors opened to a large bathroom with sparkling marble floors. A chest-height stone wall with a two-way fireplace separated a luxurious seating area with a leather sofa and two wing chairs from a large Jacuzzi tub, which was built into a glass alcove overlooking the mountains. Ty couldn't help but think that the only thing that could make the room better would be if the bed were on an outdoor deck. He loved sleeping beneath the stars with Aiyla in his arms, serenaded by sounds of nature.

Aiyla reached for Ty's hand. "I've never stayed anywhere like this before."

"Well, it won't be the last time." He began filling the tub while she used the bathroom. He couldn't wait to pamper her and help her relax.

She came out with a washcloth and dug around in her bag, withdrawing a pretty pink bottle of body wash. He took them from her hands and set them beside the tub.

"I plan on treating you right, baby, so get used to nice places."

She wrapped her arms around him and said, "I don't need luxury. I just need this. *You*, *me*, and a few less clothes."

"And here I am trying to give you a chance to settle in." He pulled her tank top over her head and tossed it on the floor, taking her in a tender kiss that quickly turned intense.

"You *love* me," she said against his lips.

"So much, baby. I never knew it was possible to love someone more with every passing minute."

He lowered his mouth to her warm, sweet lips, kissing as they stripped each other bare, then walked hand in hand into the tub.

"Careful." He helped her sit facing him and lifted her legs over his, drawing her closer. He leaned in for another kiss, feeling like a glutton and knowing he'd never get enough of them.

He wet the washcloth and poured body wash onto it, gently washing her shoulders and breastbone. Her hands slid from his shoulders to his biceps, her delicate fingers curling around them. She trapped her lower lip between her teeth, her muscles tense. She'd been more relaxed in the shower at the campsite, but that was after making love and waking up in each other's arms. He sensed she was fighting the urge to say she could bathe herself, which only made him love her more.

"Relax," he coaxed as he continued washing her. "I've got you, baby."

She exhaled a long breath and let her arms fall to the water.

"I wish I could take your pain away," he said as he washed her injured leg and kissed her knee.

"I'm okay. Two weeks of rest, ice, and elevation and I should be good to go."

He let the washcloth fall from his hands, wanting to cleanse the rest of her body with his hands. She picked up the washcloth and ran it over his arms and chest while he poured body wash into his palm and bathed her breasts. Her nipples pebbled against his fingers, and a needful sound slipped from her lips. Just being close to her could undo him, but hearing the way he affected her, combined with her soft hands running along his thighs? He was *toast.*

"Baby…"

He cupped the back of her head, guiding her mouth to his. Every stroke of her tongue made his heart beat faster, his desire run hotter. Her hands moved over his abs and he rocked his hips, wanting her to—*hell, yes.* She fisted his cock, stroking him perfectly, tight and hard, her soft palm moving slowly over the head, sending rockets of lust careening through him. He deepened the kiss, filling his hands with her hips, and lifted her. She guided him to her entrance, and he groaned with the all-consuming pleasure as her body welcomed him.

He held her there, still and tightly wrapped around him, and tangled his hand in her hair, reveling in the feel of her breasts against his chest, her thighs around his waist. He pressed his cheek to hers and said, "Don't move, baby. Just let me hold you. Let me feel *all* of you against me."

Her inner muscles tightened around his cock, and he nipped at her earlobe. "Mm. Tricky. You feel incredible, baby." He lowered his mouth to her neck, kissing and sucking, until her fingernails dug into his arms and her hips rocked. He clutched her ass, holding her still, and she whimpered.

"*Ty,*" she pleaded.

"When you say my name that way, it makes me go crazy."

He ground his hips, still buried deep inside her, and cupped one breast, slicking his tongue around her nipple. She rocked to the same rhythm as him, and he sealed his mouth over the taut peak.

She gripped his head, holding him there. *"Don't stop—"*

His favorite phrase.

He sucked harder and moved his other hand between her legs from behind, caressing the sensitive skin around her entrance. She moaned and writhed, and when he teased over her puckered flesh, her body jolted. He drew back, fearing he'd found her boundaries, but she guided his hand back to where it was and his mouth to her breast again.

"I said *don't stop.*"

He possessed *all* of her, teasing and nipping, thrusting and grinding. He pushed his finger past that tight rim of muscles, and her sex clamped around his shaft. His name flew from her lips—*"Ty!"*—as her orgasm claimed her. Her body bucked and rocked, squeezing him so tight he gritted against the need to come, wanting to extend her pleasure. But she felt too good, sounded too erotic. Heat clawed its way down his spine, throbbing through his core, and shattered his ability to think past the woman in his arms and the immense pleasures claiming more of him with every rock of her hips. When she sank her teeth into his shoulder, an explosion of sensations pulled him over the edge.

"Aiyla, *baby*—"

He held on tight, every kiss taking him higher, as their bodies took over.

They remained as one long after the last aftershock rumbled through them, their hearts twining together like strong, stable roots, anchoring and nourishing their love with every whispered promise.

Chapter Eleven

"LET'S EXPLORE," AIYLA said to Ty the next morning as they packed their belongings. They still had an hour before breakfast and the awards ceremony, and she wanted to check out the resort. She'd wanted to do it last night after they'd met Trixie and Jon for dinner, but she'd been too tired. She and Ty had cuddled up on a lounge chair on the balcony. He'd put pillows under her leg to keep it elevated, and she must have fallen right to sleep, because she'd woken up at three o'clock in the morning to pee, and Ty had insisted on carrying her to the bathroom. *No need to aggravate your leg. I've got you.*

"You sure you're up for the extra walking?"

He'd been so sweet last night and this morning. They'd made love again earlier, and after showering together, he'd massaged pain relief ointment into Aiyla's sore leg and then wrapped it. They had no idea where Jon had scrounged up the ointment, but it was thoughtful of him. Ty's touch was healing, and she knew it was probably a psychological benefit because of how close they'd become. Now, as she closed her bag, her mind traveled back in time, to when her mother was still alive. Her mother had never talked about her or Cherise's father, except to say he hadn't stuck around. She'd never seen her mother go out on a single date, which was probably why it hadn't been high on Aiyla's list of priorities. Cherise, however, had dreamed of having a *whole* family, with a husband and father for her future children, ever since she could remember. Even though her sister was happily married, Aiyla hadn't thought she was missing out on anything. Until Ty. Now she couldn't imagine going back to a life without him, and it made her wonder if her mother had ever been loved the way Ty loved her.

"Aiyla?" Ty said, pulling her from her thoughts.

"Yes, sorry. I'm okay. I want to walk around."

"You got lost there for a minute." He crossed the room with concern in his eyes and open arms.

"I was just thinking about my mom," she said as he embraced her. "We're so happy, and I don't think she ever had anything like this."

"But she had you and Cherise, baby."

"I know. I guess since I never knew what I was missing until I found you, if she never had it, she probably wouldn't have died longing for it, either."

He hugged her tight without saying a word, and it was exactly what she needed. Some questions were better left unanswered. It had been almost thirteen years since she'd lost her mother, and she didn't often wallow in the sadness of missing her. Instead, she thought of happier times, like when she and her mother and sister would watch movies and eat popcorn on Saturday nights. They may not have had enough time together, but what time they did have had been happy.

Not wanting to get mired down in memories, she took Ty's hand and pulled him toward the door. "Let's explore before our day gets crazy."

They followed the wide hallways through each wing of the

resort, and when they came to a section that was roped off, Ty explained that there had been some type of mayhem involving the accidental consumption of marijuana brownies during his cousin Josh's wedding weekend, which had resulted in damage to one of the rooms.

"Sounds like you have wild cousins."

"Not usually *that* type of wild," he said. "Luckily, another cousin, Beau, renovates historic properties. He's renovating a house on the mountain back home and then he's coming out to fix the damage and handle some other repairs for Charlotte. Who, by the way, I want you to meet."

He led her down a grand staircase to the main floor and then weaved through another maze of hallways. As they neared a set of double doors, a string of sexy sounds filtered into the hallway. They both stopped cold, sharing an *oh shit* expression. The doors were ajar, and Ty peeked into the room. Aiyla swatted his arm.

"Don't spy," she whispered.

"This is her *office*," he whispered. "I'm just making sure some other couple didn't happen upon it and decide to play office romance."

"What if it's *her?*"

He pulled back from the door. "I don't see *anyone*."

Aiyla peeked through the opening, trying to figure out where the noises were coming from. A leather couch sat a few feet in front of the door, facing an ornate wooden desk with two computer screens. The desk was littered with sticky notes, notebooks, and what looked like candy bar wrappers. Empty water bottles were strewn across a credenza and the floor. The blinds hung crooked, and the desk chair was pushed over by a bookcase.

"I don't see anyone eith—"

A woman popped up from the middle of the room, her dark hair a tangled mess. She ran to the desk and began typing feverishly. The long sleeves of the man's button-down shirt she wore flailed over her hands as her fingers flew across the keyboard—and she didn't seem to have any pants on. Aiyla stumbled backward into Ty.

"Whoa," he said too loudly.

"Shh!"

The office doors flew open and the woman grabbed Ty's hand and dragged him into the room. "Thank God it's you. Get in here." She reached for Aiyla's hand and pulled her in, too, nudging them both around the couch, bringing into view a blow-up doll lying on the floor. "You better be Aiyla or I have a bone to pick with this handsome guy."

"I am," Aiyla said, giving Ty a what-the-fuck-did-we-walk-in-on look. "Sorry to interrupt you."

"Interrupt? You're *saving* me. I'm Charlotte by the way." She pointed to Ty. "You, on your knees." She pushed down on Ty's shoulder, shoving him to the floor. "Good." She grabbed Aiyla's arm and guided her in front of him. "Come on, gorgeous, I need you to lie flat on your back."

"Um...?" Aiyla glanced at Ty, who was chuckling.

"She's an erotic romance writer," he explained. "*C. S. Sterling.*"

Aiyla felt her eyes widen. "You wrote *Crazy, Sexy, Sinful* and *Yours, Mine, and Definitely Not Ours?*" She had to work hard not to go all fan-girl crazy on her.

"The one and only." She waved her hand at the floor. "But I'm on a deadline to finish this book and I can't get the position right with this doll, so if you wouldn't mind?"

"I'm a *huge* fan," Aiyla said as she lay on her back in front of Ty. "Do you actually research *every* position?"

"You read erotic romance?" Ty arched a brow.

"Be thankful, big boy," Charlotte said to Ty. "And yes, I have to research every position. I have to make sure the mechanics are right." She handed the legs of the blow-up doll to Aiyla. "Can you please grab Charlie's thighs and hold them above your head?"

Aiyla did as she asked. "Charlie?"

"Charlie Hunnam is this week's muse." Charlotte pushed Ty's shoulders down so he was leaning over Aiyla's pelvis. "Use your left hand for balance between her legs. The idea is that you're snacking on Aiyla as she noshes on Charlie."

"Hey, hey, *hey*," Ty said in an authoritative voice. "There'll be no *noshing* on any other men."

Aiyla laughed.

"You laugh, but He-Man over here is probably serious. I doubt he wants to share a cutie like you with anyone else." Charlotte grabbed Ty's right hand and guided it to the doll's butt.

"Char!" Ty complained.

"Oh, shush. You'll offend Charlie." Charlotte stood with her hands on her hips, assessing their positions. "Good. Now stay there for a minute while I write this scene."

"Are you kidding?" Ty shook his head.

"Shh. You'll mess up my mojo." Charlotte returned to the desk, her fingers flying over the keyboard again.

For the next forty minutes they followed her every command, made sexy noises, and repositioned themselves three times. Ty snuck kisses and copped feels while Charlotte was busy typing.

"Oh, this is going to be *so* good!" Charlotte exclaimed, her eyes glued to the monitor.

Ty moved over Aiyla, nipping at her lips, and slowly lowered his body beside hers.

"You'll mess her up," she whispered.

"Shh." His lips grazed hers, and she leaned up to capture more.

He pushed the doll to the side, cradling her body with one arm, and cupped the back of her head with the other, kissing her like they were the only two people in the world, much less the room. As long as the sounds of the keyboard ticked away, it meant Charlotte was preoccupied, and the more Ty kissed her, the less Aiyla cared if Charlotte was busy or not.

She didn't know how long they lay there making out, but when Charlotte said, "Okay, you can move now," their mouths parted, leaving her dizzy with desire.

Ty brought her up to a sitting position with him, his lustful eyes locked on hers. She could barely breathe.

"Holy cow," Charlotte said as she came around the desk. "You two are going to set my office on fire."

"Sorry," they said in unison.

Ty's lips curved up in a sexy smile. Aiyla wasn't sorry. Not in the least. And when Ty leaned down and kissed her cheek, then whispered, "Let's go set our room on fire," she couldn't scramble to her feet fast enough.

Charlotte made Ty promise to give Aiyla her email address so they could chat when he was "less hot and bothered," and she all but tossed them out of the office with the excuse that she had to meet her deadline.

Ty and Aiyla made out the whole way back to their room, barely making it through the door before they tore off each other's clothes. They fell to the bed in a tangle of limbs and desperate kisses.

"If that got you this hot," she said between kisses, "I need to buy a blow-up doll."

He grabbed her hands and pinned them above her head, gazing at her with a dark expression. "You buy a blow-up doll and I swear you'll find him hanging by a noose."

Her heart was so full of him, as much as she was flattered by his jealousy, she didn't want to be the cause of that type of hurt, even if joking. With a laugh, she said, "You have me, Ty. *All* of me. I don't want any other man, plastic or real."

"I've waited so long to hear that. Tell me again."

"I love you. Only you." In his eyes she saw more love than she ever imagined possible, and when his lips met hers and their bodies came together, she said it again and again, until she knew he'd hear it in his sleep.

THEY SHOWERED—*AGAIN*—and hurried out of the resort to the awards ceremony, which was already in progress. Sponsorship banners flapped in the breeze, surrounding a crowd of competitors and spectators. Colorful flags hung above a portable podium, where Eric James, the founder of the Foundation for Whole Families, and Parker Collins, the founder of the Parker Children's Foundation, were being photographed and presented with enormous cardboard checks representing the money raised for their foundations. Ty held Aiyla's hand as they joined the others.

"Where have you guys been?" Trixie asked. Her ankle was wrapped, and she was leaning on a crutch that had the name of the resort on the side. "You missed breakfast."

"No, we didn't." Ty winked at Aiyla, and her cheeks flushed.

"You also missed the singles awards," Trixie said. "You won first place for the bike race, Ty."

"Don't worry. They just slipped in my name instead," Jon teased, and handed Ty a blue ribbon. "Congrats, dude."

"Thanks for grabbing it for me."

"No problem." Jon's gaze turned serious, morphing seamlessly from jokester to concerned physician as he turned his attention to Aiyla. "How's your leg, sweetheart?"

"It's not too bad today. Thanks for asking." She leaned into Ty and said, "He's been spoiling me rotten with lots of leg love."

"Good man," Jon said. "I checked with my office and penciled you in for an appointment late Friday afternoon. Can you work that into your schedule?"

"I hate to waste your time," she said. "Maybe we should give it a few days—"

"We *can*, and we *will*, make time Friday afternoon," Ty said firmly. Softening his tone, he added, "Better safe than sorry, especially since you're either coming with me on the climbing trip or we're going to New Zealand. Either way, we need to know what's going on with your leg."

"I can't wait to travel together," she said.

He knew she was trying to change the subject. "Good. Then we need to get your leg checked out, because we have big plans."

"We do, do we?"

"I was thinking about it." He tucked a wayward lock of hair behind her ear. She looked so pretty, she glowed. She looked...*loved*. "New Zealand is, what? An eight- or ten-week commitment, right?"

"About that."

"But if we go on the climbing trip, it's only four weeks. Then we can take some time and visit with your sister and nephews, who I definitely need to meet."

"You do?" Surprise rose in her eyes.

"Yes. I need to connect with the woman who helped raise my incredible girlfriend, and her boys are probably in desperate need of a little crazy adventure time." He leaned down for a kiss.

"Can you clone yourself, please?" Trixie asked. "But make the clone a cowboy."

"I told you, darlin', I'll wear leather chaps." Jon draped an arm over her shoulder. "Think about it. You. Me. Naked. On the back of a horse."

Trixie rolled her eyes. "Sex on a horse. Only you...You need to take notes from Ty."

Ty laughed and continued telling Aiyla about his thoughts on their upcoming travels. "After visiting your sister, I thought we'd head to Portugal to see Ms. F and hit a few of the villages you wanted to see. While we're there, we can plan our trip to South Africa for early next year."

Aiyla's eyes widened. "You really *have* thought this out, but that'll take every penny I have saved plus a lot more if I'm not working in between trips."

"I've got you covered, baby cakes." When she opened her mouth to complain, he silenced her with a kiss.

He wrapped her in his arms and said, "You have places you want to go. I want you with me. That's called *compromise*."

"Hey, Romeo and Juliet," Jon said. "They just announced

you two as the winners of the couples' rafting race. Sorry, dude, but I can't accept the ribbon for you this time."

"Thanks. We've got this. Come on, babe." Ty took Aiyla's hand, and they headed up to the podium. "Let's go collect the first of what is sure to be *many* wins as a couple."

AFTER COLLECTING THEIR ribbons and standing for pictures with the rest of the winners, Trixie and Aiyla pulled out their phones, insisting on getting their own pictures. Ty asked a woman standing nearby to take a few of all four of them, and after, she took some of just Ty and Aiyla. Ty looked forward to having hundreds of pictures of the two of them, taken all over the world. Aiyla and Trixie exchanged phone numbers so they could get together in between Ty and Aiyla's travels, and then they shared so many hugs, Ty didn't think they'd ever get on the road.

Hours later, Ty pulled into Aiyla's apartment complex and parked in front of her building. On the way home, she'd sent an email to her contact at the New Zealand resort, explaining that she wouldn't be able to come out after all, and she called her sister to let her know she was heading to Maryland. They talked for almost an hour, and though Ty tried not to eavesdrop, he enjoyed hearing Aiyla tell her sister, *Remember Ty Braden?* The giggles and cryptic answers that followed told him she'd shared something about their time together in Saint-Luc.

He came around the car and helped her out. "Careful. Your leg is probably going to be stiff."

"It is a little, but it'll stretch out. I should warn you, my place is pretty sparse."

"I should *remind* you"—he brushed the tip of his nose along her cheek—"I don't have a place of my own."

"You mean no place of your own in Peaceful Harbor?" she asked as he grabbed her bags from the trunk.

He shook his head. "Anywhere. I've never found a reason to buy one. I spend most of my time on the road." He slung her bags over his shoulder and followed her up to her apartment. Her limp was more pronounced, and he was glad Jon was going to do a full workup tomorrow. "When I'm home, I like to catch up with my family, and staying with them kills two birds with one stone. I usually stay with one of my brothers, but now that all my siblings have significant others, I hate to intrude on their privacy. If you don't mind, I made arrangements for us to stay with my parents."

"That makes sense. I'm fine with staying with your parents," she said as she unlocked the door. "I've had this apartment forever. It's close to the resorts where I used to work and close to the airport."

He followed her inside and closed the door behind them, taking in her cozy one-bedroom in a quick glance. A champagne-colored couch sat against the far wall, covered with bright throw pillows. A simple wooden coffee table was littered with travel magazines. On a shelf beneath he spied copies of a few of her books. Across the room there was a kitchen alcove beside a fireplace. On the other side of the fireplace was Aiyla's bedroom. Her mattress sat on the floor, covered with earth-toned blankets and a plethora of colorful pillows.

We really were made for each other.

He'd gotten rid of his bedframe when he was a teenager and had never missed it.

He turned, and his gaze caught on the walls behind them.

Nearly every inch was covered with photographs—black-and-whites, colors, sepia—featuring faces of the elderly. He set her bags down, drawn in by the beauty and the energy emanating from the images.

"Baby" was all he could manage as he stared at the pictures. He felt like he was in a museum. He wanted to touch each photograph—each *person*—and hear their stories. Aiyla had an eye for capturing the very essence of people. He took in one picture after another, slowing to examine deep-set eyes beneath bushy, unkempt brows and a frayed gray woolen cap. The man looked like a New England fisherman. His face was dark and aged as worn leather, his lips lost inside a thick, wiry white mustache and beard. Hanging crooked from a thumbtack beside that picture was a black-and-white image of a woman with dark creases above tiny, too-far-apart eyes and a toothless, joyful smile. Several beaded chokers circled her long neck, and enormous plates hung in her stretched earlobes. There were dozens of pictures of elderly men and women staring blankly, intensely focused, or casually, into the lens, begging to be seen. Small, round, tired eyes of an older Asian woman gazed up from beneath a giant cone-shaped straw hat. Wispy strands of black and gray hair framed her puckered lips and crow's-feet. The ball of her cheeks looked oddly soft and taut, like mountain peaks among rivers of wrinkles. She was missing an arm and half of her jaw. Ty squinted to take a better look.

"She was from Hoi An, Vietnam."

"Aiyla, these are magnificent. I own every one of your books and I haven't seen any of these pictures before."

"These are my favorites. I don't share them with the world."

He turned to face her, and his attention was drawn to a single framed photograph hanging behind her, surrounded by others held in place with colorful thumbtacks—pictures of the two of them in Saint-Luc.

She shrugged shyly, a sweet smile lifting her lips.

He crossed the room in rapt silence. She'd captured him walking away in the spray of a streetlight, snow dusting his shoulders, scarf, and knit cap. The world seemed to be moving at a fast pace around him, out of focus. Despite the blurriness of his surroundings, he recognized the telltale rounding of his shoulders as he'd walked away from her their last night in Saint-Luc. His chest constricted with the memory of how much it had hurt to leave her, not knowing if he'd ever see her again. He took in the surrounding pictures. *Happier* pictures. Pictures of two people in love, embracing in their winter coats and gloves, his arm outstretched as he held the camera. Her voice sailed through his memory, *Take one with my phone!* Beneath that picture were several more from Saint-Luc. The two of them cuddled beneath a blanket, snow falling like blessings around them, their eyes locked on each other. She wore a red hat, and he wore a black one. In another picture, they were sticking out their tongues, and in yet another, making silly faces, and one had been taken midkiss.

Emotions bubbled up inside him. He reached for her, and she came willingly into his arms, returning his embrace.

"Stalkerish?" she asked.

He couldn't even muster a laugh. It was all he could do to tip up her chin and kiss her. "You've always been mine, just like I've always been yours."

Chapter Twelve

AIYLA HAD NEVER minded flying, but she was nervous about meeting Ty's family, tired from the grueling charity challenge, and it seemed no matter how she sat, her leg hurt worse than it had before, which caused her to fidget and shift in her seat.

"Baby, come here." Ty guided her onto his lap.

"I can't sit here," she said, feeling a little silly.

Ignoring her comment, he lifted her legs over the armrest, cradling her safely and lovingly against him, the same way he'd done a hundred other gentle, caring things since they'd come back together. He plugged earbuds into his phone and put one in her ear, one in his own.

"Better?" He planted a kiss on her lips, replacing her mild embarrassment with a sense of belonging *exactly* where she was. "I've got you, babe," he reassured her. "Close your eyes and try to rest."

She must have fallen right to sleep, because the next thing she knew, he was waking her up to climb back into her seat and prepare for landing. How did he know what she needed better than she did? And when had she begun *needing* anyone?

Ty held her hand as he drove to his parents' house, and

when she began nervously fidgeting again, he lifted her hand to his lips and kissed it. She realized that letting Ty reassure her, letting him take care of her and *love* her, wasn't a sign of her becoming needy at all. It was confirmation of how much she trusted him.

"You okay?" He parked in front of an enormous Victorian house with a wraparound porch and gingerbread trim along the peak. The lawn was perfectly manicured. Beautiful gardens lined the walkway up to the front door. The house looked strong and stable, like Ty.

Her stomach churned. "Yeah, I am."

Ty leaned across the seat and cupped the back of her neck, drawing her closer. "I love you. *They'll* love you."

He pressed his lips to hers, drew away, and came back for more, taking the kiss deeper and practically crawling over the console to hold her. Greedy sounds slipped from his lungs as his hands pushed into her hair, refocusing her nervous energy into heat and excitement. Could they stay right there, kissing until morning?

A knock sounded on the window, and Aiyla jumped. Ty groaned and glared at a pretty brunette peering through the glass. Aiyla recognized her as Ty's younger sister, Shannon, from pictures he had shown her in Saint-Luc. Shannon had Ty's mischievous eyes and a hundred-kilowatt smile. Behind her stood a tall, handsome man with brown hair as shaggy as Ty's. *Steve.*

The door opened and she leaned in. "Geez, Ty. Let the girl breathe, will you? Hi. You must be Aiyla. I'm Shannon, Ty's sister." She patted the man's hand resting on her shoulder and said, "This is my fiancé, Grizz, but most people call him Steve."

"How's it going?" Steve said with a friendly smile.

MELISSA FOSTER

"Hi," Aiyla said. "It's nice to meet you."

"Hey, sis. Hey, Steve." Ty stole another kiss from Aiyla and lowered his voice. "I forgot to tell you they were staying here, too."

"It's fine. I want to meet your family."

Shannon reached for Aiyla's hand and helped her from the car. "I heard your leg was giving you trouble and you *still* kicked ass in the race."

"I don't know about kicking ass, but your brother is amazing. Without him, I'd have had to quit."

"Don't let her fool you. *Quit* is not in her vocabulary. She only let me help her because I refused not to let her." Ty came around the car and pulled Steve into a manly embrace. "We won the couples rafting race."

"That's awesome." Shannon put an arm around Aiyla and said, "You can lean on me on the way inside and tell me all about how you and Ty met in Saint-Luc."

"Shan," Ty warned.

Shannon laughed. "If he thinks I'm not going to be nosy when he brings a woman home for the first time, he has another thing coming."

Aiyla was nervous again, but she loved Shannon's outgoing personality. She glanced over her shoulder at Ty, and he blew her a kiss. He and Steve followed them toward the house, carrying their bags.

As they ascended the porch steps, the front door opened and a dark-haired man stepped out, his head held high, serious dark eyes gazing down at them. A blond woman with a mass of curls followed him out and gasped, bringing a smile to the man's face, softening all his sharp edges.

"You're here!" The woman reached for Aiyla, hugging her as

tight as Aiyla's own mother would. "What a pleasure it is to meet you. I'm Maisy, Ty's mother, and this is Ace, Ty's father."

His father opened his arms and embraced her warmly. "Welcome to our home, sweetheart."

"Thank you for allowing me to visit and crash your daughter's wedding."

"We're thrilled you could make it," Maisy said as she pulled Ty into a hug.

"Hi, Mom." Ty kissed her cheek. "Sorry we got in so late."

"Oh, baby. We wouldn't care if it was three in the morning. All that matters is you're home safe and you've brought beautiful Aiyla with you." Maisy put her arm around Aiyla, guiding her into the house as Ty embraced his father. She led Aiyla into a lovely living room with two big sofas, comfy-looking chairs, and a mix of eclectic art pieces and pretty throw blankets. An ornate mantel held a number of framed family photos, and across the room were glass doors overlooking the ocean. The whole thing—his family's warm welcome, the peaceful, homey room, and the magnificent view—took her breath away.

"Are you hungry?" Maisy asked. "Thirsty? Do you need to elevate your leg?"

"I'm fine, thank you. Does everyone know about my leg?" she asked, and just as quickly realized how close Ty's family was. Of course they'd all know.

"I told Ty I wanted to invite you to join me and the girls tomorrow. We're going shopping and then having lunch and getting our nails done for the wedding. Ty said it would depend on if your leg was hurting or not." Maisy's expression turned thoughtful. "I hope that's okay, sweetie. He was just looking out for you."

Maisy hadn't even met her and she already wanted to include her in their plans? Aiyla warmed all over. "It's fine. I was just curious."

"In case Ty didn't warn you, there are no secrets in this house," Shannon said. "The day Ty came home after his trip to Saint-Luc, I knew something had changed. *He'd* changed. Of course I had to pry the truth out of him."

"And then tell everyone else?" Ty shook his head.

"Well, yeah, of course." Shannon rolled her eyes. "It was like you'd left part of yourself behind and you didn't quite know how to manage without it."

Ty nuzzled against Aiyla's neck and said, "I did leave part of myself with you. She's right, baby. A man can't function with half a heart."

She knew his family would see her feelings for him written all over her face. There was no masking how she felt, not when he said such romantic things and made her feel so special.

"Everyone was worried about you," Shannon explained. "I was just the only one willing to push hard enough to find out what had happened."

Aiyla wondered what it must be like to have so many people who cared enough about him to push and worry.

Steve reached for Shannon and said, "Careful spilling all your family's secrets, butterfly. It took Ty forever to finally find a girlfriend and you're going to scare her off."

Butterfly. That was so sweet. She wondered why he called her that.

"*This* coming from a reclusive mountain man who has hugged more trees than women?" Ty nudged Steve's elbow.

"I love my tree hugger," Shannon said.

Maisy smiled at Ace. "It's good to see the kids so happy,

isn't it?"

"It sure is, sweetheart. But I'm afraid it's time for this old man to call it a night." He moved from one person to the next, hugging each of them and saying a few kind words.

When he reached Aiyla, he held her by the shoulders and gazed thoughtfully into her eyes. "We sure are glad you're here. And I want you to know, our house is your house. Sleep in, raid the refrigerator, enjoy the beach. We've got only one hard and fast rule."

Aiyla stood up a little straighter, expecting him to say something about sleeping in a separate room from Ty. *This must be what it's like to have a father.*

Ace's lips curved up, and in his smile she saw Ty—thirty years from now—handsome, strong, *endearing.*

"Dad...?" Ty cocked his head, stepping closer to Aiyla.

"Settle down, son." He placed one of his hands on Ty's shoulder, his eyes moving between the two of them. "Would you like to tell Aiyla what that rule is?"

"All I know," Shannon said, "is don't try sneaking out at midnight when Nate's down on the beach playing his guitar, because he'll narc on you."

Everyone laughed.

Ty laced his fingers with Aiyla's and nodded, as if to say, *Don't worry, baby. I've got you.*

"Come on now, Ace," Maisy said gently. "The kids probably want to get to bed."

"I know I do." Ty glanced at Aiyla, and she felt her cheeks burn.

His father gave him a stern look. "Our rule is simple. Once you've been part of this family, for an hour or a day, a year or a decade, you're always welcome here."

She breathed a sigh of relief, and Ty slipped his arm around her waist, pulling her against him. "Welcome to my life, baby cakes."

The love in the room was so thick she wanted to wrap herself up in it and never leave. It reminded her of the moments she'd shared with her mother and her sister, before her mother had become ill. She missed them terribly right then, and, she realized, she missed being part of a family. She didn't see her sister or nephews often enough, and she wanted to change that.

Without any hesitation or embarrassment, she put her arms around Ty's neck and said, "I think I'm going to like it here."

Chapter Thirteen

TY AWOKE TO the sound of the doors to the deck opening. Aiyla was fast asleep, curled up against his side, bundled under blankets. The sun had just begun to rise, kissing the sky with varying shades of morning light. Maisy stepped outside, looking pretty in a pair of jeans and a colorful shirt with a thin cardigan over it. Her thick curls blew around her face in the morning breeze as she sank down to the chair beside them and offered Ty her coffee mug.

He shook his head and whispered, "Thanks. I'm okay."

She glanced thoughtfully at Aiyla, and then she looked at Ty the way he'd seen her look at each of his siblings when they'd fallen in love. A very distinct look of parental relief and happiness rose in her eyes and remained there. "I can't believe you made the poor girl sleep out here."

"I didn't," he whispered. "Sleeping under the stars is sort of our thing."

"Your *thing*," his mother said. "You have no idea how good it is to hear you say that with regard to a special lady." Her gaze dropped to Aiyla again. "She's a sweetie, Ty. You said her mother is gone? It's only her and her sister?"

Sadness welled inside him. "It was. Now she has me."

"She looks at you like you hung the moon. Please don't hurt her."

His arms tightened possessively around Aiyla. "I never would, Mom. I finally understand why Sam changed for Faith and why Shannon stayed out in Colorado with Steve after never wanting to leave home. I would do anything for Aiyla."

Maisy sipped her coffee and gazed out over the water, a small smile lifting her lips, but her brows knitted.

His mother rarely held her tongue, and she sat silently for so long, he finally asked, "You aren't going to say anything?"

She looked at him with a tentative expression and said, "Our most adventurous child has found his forever love. I don't want to jinx it."

"You can't jinx it, Mom." He pressed a kiss to the top of Aiyla's head. "It's fate."

"I thought you believe we create our own destiny."

"I used to think that, but how else do you explain me and Aiyla meeting up after so many months without so much as a phone call or email?"

"Hearts have a way of speaking across miles and miles. But it takes the strongest kind of love to hear them. I think that's how you explain it." She set her mug on the deck and lay back in the lounger. "Your father and I used to sleep out here, too."

"I remember." He'd woken up many mornings when he was a boy, searching the house for his parents because he was hungry or bored, and he'd usually find them out on the deck, in much the same position he and Aiyla were now. He hadn't thought about those times in so long. Now he wondered if their love of nature had helped to inspire his.

"You were always the earliest riser. You'd come out and sneak onto the chair with us, tucking yourself into the crook of

Daddy's arm, like you didn't want to wake us up."

"I didn't."

She smiled. "You were like a whirlwind as a boy, sweetie. You'd lie there for a minute or two, and then you'd start chatting about all the things you wanted to do that day. Those mornings usually ended with you and your father on the beach exploring or taking the boat out before anyone else woke up."

"Those are some of my favorite memories. Maybe while we're here we can all go out on the boat."

"I'm sure your father would love that." She finished her coffee and pushed to her feet. "Speaking of your father, I need to go wake him up. He and your brothers are helping Nash set up for the wedding today. I can hardly believe my baby girl is getting married tomorrow. It seems like she and Nash have been together forever."

"They will be." Ty reached up and took her hand. "If Aiyla's leg doesn't hurt and she goes shopping with you, I'll go with Dad and help. But if her leg hurts, will you be upset if I stick around here with her?"

"Why would I be upset? That's proof that we did something right as parents. You're really worried about her, aren't you?"

"Yeah," he said quietly.

"Jon's a great doctor. I'm sure whatever is wrong, he'll fix her right up."

"I know he will." He trusted Jon, and Aiyla was probably right about her pain being from overuse. But that didn't stop him from worrying, which was a new experience for him. He'd worried about his family and closest friends, but he'd never been in love before, and he was amazed by the depth of his emotions. He had a feeling he'd caused a lot of worry for his parents over the years, and when his mom touched his shoulder, he reached up and put his hand over hers.

"Mom, I'm sorry for all the times I've caused you and Dad to worry."

"Are you under the misconception that you're *done* causing us to worry?" She chuckled and patted his shoulder. "Wait until you have children of your own. The worry never ends, sweetheart, and that's a good thing. It means you love them. Try to get some more sleep. We've all got a busy day ahead."

There was no more sleep to be had. Shortly after his mother disappeared into the house, his family converged on the deck. Now, nearly three hours later, Ty and Cole were busy hanging white sheers around the doors of the barn by the pond in Nash's yard. The afternoon wedding was going to be held outside, but the rustic barn made for a pretty backdrop. Sam and Nate stood on ladders, hanging mason jars with colorful solar lights from the limbs of trees. Nash had built a gorgeous wooden altar, with intricate musical notes and animals carved into the frame. Tempest and Nash both played the guitar, and Phillip loved animals. They raised chickens, goats, and had about a dozen cats running around their property. The carvings were perfect, and the altar looked beautiful by the pond.

Nash and Phillip were busy wrapping the columns with strings of white lights. Both father and son wore leather work belts and red baseball caps. Ty smiled to himself, remembering all the years he and his brothers had spent following their father around, helping in the yard, on the boat, and as they got older, at Mr. B's, the microbrewery their parents owned.

Not much had changed.

TY'S ENTIRE FAMILY had shown up for breakfast, giving Aiyla a chance to meet each of his siblings and to get to know their significant others. Cole and Nate were more serious than Ty and Sam, who horsed around endlessly. And Tempest, like Cherise, seemed like a careful, watchful older sister. Aiyla was also learning just how small the quaint seaside town was. Faith, Sam's fiancée, worked as a physician assistant in Cole's office. Both she and Cole had taken the day off to spend it with the family, preparing for the wedding. Nate's wife, Jewel, had three younger siblings, and her brother worked for Sam at his rafting company. Peaceful Harbor was bigger than her hometown, but it seemed to be closely knit, and she found that—and the open affection of his siblings—comforting. She'd noticed around the breakfast table that someone was always brushing the hand of their significant other, stealing a quick kiss, or passing a furtive glance. She'd been on her own for so long, she wondered what it would be like to be part of such a big, loving family. And this afternoon she got a good dose of just how wonderful it could be.

After shopping for most of the morning, Aiyla, Maisy, and the girls had lunch at a café. They decided to take advantage of the gorgeous sunny day and walk three blocks to the nail salon. Aiyla enjoyed getting to know everyone. They acted more like sisters than sisters-in-law, daughters-in-law, and friends. She wished Cherise could meet them. She'd get along well with everyone, and she'd probably love to talk about her boys, Danny, who was four, and David, who was two, with Leesa, who doted endlessly on little Avery, and Tempest, who gushed about Phillip.

"I can't believe I'm getting *married* tomorrow," Tempest said excitedly for the millionth time since they'd met. She brushed her hand over her cute summer skirt and said, "And my wedding dress?"

Shannon clasped her hands beneath her chin, fluttered her lashes up toward the sky, and said, "'It's stunning, dreamy, and romantic!'"

Tempest rolled her eyes. "Excuse me for being excited. You just wait. When you and Steve get married you'll do the same thing—and I'll tease you just as much."

Ty had told Aiyla that Tempest was like the wind. *She can calm you down or stir you up with the same easy demeanor, and she writes songs that'll melt your soul.* It was easy to understand why he saw her that way. She was thoughtful and easygoing, but she was no pushover.

Shannon draped an arm over Tempest's shoulder. "I look forward to it. Besides, I don't blame you. Jilly and Jax made the perfect dress for you."

Maisy explained that Jillian and Jax were their twin cousins who lived in the next town over, Pleasant Hill. They were dressmakers and each owned their own business, though Jax's specialty was wedding dresses, and Jillian tended to make dresses for every occasion.

"Ty mentioned his cousin Beau, and I met Ty's friend Trixie, who said she worked with another one of his cousins," Aiyla said. "*Nick,* I think his name was. Are they in the same family?"

"Yes, they have a big family, like us. You'll meet everyone at the wedding except Zev and Graham. They're traveling and couldn't make it back in time," Shannon said.

Aiyla was connecting the dots between cousins. She'd meet Graham, she realized, when they went on their climbing trip.

"Don't you just *love* Trixie, by the way?" Shannon added. "She's on my matchmaking list."

"Isn't every single female you know on that list?" Jewel teased. "Shannon wants *everyone* to be in love."

"Don't quote me or anything, but Jon seemed pretty sweet on Trixie," Aiyla said.

"Jon Butterscotch is sweet on everyone," Faith said. "I shouldn't say that, since he's one of my bosses, and thank goodness he's not like that in the office. But Sam and I went out for drinks at Whiskey Bro's with him, and I swear he looked like he was ready to haul Dixie Whiskey into the back room. The man *loves* women."

"He's just *taste testing*," Maisy said when they reached the corner and stopped to wait for the light to change so they could cross the street.

"That sounds dirty," Leesa said, and Jewel laughed.

"I might be a grandmother, but I'm still a woman." Maisy bent down and tickled Avery's foot, earning a cheeky smile from the baby. "Some people find their soul mates early on, but others are forced to wait until the universe brings them together. Mark my words, Jon will settle down when the right woman piques his interest. They all do."

The light changed and they made their way across the street.

"I think we should skip the nail salon and lay out on the beach until I digest that chocolate lava cake." Shannon held her belly.

"I'm all for lying in the sun," Aiyla chimed in.

"Oh, no, you don't," Jewel said as she looped her arm around Aiyla's. She was a petite blonde who knew how to take charge. "You're not getting out of this."

Aiyla had admitted that she hadn't ever had a manicure or pedicure. Her nails were short and she wasn't exactly careful with her hands or feet. "I'm not trying to get out of it, but I don't have long, pretty nails like you guys do."

She held out her hand and Maisy took it in hers and squeezed it gently. "It's not the length of the nails that matters, sweetie; it's how you use them."

"Mom!" Tempest chided her.

"Oh, please, Tempe. Do you think I don't know about loving up a man? There *are* secrets to being married as long as your father and I have been."

Tempest wrinkled her nose. "I don't want to know this about you."

"I wasn't going to share. Anyway, I'm excited that we get to be there for Aiyla's first mani-pedi," Maisy said. "Everyone needs a little pampering. And trust me, even my mountain-climbing son needs a subtle reminder that behind this strong, capable woman is a lady who deserves to be treated like one."

"He treats me better than anyone has ever treated me in my life," Aiyla said. "You raised him well."

"Thank you," Maisy said, touching the stroller as she walked beside Leesa. "We tried with all of our babies, and I hope we did a good job." She glanced at Tempest and said, "Because now my *babies* are raising babies."

Tempest smiled. "I adore Phillip."

"Cole is the best father in the world," Leesa said proudly.

"*Ahem!*" Tempest shook her head. "Not that I don't think my brother is a great father, but *Nash Morgan?* That man knows how to parent. Don't you think?"

"Oh gosh, *yes,*" Leesa said apologetically. "I just meant—"

Tempest hugged her. "They're both great dads. We're very lucky." Her gaze moved over each of them. "Actually, we're all very lucky. The question is, who's next in line to give Mom more grandbabies?"

"Steve and I aren't even married yet," Shannon pointed out.

"Well, neither are we," Faith said, "but we're thinking of starting a family right away after we get married."

"More power to you," Jewel said. "I practically raised my brother and sisters. I want a little more time to enjoy Nate before I go down that path."

Aiyla's ears perked up. "My sister raised me, too."

"Really? Did your mom work a million hours, too?" Jewel asked.

"She did, but we lost her when I was fifteen." Even after more than a decade, she bristled at the shock of sadness that accompanied thoughts of losing her mother. She could talk about her mother's *life* without getting mired down in too much sadness, but when it came to her death, she still felt like she was swallowing sand. She tried to push away the sadness and focus on her sister instead. "My sister, Cherise, was twenty-one and just married at the time. She and her husband, Caleb, moved into our mom's house with me so I could finish high school."

"I'm so sorry," Tempest said. "But I'm glad your sister was there for you. Did you have any other family that helped?"

"No. I've never known my father. But my mother was a housekeeper, and one of her clients, Ms. Farrington, who I always say was our fairy godmother, paid for Cherise and Caleb's move. Ms. F had been supporting my school sports activities for years in exchange for my traveling with her on school breaks and over summers. She's the one who taught me about photography and introduced me to the world of traveling."

"You traveled with her?" Jewel asked. "That's a sweet deal."

"Yeah. I was pretty lucky. Ms. F never married or had children, and she was in her late seventies when I started traveling with her. After my mom died, I worked anywhere I could after school, and then at sixteen I took my senior year of English in summer school, graduated early, and Ms. F helped me get a full-time job at a ski resort. Through her I've met resort owners all over the world who are happy to give me a job when I'm in their area taking pictures. Like I said, she was our fairy god-mother, but it was Cherise who was there at night when I'd cry myself to sleep, and who made sure I still functioned and went to school. I owe my sanity to my sister for sure."

Maisy touched Aiyla's shoulder. "Your mother would be very proud of both of you, and I'm so sorry you lost her."

"Thank you. I like to think she'd be proud. Cherise has two beautiful boys now, and she's an amazing mother."

"And you're an incredible person, too, sweetheart," Maisy said. "Ty showed us your photography books after Shannon spilled the beans about you a few months ago. You're a gifted photographer, and I've never seen my son happier. For that alone, I will always be thankful."

She drew Aiyla into a hug, and before Aiyla knew what was happening, all the girls were hugging her.

"I lost my father a couple of years ago," Leesa said. "I don't think our parents ever really leave us. I'm sure your mom is with you in spirit."

"And now you have our mom, too." Tempest smiled at Maisy, who nodded in agreement.

"And you've got me and Sam," Faith said.

"You have all of us," Shannon added. "And we're pretty frigging awesome if I do say so myself."

Tears welled in Aiyla's eyes. It had been a long time since she'd felt like she belonged someplace other than in her own solitary world. She'd thought Ty's love was a gift, but now she realized that what he'd said about his family was really true. She'd laid her past out before them and they'd still welcomed her with open arms.

"I lost my father and my older brother," Jewel said. "If you ever need an ear, or a shoulder to lean on, I'm here." She looked at the others and added, "And these crazy girls? They're not just spewing kind words. They mean it. We all do."

Aiyla opened her mouth to thank them, and a tear rolled down her cheek. Embarrassed, she turned away, wiping it dry. "Thank you." Her voice cracked, and when they all hugged her again, it drew more tears.

Her phone vibrated, and she was thankful for the distraction. She pulled it from her pocket, and her overworked heart sped up even more at the sight of Ty's name on the screen. They'd been apart for only a few hours, and she missed him already. She opened the text and couldn't suppress a much-needed laugh. She turned her phone for the others to see, showing them the picture of Ace and Phillip, both of them draped in white silk togas and beaming at the camera.

"Uh-oh. Looks like Papa Ace is at it again," Leesa said with a laugh.

"Why do I think my wedding decorations are going to all have grass stains?" Tempe asked.

"Breathe, baby," Maisy said. "Nash would never let that happen. I'm sure those are extras."

Maisy had so many endearments for all of them, it was easy to see why Ty's love came out in that fashion, too.

"We can stop by and do a spot check after we get our nails done," Faith offered. "We'll fix whatever the guys mess up."

Shannon leaned closer to Aiyla and whispered, "In case you

had any doubts, boys always grow up to be like their fathers. See how lucky you are?"

Lucky was exactly the word she'd use.

Chapter Fourteen

"ARE YOU NERVOUS?" Ty asked as he and Aiyla walked into the Peaceful Harbor Pain Management Center Friday afternoon. He'd been thrilled when the girls had shown up to check up on them after their nail appointments. Going several hours without seeing Aiyla was not high on his list of fun things to do, no matter how much he'd enjoyed the time with the guys.

"About the appointment with Jon?" she asked. "Not even a little. You know if it was anything horrible the pain wouldn't wax and wane, or be alleviated by Motrin and Tylenol. If you hadn't been so pushy, and if Jon hadn't been so darn nice, I would have waited to see how it felt in another week, then made an appointment with my doctor back home."

"That would have cut it very close for our climbing trip." He pushed the button for the elevator and kissed her softly. "Thank you for putting my worries to rest."

"It was the least I could do. You did carry me over the finish line."

The elevator arrived, and when they stepped inside, Aiyla went up on her toes and kissed him. "I missed you today."

"Not half as much as I missed you." He lowered his lips to hers, kissing her tenderly, because if he kissed her as passionately as he wanted to, he'd be sporting wood when they left the elevator, and Jon would never let him live that down.

The elevator doors opened, and as they stepped into the hall he said, "Tomorrow's going to be all about family, so tonight I'm kidnapping you."

"That sounds *promising*."

"You look hot in those little khaki shorts, but I bet they'll look even sexier on the floor." He pulled open the office door and smacked her butt as she walked through.

"I was hoping if I wore shorts Jon wouldn't make me wear a paper gown." She lowered her voice as they approached the reception desk. "I hate those things."

Brandy, the petite brunette receptionist who had worked for Cole and Jon for the last few years, greeted them with an eager smile. "Hi, Ty."

"How's it going, Brandy? This is my girlfriend, Aiyla Bell. She has an appointment at four."

"Yes. Dr. Butterscotch said you were coming in." She handed a clipboard and pen to Aiyla. "If you wouldn't mind filling these out, then we'll get you right back to see him."

Aiyla filled out the documentation and provided the necessary identification cards, and a few minutes later they were brought into an examination room. Even though she'd said she wasn't nervous, Ty noticed her fidgeting with the edge of her shorts.

He reached for her hand and said, "No paper gown. Must be those sexy shorts."

"Or the fact that you told the girl who brought us back not to bother leaving the paper gown."

"Yeah, it could be that."

A knock at the door sounded and Jon peeked his head in,

shielding his eyes with his hand. "I heard you two were in here. There's no hanky-panky going on, is there?"

"Unfortunately, no," Ty said.

Jon hiked a thumb over his shoulder. "Want me to come back later?"

Ty chuckled as Jon walked in and shook his hand. He looked every bit the part of a professional doctor in a dress shirt and tie, with his hair neatly brushed. He pulled a chair over to the desk and motioned to the seats beside the exam table. From that moment on, nothing about the way Jon acted resembled their race buddy *Speed*.

"Why don't you two sit down while we go over Aiyla's medical history, and then we'll do the exam." He looked over her paperwork and asked a number of routine questions. His expression softened, and he said, "I see your mother had pancreatic cancer? Has there been any other family history of cancer?"

Cancer? Ty's heart lurched, and he reached for Aiyla's hand. "I thought your mother died from a staph infection after a medical procedure."

"She did." The sadness in Aiyla's eyes was palpable. "The infection was the result of a procedure she'd had because she had cancer." She shifted her gaze to Jon and said, "No one else in my family has had cancer. Just my mom. Although I don't know my father, so I have no idea about his medical history."

Jon nodded.

Ty's heart took another hit at her confession. "Is that hereditary? Pancreatic cancer?"

"About ten percent of pancreatic cancers are thought to be related to genetic factors," Jon explained. "That means an inherited gene mutation can be passed from parents to their children. Although those genetic conditions are not known to directly cause pancreatic cancer, they can increase a person's risk for developing the disease."

Aiyla squeezed his hand and said, "Ty, I'm here for pain in my *leg*, not digestive problems. Trust me, if I thought for a second I had cancer, I'd have been in the doctor's office first thing. I watched my mom die. I wouldn't mess around."

He would give anything to go back in time and be with her when she'd lost her mother, to help bear the burden of that pain. "I know, babe. I just want to understand, that's all."

Jon asked her more questions, some of which he'd asked when he'd examined her in Colorado. *When did the pain start? Is it persistent? Does it wake you up at night?* Ty had a feeling Jon was comparing her answers to last time, just as he was. He also asked several new questions: *Any fevers? Rashes? Weight loss? Fatigue? Changes in sleep patterns?* She answered no to each one.

"Okay, Aiyla." Jon pushed to his feet. "Why don't you hop up on the exam table and we'll take a look at that leg."

He took his time, inspecting and palpating her legs, knees, and joints and checking her range of motion on each limb. He put her through a litany of flexing and raising exercises, and he explained that back pain could refer to the legs and an unbalanced gait could also cause issues. He watched her walk up and down the hallway.

Ty found himself holding his breath during each and every stage of the exam, and when they returned to the exam room, he couldn't wait any longer. He tried to temper his anxiety and asked, "What do you think, Doc?"

"It's hard to say right now. This could be nothing more than an overuse injury, as Aiyla thought. But you mentioned going on a climbing trip in two weeks. I'd like to send you over to radiology for an MRI so we cover all our bases. That way we'll know what we're dealing with. I should have results Monday morning, and I can have Brandy fit you in first thing Monday if you'd like for a follow-up."

"Yes, please," Ty said.

"Okay. Eight o'clock Monday morning. Until then," he said to Aiyla, "you said the Motrin and Tylenol are helping?"

"Yes, they seem to be."

"Then keep that up if you need to." Jon wrote up an order for an MRI and told them to head down to the radiologist's office, which was in the same building. "And if you do any heavy exercise, *ice*, *rest*, and *elevate*."

"She's not doing any heavy exercise," Ty said firmly.

Jon nodded and asked Aiyla how long she was going to be in town.

She looked at Ty. "We haven't really talked about that. A few days, maybe?"

"As long as it takes to get her healed up." Ty draped an arm over her shoulder, pulling her in close. "Are you okay with that?"

She smiled and said, "I doubt I have a choice."

BY THE TIME they finished getting her MRI, it was almost seven o'clock. They stopped for energy bars at a convenience store and headed to Ty's parents' house before going out on their special date. After throwing on her sweatshirt and taking some medicine, she found Ty in the driveway putting a cooler in the back of an old Jeep.

"Where did this come from?" She peered into the backseat

and saw a camera bag, blankets, and towels.

"The garage. It's my father's. We need four-wheel drive to get where we're going."

He opened the door and she climbed in. "That sounds interesting. Where are we going?"

"To one of my favorite spots. Think you can handle a five-minute walk?"

"I can handle an hour walk."

He ran his hands up her legs and leaned in closer, his eyes turning dark and seductive. "My brave, strong girl. I brought dinner, but we might want to skip it and go straight to dessert."

His warm lips pressed against hers and he squeezed her thighs, making her body hum. As their mouths parted, "Dessert" slipped from her lips, and he chuckled.

They drove through the small town, the wind whipping her hair across her face, as strip malls and residential streets gave way to fields and the bar Faith had mentioned Whiskey Bro's came into view. The rustic shack had blacked-out windows, and the parking lot was full of motorcycles and trucks. She couldn't imagine Faith going anywhere near that place, which only made her more curious.

"That's the bar Faith said she went to with Sam," she said as they passed. "We should go there."

"You like biker bars?"

"I've never been to one, but Faith went, so it can't be too bad, right?"

"We know the owners. They're good people. But it's definitely a biker bar. If you're afraid of long-haired, tattooed guys who look like they can rip your head off and have no filter whatsoever, you should stay away."

She couldn't resist getting a rise out of him. He was so cute when he was jealous. "I like hot bikers."

His eyes narrowed, and she leaned across the seat and kissed him. "I'm teasing. I want to check it out, but for the adventure, not for the guys." She put her hand on his thigh and inched her fingertips up, grazing his cock. "The only guy I want is right here."

He guided her hand over his growing erection. "I'm all yours, baby. There's nothing I won't do for you, including taking you to that bar, but if anyone touches my girl, you might have to bail me out of jail."

"My big, bad Bradonian is *very* possessive."

He lifted her hand and kissed it, then placed it between his legs again, sliding her a hungry look. "Hang on, sweet one, we're hitting the trail."

He turned onto a steep mountain road lined with lush plants and tall, looming trees, which shaded the road from the moonlight. The Jeep rocked and rumbled over the uneven terrain. When the road narrowed, turning to rutted, overgrown tire paths, Ty slowed to a snail's pace, barely clearing trees on either side of the vehicle.

"This feels like we're going to end up in a movie like *Wrong Turn*."

"There are no wrong turns in Peaceful Harbor."

After a mile or so the trees opened up and the road disappeared. Ty continued driving through a field of long grass, the headlights bouncing over the rugged terrain. He cut the engine, and blue-gray moonlight spilled over the wilderness. The sounds of tree frogs and crickets, animals scurrying across the forest floor, and leaves brushing in the gentle breeze surrounded them. The first few anxious and exciting moments that always came with unfamiliar territory made Aiyla's pulse quicken.

"Now I know why you brought your camera," she said. "This is gorgeous."

"This is just the beginning." He climbed from the Jeep and tossed the blankets and towels into a backpack she hadn't noticed before.

He put his camera bag over his shoulder and head, so it hung across his body, and hoisted the pack over his shoulders before grabbing the cooler. As she watched him preparing for their evening, taking care of everything, she remembered the sadness and concern in his eyes when he'd heard about how her mother had died. She knew she owed him an explanation, but he hadn't pushed for one, as if he'd known she didn't want to get caught up in it in front of Jon. And now he stood before her with his hair hanging over his eyes, his broad shoulders carrying the weight of his surprise romantic evening. He looked rugged and manly, and when he reached for her hand and pulled her in closer, touching his lips to hers, she knew it wasn't his looks that made her heart take notice. It was *all* of him. Maybe it was the emotions from spending the day with his family and feeling so welcome, or the way he cared so deeply about her well-being, or maybe it was just that she was too in love with him not to share it.

Whatever the reason, her emotions spilled out. "I never thought about what I wanted in a boyfriend, but if I had, you'd surpass anything I could dream up. I love you, Ty, and I appreciate your help during the race, and going to see Jon with me, and sharing your family with me." She looked up at the starry sky. "And tonight…" When she met his gaze again, he was smiling. "I just want you to know all of that."

His arm circled her waist and he said, "I do know. I had no idea what *love* meant before you. But now I know it means that someone else is always there. You're in my every thought, in everything I do, everything I hope for. Our stars have collided, babe, and the universe awaits our exploration."

"Then let's not keep it waiting."

Chapter Fifteen

TY AND AIYLA walked through the woods and came upon abandoned railroad tracks. Green plants and spiky grasses sprouted up between aged wooden ties overgrown with wildflowers and weeds.

"This is beautiful," she said as they walked beside the tracks.

"When I was in middle school and I got too rambunctious, my dad would take me hiking all over these mountains. I probably wouldn't have been rambunctious if you were around."

"You would have been all over me like white on rice, and then I would have been one of the Ty *harem*. Then I'd have had to find some other guy to go adventuring with and leave you in the dust."

"Girl, you are *so* wrong." He hauled her in for a kiss. "If you'd have been mine, I never would have let you go."

"I love that you think so. Tell me more about *rambunctious Ty*. Your dad used to take you here?"

"He did, and as I got older, I'd come here when I wanted peace and quiet. There was another place that Cole took me before he left for college, out by the river, where he used to go to be alone. But this was *mine*. There's a creek up ahead. That's what I wanted to show you. I took my first pictures there."

"How old were you?"

"Fourteen. I'll never forget when my parents gave me my first camera. I hadn't asked for one, but I used to spend hours going through *National Geographic* magazines. I remember feeling like those pictures were *alive*. I wanted to crawl into them and touch everything. It was like the pictures you take. Yours make me want to meet the people and hear their stories. Anyway, when my father put that camera in my hands, it was like he opened a door. I got on my bike that afternoon and came straight here. This is where I fell in love with photography."

"You rode your bike all this way? My mom would never have let me do that at fourteen."

"She let you travel without her."

"Yes, with the woman she worked for and trusted."

"Well, to be honest, my parents didn't know until I developed the pictures; then I got my ass handed to me."

She laughed. "Now, that's good parenting."

Flowers gave way to tufts of grass, and the dirt beneath their feet turned soft. Without the cover of greenery, the railroad ties appeared rotted and broken.

Ty put a hand on Aiyla's back and pointed up ahead, where the thick steel rails of the tracks were twisted and gnarled as they snaked out over a debilitated trestle. "All I wanted was to see *this* through the lens of the camera."

"Whoa," she said. Moonlight glistened off the water like silver in contrast to the rusted, tangled mess that was the railroad tracks. "That's a beautiful disaster."

"Right? Well worth being grounded as a kid." He set their bags and the cooler on the ground, fished out the blanket and spread it out. Then he handed her his camera. "Want to take a few pictures?"

"Do I ever!"

She looked through the lens, but it wasn't the mangled tracks and conflicting serenity of the water she wanted to see. She focused on Ty as he gazed out at the picturesque view. His hair was pushed back, bringing his handsome face into focus. His thick dark brows made his eyes appear even more intense. She moved around him, taking one picture after another, capturing his surprised expression—and the instant lusty look that replaced it.

He stepped closer, reaching for her, and she stepped back, taking pictures as she went. When he caught her around the waist, her face tipped up, and she caught sight of a house on the hill behind him.

"Ty, there's a house."

He carefully lowered the camera and kissed her. "Mm-hm."

He kissed her neck as she lifted the camera again, peering through the lens, trying to get a better look at the house.

"Who lives there?"

"No one," he said, continuing to nibble on her like she was dinner. "That's the house Beau's renovating. It was abandoned forever before he bought it."

"There's a light on inside."

"Beau must be there," he said, and kissed her neck. "But *I'm* right here—"

"Let's go see it," she said excitedly, and headed up the hill.

"Why did I have to fall for a woman who loves old things?" he teased as he put a hand on her lower back.

"Because you'd be bored with someone who was predicta-ble, *and* you know I adore your kisses and I'll more than make up for it later." She planted a kiss on his lips. "*Promise.*"

As the house came into clearer view, her pulse quickened at the spectacularly unique and desperately-in-need-of-love property. "Oh my gosh, look! The porch is *round*, and look at all the windows! Can you imagine the view they have of the water?"

"Yes," he said with a laugh. "I have a million pictures taken from the porch. It's a gorgeous view."

They circled the small one-story home, admiring the uniqueness of the round porch, which circled the entire house. The paint and siding were chipped, and pieces were missing in some places. The clay-colored cone-shaped roof sagged over the front door, and several enormous picture windows were cracked or boarded up. Brick piers stood beneath aged wooden columns around the perimeter, holding up the porch roof.

"Yup. Beau's here." Ty pointed toward a shiny black truck out front.

Aiyla handed Ty the camera. "I *have* to peek inside. Do you think he'll let us in?" She peered through the window. "There he is! I see him."

Beau must have heard her, because he looked right at the window with a fierce expression.

She jumped back. "Oops. He saw me, and didn't look happy."

The front door opened and a big man walked out, his jaw tight, eyes serious as they landed on Aiyla. She lifted her hand in nervous wave. "Hi."

"How's it going, Beau?" Ty stepped onto the porch, and a surprised smile softened his cousin's expression.

"Hey, cuz. What're you doing out this way?"

"I was showing my girlfriend, Aiyla, the old tracks, and she saw your lights on and got curious. Aiyla, this is Beau. Beau, Aiyla."

Beau nodded at her. "Nice to meet you."

"You too. Sorry to peek in your window."

"No, you're not," Beau said casually.

Ty laughed. "He's got you nailed, babe."

Her nerves eased, and she had to smile at his direct nature. "You caught me. I have a thing for old houses."

"And mountain climbers, apparently," Beau said. "Come on in and take a look around."

"What are you doing out here so late?" Ty asked as they walked inside.

Beau looked down at his dusty shirt and jeans and splayed his hands. "I was gutting the kitchen, but I just finished cleaning up and I was getting ready to leave." He glanced into the yard. "Did you walk here?"

"We came in the back way and walked along the tracks," Ty answered.

Aiyla stood in the foyer feeling a wave of nostalgia. The home she'd grown up in was surrounded by woods and about this size, with similar worn hardwood floors, high ceilings, and dark crown molding. Her childhood home didn't have interior columns like the ones separating the foyer from the two small rooms on either side of the home, but she remembered telling her mother they should knock down the walls. It had become a running joke between them. Whenever Aiyla or Cherise would suggest making a change to anything, her mother would say, *We should consult Sledgehammer Sally*, which was what her mother called her in those instances.

Smiling at the memory, she admired the room to the right, with a built-in bench that ran beneath two large windows and a built-in bookshelf in the corner. She imagined covering the bench with fluffy pillows and watching the rain fall in the spring, or snow fall in the winter.

"There's not much to see yet," Beau said.

"Are you kidding?" she said. "This place is full of character. The house I grew up in was about this size, although it didn't have a round porch or the spectacular view of a creek. But we did have woods, and I have great memories of playing in them."

Ty took her hand as they walked into the living room. The floor was covered with tarps and tools, but even with the chaos of refinishing, she could see how beautiful the home could be. A wall of windows faced the creek, and an old stone fireplace sat off to the right between two smaller rooms, which she assumed were bedrooms. Across from the fireplace was what would be the kitchen area.

"This is gorgeous," she said, taking it all in. "Can you imagine if you put a whole wall of glass doors here and exposed the rafters in the ceiling? You could carry the stone from the fireplace across the wall, maybe throw in a few built-in bookshelves. And that roof over the porch? What a *perfect* sleeping deck." She imagined sitting on the porch with Ty, watching the sun come up over the creek.

"A sleeping deck?" Beau said. "I hadn't thought about that."

"Really? I'd rather sleep outdoors any day. And with that view, and the sound of the water? People pay a lot of money for sound machines that imitate what you have right here at your fingertips."

"That's a great selling point," Beau said. "I'm flipping this property. Are you a decorator? An architect?"

"No. I just love old houses." She felt Ty's gaze on her as she walked around. "The open kitchen is wonderful. Please tell me you're not going to wall it off. This is so cozy and welcoming."

"Babe." Ty smiled and shook his head. "Beau's been doing this a long time. I think he knows what'll sell best."

"Oh gosh, I'm sorry," she said. "I don't mean to tell you how to do your job. I just got excited."

"No worries. I'm not going to wall off the kitchen. I think it's better for entertaining this way." Beau went to the windows and gazed outside. "And I like your sleeping porch idea."

"You do?" She joined him by the windows. "I saw one once that had open archways, no screens or anything, but they'd draped one of those mosquito nets around the bed. It was so pretty."

The three of them walked through each room tossing out design ideas. Ty suggested adding accent lights around the edges of the ceiling if Beau exposed the rafters, and Aiyla imagined how romantic that would look at night. After they'd gone through each room, Aiyla thanked Beau for letting them traipse through.

"Anytime. I've enjoyed brainstorming with you. Ty, are you and Graham still planning your climbing trip?"

"Definitely. Aiyla's coming with us," Ty said. "Graham's supposed to be back in town a few days before we leave. We should try to get everyone together for dinner before we head out."

"That'd be great. Speaking of heading out, I've got to get a move on," Beau said. "Zev is Skyping everyone tonight, and I want to catch up with him before he goes off the grid again."

"Zev is Beau's younger brother," Ty explained. "He's a treasure hunter, and he travels more than we do."

"Seriously?" she asked. "Like pirate treasures? What a cool job."

"Cool, yes, but not often fruitful. I swear he must live on twigs and berries," Beau said as they walked outside and he locked up. "I'm glad I had a chance to meet you, Aiyla." He brushed the dust from his shirt and hugged her. "Let me know about dinner, because by the time you get back from your cross-country trip, I'll be in Colorado renovating the Sterling House."

"We were just there for the Mad Prix. It's a gorgeous old inn," Aiyla said.

"It will be," Beau said. "I'm on cleanup duty after our cousins trashed the place."

They talked for a few more minutes, and after Beau left, Aiyla and Ty stood on the back porch gazing out over the creek. It was warm and breezy, and the creek looked inviting.

"Are you hungry?" Ty asked.

"Not really." She stepped from the porch and pulled off her sweatshirt. "Are there other houses around here?"

He followed her down the hill. "No, not for miles."

"So…we're *totally* alone?"

"As far as I know."

"Let's go skinny-dipping!" She limped down the hill, pulling off her shirt and laughing as she tossed it at Ty.

"Skinny-dip—" Her shirt hit him in the face as her bra fell to the ground.

She kicked off her boots and tugged off her socks. "Come on!" she hollered, wiggling out of her shorts and panties. She turned to face Ty, only then realizing he was looking at her through the lens of the camera. Her arms shot across her body. "Don't you dare!" She turned and ran into the creek.

"Aiyla, wait!"

She tiptoe-ran through ankle-deep water. "Hurry up!" She ran to the middle of the creek and realized she was only in *calf-*

deep water.

Ty doubled over in laughter.

"You *knew* it was this shallow?" she yelled.

"I tried to tell you."

She crossed her arms over her chest. "Ty!"

He took off his shirt and set his camera on it, yanked off his boots and socks, and shimmied out of his jeans and briefs.

Holy frigging hotness. "You're coming in?"

Six-plus feet of naked Ty Braden strode through the water with a wide grin and a dark look in his eyes. "Damn right I'm coming in, so you'd better be ready."

"For?" She stepped backward, her pulse quickening as he neared.

"For your *man*."

He reached for her and she squealed and darted away, splashing them both. He caught her around the waist and hauled her against him as she shrieked.

"You're not getting away that easily, my sweet *naked* girl."

She wrapped her arms around his neck, feeling his hard length against her belly, and her entire body ignited. "Getting away is the *last* thing on my mind."

TY LOWERED HIS mouth to Aiyla's, kissing her until she rose onto her toes, trying to scale him like a mountain. He lifted her into his arms, smiling against her lips as he carried her to the shore. He'd gone into some sort of a trance inside the house, watching her eyes light up as she'd gone through each room talking about how it reminded her of home and what she'd change. He'd never given a house a second thought, but he began to imagine what it might be like to put down roots with Aiyla, to have a home to come back to and call their own. And when she'd limped down to the water with that sexy smile and sassy attitude, he'd been struck dumb with love.

"You tricked me," she said happily as he laid her on the blanket.

"No, babe. I was too busy *enjoying* you to even think about tricking you."

She lay beneath him, drops of water glistening off her skin as he covered her shoulders and chest with kisses, loving the way she breathed harder with each one. He'd learned her pleasure points, how to tease her and make her go wild. As he ran his tongue around her nipples, over the tips, and lavished each beautiful breast with openmouthed kisses, she squirmed and made those sexy, needful sounds that drove him out of his mind. He followed the curves of her body with his mouth, sinking his teeth into her hip, slicking his tongue along the juncture of her thighs, tasting her sweetness.

"*Ty*," she pleaded. Her fingers pushed into his hair, her hips rocking against his mouth.

He wanted her out of her mind with desire. He moved lower, one hand on either side of her injured leg, kissing a path down her thigh, covering every spec of flesh until he reached her shin. His heart ached with the memory of the sadness in her eyes when she'd spoken of her mother's illness. He reached for her hand, needing to feel even more connected, and held it as he kissed her from shin to ankle, tasting the creek water, and more intensely, the love he had for her. As he kissed his way up her other leg, the scent of her arousal drew him in. He licked and teased her swollen sex until it glistened, and she begged for more. He pushed her thighs open wider, pressing them into the ground as he devoured her, thrusting his tongue in deep, then teasing her with light flicks over her most sensitive nerves. She writhed and moaned, digging her heels into the blanket. He teased her with his fingers and pushed them into her sex, seeking the spot that curled her fingers into fists. He stayed with her, loving her with his mouth and hand until her body shook and bucked, a string of indiscernible, sinful sounds sailing from her lips. Just hearing them nearly pulled him over the edge.

"Need you," he ground out, overcome with lust and love.

He aligned their bodies, feeling her slick heat against the head of his cock. Wanting to feel her heart beating against his, he cradled her against him as their mouths, and their bodies, became one. Every thrust earned another moan, a claw of her nails. Heat and desire rushed through him, and he fisted his hands in her hair, tearing his mouth away with the need to *see* her. To see what their love did to her. And it was all right there, in the flush of her cheeks, her heavy breathing, and the alluring mix of white-hot vixen and sweet, loving woman gazing up at him.

He searched for words that could express the depth of his emotions, but his mind was whirling like a tornado, and only one word came: "Forever."

As their mouths crashed together and their bodies took over, they succumbed to the domination of their love, and as they crested the peak, he knew words could never be enough.

They lay together afterward, Aiyla's sated body draped over his side, her fingers absently drawing circles on his chest. "I like it here," she said. "It reminds me of home, and of my mom."

"I'm glad, babe. Can I ask you something about her? If you'd rather I didn't, I understand."

She leaned her chin on his chest, her eyes shadowed with

sadness again. "I'm sorry I didn't tell you she was sick. For some reason it makes me less sad to say she died of a staph infection than talking about the disease. It was the staph infection that killed her, although if that hadn't, the cancer would have."

He rolled onto his side, holding her close. "Does it scare you? Because Jon made it sound like even if you did inherit the mutated genes it doesn't mean you'll end up with the disease."

"It's not that I'm scared. Her doctors explained all of that to me and Cherise. She suffered a lot, and the cancer took over so fast. It's not something I like to think about, and it just makes me sad to talk about it, that's all."

"I understand. If Nate's experience with losing his best friend is any indication of the power of grief, then I know it can eat you up if you keep it in and it can tear you apart when you let it out. But with love and support, all those broken pieces can be put back together in a way that they no longer feel like shards of broken glass. We don't have to talk about how you lost your mom, but if you ever want to, I'm here. And if you break down and cry, or get angry with the world, you don't have to worry about your broken pieces. I'll pick up each and every one, and I'll love them until you're whole again."

Chapter Sixteen

SATURDAY ARRIVED WITH sunshine and love in the air, the perfect day for Tempest and Nash's bohemian-style picnic wedding. Colorful blankets and quilts surrounded the pond, each covered with mismatched, oversized throw pillows Tempest and the girls had bought over the last few weeks. Each blanket included place settings, a picnic basket filled with food, and a small tray Nash had made out of repurposed materials, beneath beautiful floral centerpieces. They'd strung enormous paper flowers from the trees and around the roof of the altar, where Nash and Phillip now stood. They wore matching light gray linen pants and short-sleeved white dress shirts with suspenders, though Nash's pants were long, and Phillip wore shorts.

Nash played the guitar as he and Phillip sang "I Choose You" by Sara Bareilles, singing about how they chose Tempest and they were ready to tell the world they finally got it all right. Ty's mother had told him that Nash and Phillip had been practicing since the day Nash had proposed.

Tempest and Ace stood at the entrance to the barn, beneath the silk drapes. Ty moved stealthily, taking pictures of Tempest and their father as they made their way along the rose-petal aisle toward the altar.

As Nash sang about his whole heart belonging to Tempest, Ty's camera landed on Aiyla. She looked gorgeous in a short lavender dress and a pair of strappy sandals that showed off her long legs. They'd spent the night at the creek, waking with the sun. After wading in the cool creek and taking more pictures, Aiyla had insisted on taking one more peek through the windows of Beau's house, and Ty had caught her excitement on film.

Cole nudged him, motioning toward Tempest and their father, reminding him he was looking at the *wrong* beautiful woman. Aiyla blew him a kiss as he passed by, and he mouthed, *I love you*, then swiftly moved off to the side so he could catch pictures of his father kissing Tempest's cheek as he placed her hand in Nash's. Tempest had tears in her eyes, but that wide smile that she was known for tugged on Ty's heartstrings. He was happy for his sister, and equally so for Nash and Phillip. In a few minutes, Tempest would have a new family, a new name. A new *forever*.

As she and Nash recited their vows, Ty took more pictures, catching the moment when Phillip, in all his curly-haired glory, held up a black velvet box with their rings in it.

"Put it on her, Daddy! Make her my mommy," he said loudly, and everyone laughed, except Tempest, who cried happy tears.

Ty took pictures of Nash's mother and her new boyfriend holding hands and his cousins Jillian and Jax and the rest of their family all watching in various stages of joy. Even Jon looked teary-eyed. Ty caught the very moment Tempest and Nash were pronounced man and wife, and the long, steamy kiss that went on so long everyone yelled, "Get a room!"

Phillip wiggled between them, thrusting his arms up toward Tempest. "My turn, Mama!"

Tempest swept him into her arms and kissed him. "I love you, sweet boy."

"I love you, too, Mama."

Nash kissed them both. "My sweet angel, my *wife*. I adore you."

Ty caught the kisses, and hearing the pride in his brother-in-law's voice unleashed something inside of him. He lowered the camera, his eyes landing on his beautiful Aiyla. The love of his life. She glanced over, and their eyes locked. As everyone cheered and congratulated the happy couple, Ty made his way across the lawn toward her. His heart beat so hard, he was sure she could feel it thrumming in the space between them as he took her hand in his and said, "I want this with you."

Her brows knitted. "What? A farmette with a pond?"

"No. A *wedding*," he said, surprising himself as much as her.

Her eyes widened.

"I never want to be apart again. I want to know we're always going to be there for each other. In good times and in bad. Marry me, Aiyla. Be my bride, my wife, my *forever*."

Tears spilled from her eyes. "Ty...?"

He watched a thousand emotions roll over her face, each one surer than the next that this was right. That *they* were right. "It's fate, baby. You know it is. We're the same adventure-seeking, earth-loving, unstoppable best friends we were in Saint-Luc. They say absence makes the heart grow fonder. I say the hell with that. We've had a lifetime worth of growing fonder. I want more than fondness. I want unyielding, all-consuming, *forever* love. I want to love you and to make your life so great you'll never regret a second of our life together."

"Ty, pictures, man," Nate said as he stepped up beside him. He took one look at Aiyla's tears and scowled at Ty. "Goddamn it. What did you do?"

"Proposed," Ty said anxiously, still holding Aiyla's gaze. She was smiling through her tears, and he was hanging on her every breath, awaiting what he hoped would be a *yes*.

"Holy shit," Nate said under his breath.

Ty didn't have to look—couldn't look away from his future bride—to know Nate was smiling.

"Baby?" Ty urged.

Tears streamed down her cheeks as she nodded. "Yes. Of course, yes!"

She threw herself into his arms and he spun her around, kissing her as her words played in his mind. *Yes. Of course, yes!*

"I love you, baby cakes," he said. "I have loved you since day one."

"You were supposed to be taking pictures, not *proposing*," she said giddily. "I love you so much, but no one will ever trust you to take pictures again!"

"I don't think that's going to be a problem. You said *yes*. My proposal days are over."

He kissed her again, and as he set her on her feet, he realized the cheers and congratulations sounding out around them were no longer for Tempest and Nash, but for them.

AIYLA SPENT THE afternoon with her head in the clouds. Nate absconded with the camera, taking pictures of her and Ty, and then of everyone else he claimed Ty had lost sight of. She and Ty sent selfies to Trixie and Cherise with the caption *We're*

engaged! which spurred long, congratulatory phone calls. As the afternoon turned to early evening and the excitement of the day settled, Aiyla snuck away and called Ms. F to give her their happy news. She was thrilled for them, and even happier to hear that they were hoping to visit her later in the year.

After the call, Aiyla returned to the party, where Maisy and the girls were sitting on blankets chatting. Tempest sat beside her mother, smiling as she had been all day. Her dress was just as dreamy as she'd described. Jillian and Jax sure knew what they were doing. They'd transformed vintage lace and silk slips into long, delicate layered panels perfect for her bohemian wedding. Retro-inspired moonstone-style beading accented the empire waist, and lace spaghetti straps accentuated Tempest's natural femininity. She wore baby's breath in her long blond hair and had gathered it over one shoulder with a simple silk bow. She looked happy and beautiful.

Maisy tucked a strand of hair behind Tempest's ear and squeezed her hand. There was nothing like the love between a mother and daughter, and as Aiyla watched them, sadness swallowed her. She turned away and found Ty kneeling before Phillip, showing him how to weave dandelion stems together. Her heart was so full, she felt on the verge of tears again.

"Oh, no, you don't." Shannon took her hand and led her toward the blanket with the girls. "You're going to have a lifetime with my brother. Right now we have something very important to discuss."

They sat on the blanket, and Maisy reached for her hand. "Congratulations again, honey. I'm still reeling from Ty's proposal."

"You and I both," Aiyla admitted. "It was totally unexpected."

"They usually are. When love hits, you *know*." Maisy glanced across the lawn at Ace and said, "You may not realize this, but Ty is a lot like his father. I know on the outside, Ace looks calm, cool, and collected. But when he sets his sights on something, it's because he knows it's exactly what he needs, wants, and *must* have. Ty is the same way. I know some people think he's impulsive—"

"He's not *impulsive*, Mom," Shannon said. "He's *extreme*. There's a difference."

Maisy laughed softly. "Yes, sweet impulsive daughter of mine whom I love to the ends of the earth. If you'd have let me finish my sentence, you'd have heard my explanation. Shannon is spontaneous. She's not afraid to make quick decisions led by her heart. And I love that about her. Tempe," she said, eyeing her daughter, "is more cautious, and will think through the ramifications of every little thing. But when she makes a decision, she's as sure as a person can be. And Ty is a mix of both. *Extreme* is the perfect way to describe him. He's intense and doesn't do anything halfway. When he fell in love with you, you changed him for the better. He's more focused and driven than ever. And this proposal was his way of telling the world— telling his *family*—that you are now his entire universe."

If she had any worries about his family being upset over Ty's quick proposal or his proposing during Tempest's wedding, they were all laid to rest at that very moment as Maisy pulled her into her arms and embraced her, drawing more tears.

"Honey," Maisy said, "there's no pressure for setting a wedding date, but we want you to know that we are happy to go to wherever your sister is for the wedding, if you'd rather have it there. Or we'll fly her family in. We don't want you to feel any pressure from our mad clan to have the wedding here."

"Thank you. We haven't gotten that far yet. We're still in the floating-in-the-clouds stage."

"Well, when you come back down to earth, I hope you'll let me and Jax make your dress!" Jillian chimed in. Energy radiated off Ty's petite, burgundy-haired, effervescent cousin. She was the complete opposite of her brawny, blond, reserved twin, Jax. "No charge, of course. It'll be our wedding present to you and Ty."

"Oh my gosh. Really?" She looked around at the girls, who were all nodding. "How can I say no to that? Thank you."

The girls immediately launched into a discussion about wedding dresses. *Wedding dresses!* Was she really getting married? As the girls talked, Aiyla caught sight of Ty heading her way. Her pulse quickened like a jackrabbit. He looked handsome in his dark slacks and button-down shirt. She'd never seen him dressed up, and as gorgeous as he looked in his dress clothes, she still wanted to tear them right off of him. She felt her cheeks burn and shifted her eyes away from her hunky fiancé to his brothers and Nash, who were following him over. Sam carried a guitar in each hand.

Fiancé. She loved the sound of that.

Ace and Steve approached from the other side of the yard.

"We're surrounded," Maisy said. "What is going on?"

"We finally figured out why you and Dad made us learn to play instruments." Sam handed one guitar to Ty, and the two of them began playing "Amazed," by Lonestar.

While the men each sang to their significant other, Ty's cousins and the rest of their family and friends gathered around. Nash lifted Phillip into his arms as he serenaded his new wife.

Aiyla's heart swelled at the show of love. As Ty sang about the smell of her skin and the taste of her kiss, it didn't matter that this was a group serenade. She knew he meant every word just for her.

When they finished singing, Ty gathered her in his arms and said, "I love you."

Beau took the guitar from Ty, and Nick reached for Sam's.

"Dance with your girls," Beau said. "We've got this."

Beau and Nick began singing a country song Aiyla wasn't familiar with, but it didn't matter. She was in Ty's arms, his heart beating against hers, as he gazed deeply into her eyes, and everyone else—*every other thought*—disappeared.

Chapter Seventeen

SUNDAY ARRIVED WITH a flurry of activity. Phillip was staying with Maisy and Ace while Nash and Tempest were on their honeymoon, and the little guy was up at the crack of dawn. He and Papa Ace had gone to feed the animals at Phillip's house, and when they came back, they made pancakes for everyone. Ty suggested they go for a sail, and several hours later, as the afternoon sun smiled down on them, he stood between his father and Steve near the cabin of their boat, where his mother and Phillip had gone in search of fruit. Ty watched Aiyla as she lay sunbathing on the deck with Shannon, and his mind drifted back to last night. After he'd proposed, Sam had told him about a custom jeweler named Sterling Silver, who made jewelry based on people's personalities and their lives. This morning, while Aiyla had showered, he'd called Sterling and discussed the design for Aiyla's ring. Sterling usually spent weeks getting to know the person he was making the jewelry for, but in this case Ty already knew exactly what he wanted. He couldn't wait to put a ring on Aiyla's finger so she would know that she'd never be alone again.

Aiyla laughed, pulling him from his reverie. She looked fresh as the summer sun. There was no better view than his beautiful fiancée in a skimpy, sky-blue polka-dot bikini, with her hair fanned out around her face and the sweetest hint of a smile on her pretty lips.

"You're liable to burn her image into your brain that way," Maisy said as she came up from the cabin with Phillip. Her blond hair was tied back in a thick ponytail, and Phillip's mop of dark spiral curls whipped in the wind as he bit into an apple.

"Who's gonna burn Uncle Ty's bwain?" Phillip asked, his dark eyes as serious as a boy's could get. He still had trouble with his *r*'s.

Maisy sat down and pulled Phillip onto her lap. "Nothing is going to burn Uncle Ty's brain. I was teasing him because he's staring at Aiyla. Uncle Ty thinks she's beautiful."

"My daddy does the same thing to my mom," Phillip said. "Sometimes, when Mommy is playing her guitar, I have to do this to my dad so he'll hear me." He pressed his little nose against Maisy's and said, "*Then* he hears me."

Ty laughed. "As you get older, you'll learn that women have strange powers. They can change your world."

"You've got that right," Steve said, eyeing Shannon with an appreciative gaze. "Shannon's made my life infinitely better. *Louder* and *more complicated*, but definitely *better*."

"Shannon's a trip," Ty said. "I'm glad she and Aiyla are getting along so well. But I think I need to intervene and find out what kind of lies my sister is spreading about me."

"You shouldn't lie," Phillip chimed in. "It's bad."

"You're right, buddy." Ty crouched before him, taking in his curious brown eyes and pure innocence. "See that girl down there?"

Phillip looked at Shannon and Aiyla. "*Two* girls."

Maisy patted his shoulder. "That's right, smarty-pants."

"Aiyla's going to be your auntie someday soon." As Ty said the words, his heart filled up even more, and his mind traveled to Aiyla's other nephews. He suddenly wanted to meet them even more than he had before. He'd grown up with so many cousins and siblings, and he wanted that for Phillip and, he realized, for his and Aiyla's future children.

The realization hit him with such force, he momentarily lost his train of thought.

"Can I carry the *wings* at your wedding, too?" Phillip asked, bringing Ty's mind back to the moment.

"You know what, buddy? We have two other little boys who also might want to help. I think we'll be able to find jobs for all three of you." He pushed to his feet, still stuck on his thoughts about having a family. Not now, and maybe not in the next few years, because they had a lot of traveling to do. But one day he definitely wanted a family with Aiyla.

Steve slung an arm over Ty's shoulder and said, "Let's go crash the hen party. I'm in need of some make-out time with my girl."

"Dude, she's still my sister," Ty said as they headed toward the girls.

"And she's *almost* my wife."

Ty recognized the pride in Steve's voice. It was exactly the same way he felt about marrying Aiyla.

AIYLA HEARD TY and Steve talking and her pulse kicked up. She felt Shannon's finger touch hers, as if to say, *Shh, here they come.* She'd told Shannon about the day she'd first met Ty, and the way his smile and his sexy smart-ass comments had drawn her in, and how his beautiful, mischievous eyes had held her captive for the next five days. Shannon had asked a million questions, and it had allowed Aiyla to relive every happy moment she and Ty had shared in Saint-Luc. Shannon told her about when she and Steve had first gotten together. They'd known each other for years, and she'd had a crush on him forever. Aiyla wished she'd known Ty that long. She'd love to have that much history with him, and to have seen him changing as he grew up. But part of her wondered if they'd have been best friends when they were younger, and if that friendship would have grown to what they had now, or if he'd needed to sow those wild oats of his in order to be ready to give their relationship his all.

She squinted up at Ty as he dropped to his hands and knees and perched above her. His hair was tousled and shaded his eyes. His skin glistened with the sheen of a new tan, accentuating his athletic arms. He had such a playful look in his eyes, it was easy to imagine what he must have been like as a rambunctious teenager. She knew she would have fallen hard for him at any age. At that moment, as he gazed into her eyes, she was still falling deeper in love with him—even as she became aware of the precarious position in which he had her trapped.

"Ty," she said softly. "Your parents are *right* there."

"And I'm right *here*." He touched his lips to hers. "What kind of lies is Shannon telling you about me?"

"Oh, please," Shannon said. "*Girl code*." She sat up and handed the bottle of suntan lotion to Steve. "Would you mind doing my back?"

"Baby, I never mind doing any part of you." Steve leaned in for a kiss.

"Christ, Johnson," Ty said. "*Sister*, remember?"

Aiyla laughed. What was it like to have overprotective brothers like Ty? She had a feeling she would have been a lot like Shannon, strong and determined to be autonomous. But Shannon didn't fool Aiyla. Even with her eye rolls and snappy comments, the admiration she had for her older siblings was obvious.

She glanced at Shannon and Steve as Steve put lotion on her back. They were leaving at the crack of dawn tomorrow morning, and Aiyla would miss them. She felt a sisterly kinship to Shannon. But they lived less than an hour from her apartment in Colorado, and she took comfort in knowing she could see them when she was there.

When we *are there.*

Steve leaned down and whispered something to Shannon that made her laugh. Then to Ty he said, "She's not kidding about the girl code thing. I caught her and my sister, Jade, whispering on the phone the other night, and neither of them would spill a word."

Ty's eyes narrowed. "Is this true?"

"The girl code thing?" Aiyla loved toying with him. "Isn't there a boy code?"

Ty shifted his gaze to Steve, who shrugged.

"Maybe." Ty suddenly looked confused. "But not about anything important."

"Ah, I see." She closed her eyes without answering, knowing her silence would drive him crazy.

He grabbed her ribs and she squealed, pushing at his hands and futilely trying to turn out of his reach. He was laughing now, too, and when he said, "We're not supposed to have secrets; just ask Phillip," even Shannon and Steve started laughing.

"Why do you care what I told her?" Shannon asked as Ty pulled Aiyla into his arms.

"Because you've been known to tell horrible lies that get me in trouble." He set a serious gaze on her and said, "Stolen candy bar. Need I say more?"

"I was eight years old!" Shannon snapped. She looked at Aiyla and said, "I stole a Snickers bar from a convenience store and said he did it."

Aiyla laughed. "Was it delicious? Worth the wrath of Ty?"

"I didn't do a damn thing to her," Ty said. "I took the punishment, because that's what we do. We protect each other."

Shannon's gaze softened. "Then what on earth would make you think that I'd say anything that could come between you and Aiyla? I *like* her. I have no idea how you landed such an amazing woman."

Ty lunged toward Shannon as if he were going to tickle her, and she scrambled behind Steve.

Steve put his arms out to his sides, a protective wall around his fiancée, and glared at Ty. "You know I'll toss you right in the ocean."

"My ass. I could take you on any day." Ty brushed Aiyla's hair from her face and tucked it behind her ears. "What's the big deal, she asks? I finally got the woman of my dreams in my arms, and I won't survive losing her again."

Aiyla melted right there on the spot. She was surprised she didn't pour off the edge of the boat and drip into the water. "Short of telling me that you're a serial killer, nothing anyone could ever say would change my mind about us."

"Well, there was that one time..." Shannon said, and Ty leapt to his feet, chasing Shannon around the deck as his parents hollered for them to be careful.

Aiyla and Steve burst out laughing. Shannon doubled back and Ty grabbed her around the waist, holding her like a football against his side while she thrashed. "Let me tell you about the *man* code." He nodded to Steve, who turned toward Aiyla.

Aiyla realized what was happening and tried to run, but Steve was too fast, and snagged her around her waist, her arms and legs flailing.

"Don't you dare!" Shannon warned as Ty dangled her over the side of the boat.

Steve did the same with Aiyla, and she clung to his arms. "No, please, Steve, *don't.*"

"Grizz!" Shannon hollered. "Don't let him do this!"

"Man code, baby," Steve said stoically.

"One. Two." Ty swung Shannon over the edge of the boat, and Steve did the same to Aiyla, causing both girls to scream. "Three!"

The girls screamed as their feet landed on the deck. Aiyla looked down, unable to believe she hadn't gotten tossed in the water. And then she was in Ty's arms—and Shannon was in Steve's—and Ty kissed her. His parents and Phillip cheered them on.

"The girl code means you keep secrets. The man code means you protect the woman you love."

"Aw, Ty."

"That's only half the man code, baby. You go down, I go down." He leapt off the side of the boat with Aiyla in his arms. She caught a glimpse of Steve doing the same with Shannon seconds before she and Ty crashed into the water.

She swam for all she was worth toward the sunlight, but she needn't have. Ty's strong arms and legs carried them both right up to the surface. She gasped for air, clinging to him, her legs kicking wildly.

"I could have drowned!"

"No, you couldn't have. I had you, baby cakes. I wasn't about to let go."

"What if there are sharks?"

"I'd let them eat me first." He kissed her and they began to sink. She made a pleading sound and he tore his mouth away, bringing them right back up to the surface. "I've got you, baby. Always."

Chapter Eighteen

"I'M DELAYING THE trip," Ty said Monday morning as he and Aiyla sat in Jon's office waiting for him to see them.

The pain in Aiyla's leg hadn't eased, and though she'd thought the fatigue in her injured leg would go away after the race, it still tired quicker than her right leg. She'd made the mistake of mentioning it to Ty.

"No, you're *not*. We agreed that neither of us would miss out on anything, and I'll be damned if I'll be the one to break that agreement. You're *going* on that trip. I'll go on the next one with you." Her stomach knotted. How could she convince Ty not to give up his trip for her? She didn't want to become the girlfriend—fiancée—who held him back. It would only make him resent her in the long run.

"Graham and I have done this trip before. It's not like I'm missing out on anything new."

Frustrated, she exhaled loudly. "I love you for caring enough to give it up, but please don't."

"Good morning," Jon said as he walked in. "How's one of my favorite engaged couples?" His words were joyful, but his expression was serious as he sat behind his desk.

Ty reached for Aiyla's hand. "We're great, thanks."

"That's good," he said with a smile that seemed forced. "I've got the results of the imaging." His gaze moved between her and Ty. "Aiyla, there is a suspicious mass in your tibia, and I'd like to do further testing."

"Suspicious...?" Aiyla asked. "Like, arthritis or something?"

Ty squeezed her hand. "Arthritis isn't suspicious. Jon?"

Jon looked directly at Ty, then at Aiyla and said, "There is a lesion about the size of a strawberry in your proximal tibia. I don't think we can rule out sarcoma."

Sarcoma. The word swelled and ricocheted in her head.

"What is that?" Ty asked.

Cancer. She couldn't say it. Couldn't force the word from her lips, because if she did, it would make it real. She ground her teeth together, fighting tears. She felt like she was underwater, trying to find the surface in the middle of the night, with nothing to guide her. *It's not cancer. It's not cancer.* Her body trembled and shook. *Goddamn it,* she wasn't going to let a fucking word scare her into silence.

"Cancer" flew from her lungs, full of venom at the same time Jon said, "Bone cancer."

"Bone cancer?" Ty reached for her, the disbelief and fear in his voice as real as his hand holding her tight. "How can that be? She's not sick. That doesn't make sense."

She tried to concentrate on Ty squeezing her shoulder, the smell of him, his leg pushing against hers—anything other than the voice in her head repeating, *No. God, please no.*

"I'm sorry," Jon said. "Sarcomas are not a common group of cancers. They arise in the bone and connective tissues, and in most cases they're found by accident, when looking for other causes of aches and pains. I'd like to do bloodwork and a biopsy so we know exactly what we're dealing with."

"A biopsy?" Ty asked, tightening his hold on Aiyla. "What does that involve?"

As Jon explained the outpatient procedure, Aiyla caught only a few words: *numb the area...needle...ten-minute procedure...guided by fluoroscopy...* Her heart hammered against her ribs, and fear swamped her so badly she could barely breathe. "Can we do it now? The biopsy? *Right now?*"

"Aiyla, don't you want time to think it over?" Ty asked.

"No. He just said I need a biopsy. You trust him, right?" Tears welled in her eyes, and she was shaking all over, but she refused to let her tears fall. Jon was wrong. She was sure of it. She ran, and swam, and biked, and skied. She didn't have cancer.

"Of course," Ty said, "but—"

"Then I want to get it over with." The sadness and fear in Ty's eyes nearly did her in, but she had to focus. Had to get through this so they could prove it wasn't cancer. *Cancer?* Her mind was spinning, making her feel sick and terrified. She wanted to run as far and as fast as she could. To escape the fear and make it all go away. She pressed her left foot into the floor, hating the pain it caused. Her body had betrayed her. *You can't outrun fate.*

A tear slid down her cheek and she turned away from Ty, swiping it away as Jon pushed a box of tissues across the desk. She ignored them, refused to give in and be weak, and willed the rest of her tears to remain at bay.

"I want to do it right away, please," she said, steeling herself against the fear consuming her.

"I thought you might want to do that," Jon said. "I've cleared my morning schedule. Our surgery center is right downstairs, and we can do it there. As I mentioned, it's an outpatient procedure. You'll be sore afterward, but over-the-counter medications will alleviate the pain."

"Surgery?" Ty asked.

"We're not doing surgery. It's a core-needle biopsy, and I'll need the CT scan to guide me to make sure I biopsy the right area. Otherwise I could do it here in my office."

"And the results?" she asked. "How fast can we get them?"

"I'll talk to pathology and put a rush on it," Jon assured her. "Hopefully we'll have the results by the end of the day."

Aiyla didn't hear a word of the instructions Jon gave to Ty about the procedure and aftercare. She left the office on autopilot, guided by Ty to the surgical center. She felt detached from the situation, like it was happening to someone else, out of her control. She mechanically filled out the paperwork, answered the necessary questions, and changed into a patient gown. The patient gown she had hated now seemed like the least of her problems. She was aware Ty was saying reassuring things the whole time, but she couldn't process a single sentence. She was mentally gone, the same way she'd been when her mother was at death's door. It was the only way to survive the all-consuming fear that lay in wait, like a villain ready to swallow her whole.

Nurses came in and told Ty they had to take her now. *Take her.* It sounded so ominous.

She struggled to remain strong, for Ty, for herself. For Cherise. *Oh God, Cherise.*

She couldn't have cancer. Her sister couldn't lose her, too. Ty hugged her, kissed her, and as he left the room, she felt like her heart was being ripped out.

"Ty—" flew desperately from her lips. In her next breath, he was holding her tight.

"I'm right here, baby." Tears welled in his eyes, and he gritted his teeth, blinking them away. "You're going to be fine. I'm right here. We don't have to do this now if you're not ready. We can ask Jon to give you a few days."

She clung to him, refusing to let her own tears fall. "No. I have to do it right now. I just need *this*." She wrapped her arms around him, soaking in the feel of his heart beating sure and steady against her own.

"I'm sorry, Aiyla," the nurse said, "but we have to go to the procedure room now."

Ty pressed his warm hands to her cheeks and gazed at her with an expression of strength and love. "We'll get through this, baby cakes. There's nothing we can't handle."

"It's not cancer," she said emphatically, silently praying she was right. As she watched him walk out of the room, a flood of tears streamed down her cheeks.

TY PACED THE waiting room, hurt and anger waging a full-on war inside him. He wanted to be in that room with Aiyla, to take the fear and the pain away, to switch places with her. To make this whole nightmare go away. He sank down to a chair, elbows on knees, and clutched the sides of his head, bent over in frustration, filled with too much fear to see straight. He felt a hand on his back and lifted his eyes, tears welling again at the sight of his eldest brother, Cole.

"Goddamn it," Ty ground out as he rose to his feet and his brother embraced him.

"What's going on? I was looking for you after your appointment and Brandy said I could find you here." Cole's dark eyes searched his, and he knew his brother saw all the hurt and fear in them.

"Aiyla's having a biopsy on her leg." Hurt clawed its way up his chest. "The MRI showed a suspicious mass. Jon said he can't rule out cancer."

"Jesus, Ty." Cole embraced him again. "I'm sorry."

They sat down, and Ty filled him in on the information Jon had shared: the size of the mass, what Aiyla could expect after the procedure. "He said he'd push to get results today, but I just don't know what to do." He stared at the doors to the procedure areas. "I want to be in there with her. I want to be the one *on* the fucking table. I'm sitting here praying the MRI was wrong, that this is all some big mistake, and I know that's an impossibility. Cole, she's my whole world. What can I do to help her?"

"Exactly what you're doing," Cole said empathetically. "Be here for her."

"It would take a fucking act of God to pry me away from her."

"I know," Cole said. "How is she holding up?"

Too anxious to sit still, Ty pushed to his feet again. "She's so damn strong, but she lost her mother to cancer—she has to be scared out of her mind. I will be there every second for her. I will be her rock. I'll be her fucking mountain. But goddamn it…" His throat thickened, swallowing his voice.

"Dr. Braden?" the receptionist called out, and Cole looked over. "Brandy is on the phone. She said you have two patients waiting."

"Thank you. I'll go right up." Cole put his hands on Ty's shoulders, like their father had done a million times, his compassionate gaze as reassuring as it was worrying. "Listen to me. If it is bone cancer, you're in the best hands you could be. Jon's a specialist, an orthopedic oncologist. Once he gets the results, then we'll know what we're dealing with. I know we're family, but we maintain doctor-patient confidentiality. You need to tell Jon he can fill me in so I can be there for you both, but only if Aiyla wants that. I'll come by Mom's after work, but if you or Aiyla need me, text and I'll be there, got it?"

"I appreciate it, but hold off on coming to Mom's until I talk to Aiyla. I don't know if she'll be up to seeing family, or talking, or...fuck, Cole. Cancer? That wasn't even on my radar screen."

"It never is." Cole embraced him again. "You're not alone in this, Ty, and neither is Aiyla. Not by a long shot. Give her my love, and let me know what Jon says."

As Cole left and the sense of being alone settled in, despite knowing his brother would be there for them, he knew the fear Aiyla was feeling had to be even worse.

After the longest wait of Ty's life, Jon finally came through the double doors. Ty rushed over to him, trying to read his face, but he wore the expression of a cautious professional who did this type of thing every day.

"She did great," Jon assured him. "She's changing her clothes, and then you can take her home. She's going to be sore for a day or two, and although we didn't give her any sedatives, she'll probably be exhausted from the emotional drain of the situation."

"Right, okay. I know. But can you tell me anything more?" *Like she doesn't have cancer?*

Jon shook his head. "Not yet. But hopefully I will know more later today."

"Thank you for getting her in so quickly, and for rushing

the results. Can I see her?"

"Yes. I have to go see my other patients, but the nurse can show you where she is. I'll call Aiyla as soon as I know something. And, Ty, I'm really sorry she's going through this. She's a sweetheart, and she was a trooper in there."

"Thanks." Ty bolted through the doors, and the nurse brought him back to see Aiyla.

He found her sitting on an exam table, her fingers curled tightly around the edge. She was dressed in her own clothes, with a bandage on her leg. Her shoulders were slumped, and as she lifted a terrified gaze to his, spears of pain sliced through his chest. He went to her, carefully stepping between her legs, and gathered her in his arms.

"I'm here my beautiful, brave girl. I'm right here, and I'm not going anywhere."

He wanted to wrap her up and sweep her away from the pain and the worry and never let anything bad touch her again.

She rested her cheek in the crook of his neck, and her tears slid over his skin, telling him everything she couldn't manage to say. He held her tighter, one hand on her back, the other holding her head, in an endless embrace.

Chapter Nineteen

TY HELD AIYLA in the surgery center until the nurse came in and told them that they needed the room. Aiyla would have remained right there, safe and loved in his arms forever, if they would have let her. She was still in shock, moving on autopilot as they climbed into the Jeep, and that terrified her. But what scared her even more was the look in Ty's eyes. He was trying to be strong, but she knew him well enough to see through the facade to the fear he was trying to tamp down.

"We'll go to my parents' house and watch a movie or something," Ty said as he climbed into the driver's seat of the Jeep.

She vowed to herself to remain detached from the entire medical situation—the procedure, the looming diagnosis, all of it. She needed to remain strong or she'd lose her mind. She'd been so scared during the procedure, she'd thought about the creek to calm herself down. She remembered the peacefulness of the gentle breeze and the beauty of the mangled tracks. She'd closed her eyes and relived the feel of the water on her toes, the rush of love as Ty had stripped naked and chased her. And when the pressure became uncomfortable during the procedure, she'd disappeared into the memories of making love with Ty on the shore. That creek had become theirs, and she wanted to be in *their* world right now, not anyone else's.

"Would you mind if we didn't? I love your family, but I'm not sure I can focus on anyone or anything right now. I need some time alone with you to process everything."

"Anything you want, babe. Are you hungry? Do you want to get something to eat or just go find someplace to be alone?"

She glanced in the back of the Jeep, where the blankets and towels had fallen to the floor. "Can we stop for energy bars and maybe some juice? Something easy and quick, and then go to the creek?"

Half an hour later, Ty parked by the tracks and insisted on carrying Aiyla to the creek. He cradled her against his warm body, and she carried the food and blanket as he made his way down to the water. It was just as beautiful as she remembered. Ty was careful as he set her on the grass so he could spread out the blanket. They didn't talk, but the silence wasn't uncomfortable or oppressive. It was exactly what she needed. And when she lay on her back and Ty wrapped her in his arms, resting his head on her chest and pressing a kiss to her breastbone every now and again, it was also what she needed.

He was what she needed.

His love, his strength, his innate understanding.

She ran her fingers through his hair and closed her eyes. Her mind began wandering down a dark *what if* path. *What if I have cancer?* Memories of her mother's battle with the disease slammed into her. She breathed deeply, trying to will the memories away, but they crashed over her one after another.

"Baby cakes?" Ty lifted his head and gazed down at her. "What is it?"

She turned away, closing her eyes tight against an onslaught of tears.

He guided her chin back toward him with a gentle touch and pressed his lips to her forehead and cheeks. "It's okay, sweet girl. Together we can deal with anything."

Even with her eyes closed, tears poured out. "I'm so scared" came out in a bubble of sobs. "I feel like I can't breathe."

He gathered her in his arms and held her. "I know, baby. I am, too, but we can get through anything. *Anything.*"

"What if it *is* cancer?" *Oh God! Please don't let it be cancer.*

"Then we'll deal with it."

"You don't know," she said between sobs, "how awful and hard cancer is."

He held her tighter, kissing her cheek over and over. "Nothing is too hard for us."

"I watched my mom die!" she cried, clinging to him as if he could save her from the heartache bowling her over one memory at a time. "Chemo, radiation. It was horrible. She was sick and frail and—" She buried her face in his neck. "I'm scared, Ty. I'm so scared I want to run away and keep running until there's nothing left."

"Nothing left?" He drew back with tears in his eyes. "Baby...? You run, I run. I'll fucking carry you."

She laughed through her tears. "I don't mean run from you. I mean run from whatever this is in my leg."

He brushed her tears away, then kissed her softly. "We don't run. We *deal.* We conquer. We move forward. *Together.*"

She tried to swallow past the lump in her throat, but it was impossible. A spear of panic shot through her and she closed her eyes, concentrating on what he'd said and trying to regain control of her emotions. She was trembling, and tired. *So damn tired.* Fear gnawed at her, keeping her on edge and draining her energy. She gazed into Ty's loving eyes, and she knew with him, it was okay to let down all her defenses.

She collapsed against him, tears flowing, heart hurting, and more sobs tumbled out. His body surrounded her like a protective shield as he stroked her hair away from her face and pressed tender kisses to her cheek.

"That's it, sweet girl. *Breathe*, baby. Let it all go."

She drew in one ragged breath after another until her sobs slowed and eventually abated, until all that was left was Ty's sweet whispers lulling her to sleep.

AIYLA SLEPT FOR several hours, some of it fitful, her body jerking and mewling sounds escaping. Ty soothed his hand down over her back, reassuring her in whispers and kisses, until she slept soundly again. Was she dreaming about the procedure or about losing her mother? Was she in pain? He'd never experienced love so intense that he ached right along with a person. And now it was like there was no separation between them. She hurt, he hurt. She smiled, he smiled. He welcomed those feelings, but they were unfair. He should be able to endure her pain *for* her.

As the late-afternoon sun dipped, taking the heat of the day with it, he pressed his lips to her forehead and closed his eyes, praying with every iota of his being that she would be okay.

"Mm." Her lips curved up in a sweet smile as she blinked away the fog of sleep. "Sorry. I didn't mean to conk out like that."

"You needed it. How's your leg?"

"Achy. What time is it?" She sat up as he checked the time on his phone.

"Almost five. We should head back to the Jeep so you can take some pain medicine."

They gathered their things, and he carried her back the way they'd come. "By the time we get married, I'm going to be an old pro at this. Carrying you over the threshold will be a piece of cake."

"Unless I get so stressed that I start chowing down on cake," she teased.

Damn, it was good to see her smile.

"You could gain a hundred pounds and I'll still love you *and* carry you."

Aiyla took pain medication as they drove down the mountain. "Thank you for being there with me today. And for letting me bawl like a baby and fall asleep on you."

He laughed. "I love you, babe—"

Her phone rang, and fear flashed like a lightbulb in her eyes, cutting him to his core. He pulled over to the side of the road and took her hand in his, giving her his full attention. "It's okay, baby. I'm right here."

She lifted the phone to her ear with a shaky hand. "Hello?" She mouthed, *Jon.*

Ty's pulse kicked up.

"Sore, but okay," she said in a tremulous voice.

Each pause as she listened to Jon brought a jolt of panic in Ty.

"Yes," she said softly. "When?"

Aiyla bit her lower lip, and Ty's heart sank. He ground his teeth together, praying for the best and fearing the worst.

"Okay, thank you." Tears welled in her eyes as she ended the call. "We have to go to his office right now."

Ty pulled her into his arms, and she pushed out. "*Now,* Ty.

Sorry, but he's waiting for us, and if you hug me, I'm going to break down."

"Okay, babe." He pulled onto the road, his thoughts reeling. "What did he say?"

"Just that he had the results. But if the results were good, he'd have told me, right? He wouldn't wait or need us to see him in his office."

She turned hopeful eyes to him, and it was all he could do to say, "We don't know that. He might be asking us to come in so he can go over treatment plans, or anything. Don't go there in your head, Aiyla. Not now. Not yet, and hopefully not ever."

She nodded absently.

When they got to Jon's office, Ty helped her from the Jeep and held her again. "No matter what happens in here, I'm with you, Aiyla. Do you hear me?"

She blinked several times, swallowing hard, clearly struggling to keep herself in check as she nodded.

He cradled her face in his hands and gazed into her worried eyes. "I love you, baby. *Unconditionally.*"

His lips came down over hers softly, but he felt too much, loved her too intensely to let her go with anything short of a kiss that left no room for doubt about the strength of his emotions. He took the kiss deeper, forcing all his fears to the back burner and pouring all his strength, all his positive energy, into their connection, hoping she would soak it up.

He slid his hand to the nape of her neck, drawing away slowly. "You okay, babe?"

"I am now," she said breathlessly.

He held her close as they went up to Jon's office. Every step brought another pulse of worry. They were taken directly to Jon. He was pacing by the windows when they walked in, and the look on his face made Ty's gut twist, and every muscle in his body flexed. Aiyla pushed herself deeper into his side, as if she wanted to crawl inside him for protection. His fingers tightened around her waist. Now he was the one with the urge to run—to pick her up and carry her off so whatever news about to come out of Jon's mouth would never be heard.

"Ty, Aiyla, thank you for coming in." Jon waved to the chairs across from his desk, his eyes apologetic, his tone too professional.

No fucking way. Ty felt sick to his stomach. He sat in a chair and brought Aiyla down on his lap, his arms around her, hoping he was reading Jon wrong—and needing to absorb the impact and keep Aiyla safe if he wasn't.

Jon sat in the chair beside them, his gaze passing a silent message to Ty that seemed to say, *Brace yourself.* He could feel Aiyla's heart beating too fast, and the fear in her eyes told him that she'd noticed that look, too. In that split second, something dark and visceral clawed up from the depths of his soul. *Hatred.* It boiled in his blood, making him want to slam Jon against the wall, to shut him up before another word left his mouth. He knew it was wrong, knew it was misdirected, but darkness consumed him. There was no escaping it. He struggled to push those emotions away, but it lingered right beneath the surface.

"Aiyla, there's no easy way to say this, so I'm just going to give it to you straight. The biopsy confirmed that you have chondrosarcoma, which is a type of bone cancer that develops in cartilage cells. It's the second most common type of primary bone tumor. Hopefully we have found it early enough that it hasn't spread."

Ty felt gutted. The color drained from Aiyla's face. Her lower lip trembled, and tears rose in her eyes, making Ty's eyes burn with his own. He fought them hard. He would *not* break down when Aiyla needed him most. *Chondrofuckingsarcoma?* No disease was going to take Aiyla from him. They would fight this son of a bitch. Do whatever it takes.

He put his hand on the side of her head and pressed his lips to her temple. "It's okay, babe. We'll fight it."

She pressed her mouth shut and nodded, visibly struggling to hold it together. The hatred inside Ty surged, redirecting toward the disease instead of the bearer of the news, and he forced himself to put the disease into a form he could relate to and conquer, like the worst fucking mountain in the world. Envisioning it that way allowed him to concentrate on the goal—*beating the life out of the disease*—and focus on coming up with a solid attack plan.

"What's our next step, Jon?" he asked. "How do we fight this?"

"The first thing we need to do is get a PET scan to determine if the disease has spread, and stage it. Once we have those results, Aiyla, you'll need to decide if you want to treat it here, or someplace else, and then we can take the next step."

Ty looked at Aiyla, who appeared shell-shocked. "Do you want to go back to Colorado? We can deal with it there, in Oregon where your sister lives, or here. Wherever you want, I'll be there with you."

A tear tumbled down her cheeks. "I can't put this on Cherise. She has two little boys, and she doesn't need…" Sobs stole her voice.

"Shh. It's okay." He embraced her. "It's okay. Do you want to do it here?"

"You don't have to decide right now," Jon said. "This is a lot to process. If you decide to seek treatment here, I'd like to put together a multidisciplinary meeting with a leading oncologist and radiologist, and we'll discuss treatment options."

"But you're an orthopedic oncologist. Why do we need to see another oncologist?" Ty couldn't believe they were talking about oncologists and cancer treatments.

"This is a complicated disease, and depending on what we find with the PET scan, we want to be sure Aiyla is covered on all levels." Jon turned his attention to Aiyla and said, "You should have as much information as possible before making any treatment decisions. If the cancer has spread, you'll need a medical oncologist to oversee chemotherapy and manage side effects. You might also consider speaking with a psychologist or a social worker to help deal with the emotional impact of the diagnosis."

If the cancer has spread, hit Ty with the force of a bullet, magnifying in his head and drilling the reality into his heart.

"Thank you," Aiyla said softly, then a little stronger, "Can we get the PET scan right away? I need to know what's happening inside my body."

"The office needs to process the paperwork through your insurance company first, which can take some time," Jon explained. "Once we have approval, they'll try to get you in for the next available appointment, but it could take a week or two for the insurance to clear."

Ty didn't know squat about this type of cancer, but he knew enough to realize that any kind of cancer was a ticking time bomb, and he wasn't about to wait around for her wick to grow short. "We'll pay cash. Let's get her in fast, please. Whatever it takes, you know I'm good for it. I don't want Aiyla worrying any longer than she has to."

She shook her head. "Ty, I can't pay—"

"I can," he assured her. "Now is not the time to let your pride get in the way, baby. Let's get this done so we know what we're facing."

"Aiyla?" Jon said. "It's your call."

Her brows knitted, and for a second Ty worried she'd fight him on it, and when she nodded and said, "Okay," relief rushed through him. One less obstacle to overcome.

Jon gave them several pamphlets about dealing with cancer and in particular chondrosarcoma. "I would advise that you hold off on reading too much on the Internet. There's a lot of misinformation out there that can do more harm than good."

"I know," she said softly. "We learned that when my mom was sick."

"There's one more thing. Pathological fractures are common with this type and size of tumor because the disease weakens the bone. In fact, many tumors such as these are found accidentally when we think we're looking for a fracture. Now that we know what we're dealing with, tread carefully, okay? And, Aiyla, I'm one of a few hundred doctors who specialize in sarcomas. You're in good hands with me, but if you choose to seek treatment elsewhere, I'll find you a specialist who can do an equally excellent job."

"Thank you," Ty said.

"Do you have any other questions that I can answer before I call and schedule the PET scan?"

Aiyla shook her head. "I might later, but right now I just want to get that test so we know…" Her voice trailed off, her unspoken worries hanging in the silence.

"I'll call radiology and see what I can set up," Jon said. "Are you open to going in very early or late in the day if that's the only way they can squeeze you in quickly?"

"Yes," Aiyla said.

"Okay. I'll call you as soon as I have it scheduled, and in the meantime, Ty has my cell phone number. If you have questions, please feel free to call."

"Thank you." Aiyla pushed to her feet. Her eyes suddenly had dark circles under them. She was so pale, Ty worried she'd pass out. He put an arm around her. "I know you work with Ty's brother and Faith, but can you please not say anything to them until we have the results of the PET scan and we have time to think things through? I don't want to deal with questions until we know everything there is to know."

Damn it. Ty had forgotten to tell her he'd seen Cole earlier. "Aiyla, Cole knows about the biopsy. He was looking for us after our appointment and Brandy told him we were in the surgery center. He didn't know you were having the procedure when he first got there, but I told him. I'm sorry. He's going to worry if I don't fill him in."

"Can we ask him not to say anything to your family?" she asked.

"Of course. Yes."

"Aiyla," Jon said, "I'd never say anything without your permission, but if you want me to explain this to Cole and tell him how you feel, I can do that before he leaves the office today."

She turned pleading eyes to Ty. "Do you want to talk to him yourself? I will fall apart if I have to talk about it right now."

Ty wanted to talk to his brother, but not more than he needed to be there for Aiyla. "Why don't we have Jon talk to him and explain the situation. I want to be with you."

A small smile lifted her lips. "Thank you."

"I'll take care of it," Jon said. "Now, if you don't mind, I'd like to take my doctor hat off for a minute and slip into friend mode." He rolled his shoulders back, and his gaze softened as he took Aiyla's hand. "I'm so sorry you're going through this, but you have a hell of a man by your side, and I'll make sure you get top-notch treatment. Whatever you need, whatever questions you have, you let me know. And when we have the full diagnosis, if you need help talking to your family, I'm happy to do so."

He embraced her, and Ty heard Aiyla sniffling as she thanked him.

Jon reached for Ty and said, "I've got your backs, buddy. We'll fight this all the way."

Damn right we will.

Chapter Twenty

AIYLA SAT ON the beach behind Ty's parents' house Monday evening listening to the waves roll in and to Phillip's sweet giggles. Maisy and Ace were barbecuing by a bonfire in their backyard, while Phillip played nearby. Ty was pacing the beach a few feet away from Aiyla, talking with his cousin Graham about canceling their climbing trip. She didn't even try to get him not to. Guilt swamped her that she needed him so badly. Was she being selfish by not cutting Ty loose from the tethers of a disease that could kill her? Should she make it easier for him? Push him away? In her heart, she knew that wasn't something she could ever do, but she was so scared and so confused and hurting so badly, she couldn't make heads or tails of anything. Jon had called shortly after they'd left his office. He'd pulled some strings and scheduled her PET scan for Thursday morning. She was in limbo until they had those results, and it was a horrifying place to be.

Ty blew her a kiss, and she reached for the simple thoughts she'd had just days before about how hot he was and how lucky they were to have found each other again. How fate had worked its magic. She held on to the belief that they were the lucky ones. Weren't they? There were billions of people in the world, and she and Ty had landed at the same place at the same time. *Twice.* But as she tried to hold on to those simple, lighter thoughts—*the thoughts of a twenty-seven-year-old woman who didn't have cancer*—they evaded her. Was there even a world outside of the worries scrambling around in her head? She hadn't been able to hold on to anything other than overwhelming fear since they'd learned of her diagnosis.

Ty ended his call, and as he closed the distance between them, her heart sped up. But it was the quickening of a *worried* love. He stretched his long legs out beside her and draped an arm over her shoulder.

"How's my beautiful girl?" He touched his lips to hers and she felt him smile.

Her stomach fluttered and she didn't move. She needed reassurance that she was still the same woman he'd fallen in love with. Still capable of all the same emotions, and strong. She needed to know that the diagnosis hadn't turned her into something less.

"Are you okay?"

"Mm-hm." They hadn't talked much after leaving Jon's office. She couldn't. Every time she tried to, her throat closed up.

"Want a foot massage?" he offered.

She shook her head. "Want me to give you one?"

"I have another body part that needs some attention." He brushed his lips over hers and said, "My heart needs to know you're okay, baby. I know you don't want to talk, but I need to know what's going on in your head."

"I'm okay." She wound her arms around his neck and crawled into his lap. "Don't think I'm a damsel in a distress, because that's not why I'm doing this."

"Of course not. You're saving *me* from a broken heart."

She smiled and kissed him. She believed in Ty's love for her, and she was thankful for it. But that didn't mean she was okay knowing that because of her, his life would probably change dramatically. If the cancer had spread, who knew how long she'd have left, or what that time would be like? And if it hadn't spread, she'd surely have some sort of treatments to go through. Either way, his carefree, vagabond lifestyle had changed in an instant because of her.

"I love you so much, Ty. I'm not okay, but you know that. I just can't talk about it yet. I'm too scared. But I need you to know that if this is too much for you, you don't have to—"

"*Don't*, Aiyla," he said angrily, nostrils flaring. "Don't make this disease bigger than our love. It's not. It could never be. And it will *never* chase me away. Do you understand?"

The tears she'd been holding back all evening broke free. She nodded, her chest too tight to speak.

He pushed his hands into her hair, holding her face directly in front of his, his eyes damp. "You believe in fate, remember?"

She nodded, and he said, "I *didn't* believe in it. I didn't understand why *you* did when you'd lost your mother at such a young age. It didn't make sense to me. But you told me that fate was bigger than anything, stronger than *anyone's* will. You said fate had taken your mother and nothing could have stopped that, but it had also brought you to Ms. F. You said fate had brought Cherise and her husband together. Don't start going back on your beliefs now, because Aiyla Lillian *Soon-to-Be*-Braden, the race was *fate*. Jon being at the race? *Fate*. My pushing you into going in for the appointment? *Fate*."

Every time he said *fate* he tightened his fingers in her hair. "The universe isn't going to put you through all of that just to steal you away from us. Away from *this*—"

He crashed his mouth to hers, and her entire body inhaled his love, his strength, his *belief.* Lust coiled deep inside her, spreading up her chest, through her limbs, and binding them together, stirring all the emotions that had been overridden by fear and sadness. This was *real. Unbreakable.* This was true, persevere-through-anything *love.*

"Don't push me away," he demanded. "Not now. Not ev-er."

"I won't, and I'm sorry—"

Her words were lost on the press of his greedy lips. They kissed feverishly, whispering I love yous and other sweet words of togetherness.

THEY ATE DINNER on the back deck with Phillip and Ty's parents, and afterward Ty refused to let Aiyla help carry the dishes inside. She sat on the back steps, listening as Phillip told her all about caring for his two goats, Big and Little.

"If you don't shut the gate, Dad has to chase the goats for a *long* time, and he doesn't like that. Mommy says it's good for the goats to run around, but Daddy says she just likes to watch him chase them." A rascally smile appeared on his face, and he said, "You shouldn't let goats in your house. They poop *everywhere*, and they eat the curtains, and then Mom chases them outside and Dad has to run after them again. Do you want to know about the chickens?"

"Absolutely." As Phillip told her about feedings and check-ing for eggs, she imagined the fun they must have on their farmette. For a moment she even forgot about her worries, but when Phillip finished his story, her mind found them again in the silence. It was strange to be talking about goats and chickens when there was a disease growing inside her. She was glad Ty hadn't pushed her to tell his family what was going on. They'd told them that she'd fallen and scraped her leg. She hated lying, but it was better than falling apart and not having the details they'd surely want to know. The details she *didn't want* to know, like had it spread and did her life now have an expiration date?

She gazed out over the water, shoving those worries as deep down as she could, making way for other troublesome thoughts, like what impact would this have on Ty?

"Who's ready for treats?" Ty came outside with a plate of goodies.

The shadow of sadness in his eyes was a sure giveaway that something was wrong. Had his family noticed? She tried to push away the guilt that came with knowing she was the cause of it, but there was no more room to bury anything inside her.

Ty put a hand on her shoulder, crouching beside her. "Want to come down to the fire and make s'mores?"

"I do!" Phillip exclaimed.

"Climb on, little buddy." Ty patted his thigh, and Phillip climbed into his arms. "Come on, babe."

Aiyla wasn't hungry, but she pushed to her feet and followed them down to the blankets by the fire, still trying to bury the guilt she knew he didn't want her to feel. The dull ache in her leg was constant, but knowing it was cancer made the pain inconsequential.

Maisy and Ace joined them a few minutes later and jumped right into the s'more-making fun. Ty placed the graham crackers and Hershey bars beside the bag of marshmallows while

Phillip and Ace walked to the woods at the edge of the property in hunt of twigs to use for roasting marshmallows. Ace looked even bigger and broader walking with little Phillip. He crouched beside his grandson, pointing to something in the woods.

"Adorable, aren't they?" Maisy sat beside Aiyla, bringing with her the scent of motherly love.

It was a scent Aiyla missed terribly. She wondered who her mother had confided in when she was first diagnosed with cancer. She knew from Ms. F that her mother had shared her diagnosis with her early on, but at the very moment she was told, was she alone? Did she have anyone to lean on? A lump rose in Aiyla's throat. She would give anything to walk into her arms one last time and feel the sense of love and safety that only a mother could bring.

"I remember when your guy was Phillip's age," Maisy said, bringing Aiyla back to the moment. Maisy looked at Ty, who was crossing the lawn toward Ace and Phillip. "He used to gobble up the Hershey bars without any marshmallows or graham crackers."

"I know. He told me when we were in Saint-Luc." She remembered the snowy night when they'd joined a group of friends she knew from the resort. They'd sat around a bonfire, much like this one, bundled up in blankets, sharing childhood memories. She'd told Ty about movie nights and working in the garden with her mother on the weekends, and he told her about going sailing, bonfires, and getting into trouble with his siblings.

Smiling with the memory, Aiyla said, "He said the marshmallows took over."

Maisy reached into the pocket of her sweater and withdrew a package of Reese's Peanut Butter Cups. "And you must have been the one who introduced him to s'mores made with these."

Aiyla looked at the orange candy wrapper, her chest constricting more than it probably should have over Ty telling his mother about that special night. "I can't believe he told you about that."

"He didn't. But after he got back from that trip, he brought them to a bonfire." She handed the candy to Aiyla and said, "Men are creatures of habit, and it's the small changes that mean the most. The changes they don't think anyone else notices, like candy at a bonfire. He has two of these in his pocket right now. Mothers notice these things."

Aiyla didn't know if that was Maisy's way of telling her she'd noticed that something was *off* with Ty tonight, but it didn't matter if it wasn't. Aiyla suddenly wanted to share her secret with her. She wrestled with the selfishness of doing so. Maisy would surely worry about her, and about Ty. Wasn't that what mothers were supposed to do? Worry about their children? Tears welled in her eyes, and she struggled to hold them back, but as she watched Ace hand Ty and Phillip twigs, a new worry settled in. What if the cancer treatments made it hard for her to have children? She knew Ty wanted a big family. They'd talked about it in Saint-Luc, and even if they hadn't, it was evident in the way he looked at Phillip and loved his siblings.

"Maisy" came out shakily.

Maisy glanced over, her smile instantly fading. "What is it, sweetie?"

"I have..." She swallowed hard, swiping at tears spilling from her eyes, and forced herself to say the words. "I have *cancer*." She gasped a breath, and her confession fell from her lips. "I didn't fall or scratch my leg. I had a biopsy."

"Oh, my sweet girl." Maisy wrapped her in her arms, gathering Aiyla's hair over her shoulder as her mother used to when she embraced her. "It's okay. Let it all out, honey."

Her kindness only made Aiyla cry harder. "I'm sorry we lied to you. It was my fault, not Ty's. I couldn't..."

"It's okay. Shh. Don't fret over that." Maisy held her tighter.

Aiyla spotted Ty guiding Phillip down by the water. He must have figured out that she'd told his mother and didn't want Phillip to see her crying. She drew back from Maisy's warm embrace, instantly missing it, and wiped her eyes.

"I'm sorry. I didn't mean to break down or to spring that on you."

"Oh, honey. I knew something was wrong, but I also knew you and Ty would tell us when you were ready." Her compassionate gaze drew more tears, and Maisy held her again. "Cry it out, sweetie."

Maisy held her for a long while, reassuring her. She didn't rush her or make her feel uncomfortable. She made her feel...*loved. Safe.*

When Aiyla finally pulled herself together enough to move from the circle of her embrace, Maisy smiled and reached for her hand.

"Do you want to talk about it?"

Her mind screamed, *No!* but she felt herself nodding. "I'm terrified, and I don't want to make Ty's life harder, or make my sister worry." Sobs bubbled out, and she forced herself to continue. "We don't know anything yet, other than that I have a tumor in my tibia." Her voice cracked. "I'm having a PET scan Thursday morning, and then we'll know more." A flood of tears fell as she croaked out, "I feel like I'm skiing down this never-ending slope, and I keep picking up speed." *Gasp. Gasp.*

She couldn't breathe, but she had to get this out before it tore her apart. "Part of me wants to rush to the finish line, which in my head is getting the PET scan results so I'll know what I'm facing. But then I see visions of my mom"—she clenched her eyes shut, sobbing with the memories—"and what she went through. I keep looking for a hidden trail where I can circumvent that finish line."

"Oh, honey." Maisy embraced her again.

"I don't know where to have treatments, or how to tell my sister. I'm so sorry," she cried. "I shouldn't dump this on you. I was just watching Ty with Phillip, and"—she gulped in air—"I realized that if by some grace of God the cancer hasn't spread, then treatments could make it so I can't have children. And then..." Sobs buried her voice again, but her fears were too big to hold back. "Ty" was all she could manage.

Maisy drew back, holding her hands. "This disease does not change anything. Ty loves you, and there are plenty of other ways to make a family. And as for dumping? Honey, I'm a mother to six children *and* to all of their significant others. Including *you*." She tucked Aiyla's hair behind her ear. "A mother's job is to be dumped on. We live for it, so we can help the people we love through the hard times and celebrate the good times. Do you know what that means?"

Aiyla dropped her gaze, tears pouring down her cheeks.

Maisy lifted Aiyla's chin, smiling warmly. "That means *we* will get through this. All of us. And then we'll celebrate."

"But what if...?" *I don't live through it?* "What if...?" She couldn't say the words.

"We are *not* going to think like that," Maisy said firmly. "We are going to have faith. And wherever you decide to have treatments, please know you are welcome here for as long as it takes and however long you want to stay afterward. And if you go back home, then you're going to have a lot of Bradens there with you, because once you share—*if* you share—this news with the others, you are going to have more love and support than you ever imagined possible."

It felt so good to get her secret out, she cried harder—and she felt infinitely better. "I will tell the others after we have the results of the scan. But you can tell Ace if you'd like."

"Thank you. Do you want me to come with you when you get the scan?" Maisy asked.

"No. It's okay." She glanced at Ty, who was watching them with a concerned expression. "Actually, Ty might need you there. If you wouldn't mind? He's been so strong for me, but—"

"Ty is as strong as the mountains he climbs, but he's also human. I'll be there, honey. Don't you worry. I'll take care of him while he's busy taking care of you. That's what family is for."

Chapter Twenty-One

AFTER A SLEEPLESS night, Ty lay awake long before the sun rose Thursday morning. He pressed a kiss to Aiyla's forehead as she lay sleeping on his chest. She looked so peaceful, it broke his heart to know there was a disease poisoning her. She was the sweetest, strongest woman he knew, and she didn't deserve to be dealt this hand. Anger simmered inside him. It had become his constant companion over the past few days, and he'd given up trying to fight it. He was supposed to be the man Aiyla could count on to protect her from *anything*, and he was powerless against this disease. He couldn't rip it from her body and beat it until it was nonexistent. And he knew if rage stacked up inside him every time he thought about it, it was probably ten times as difficult for Aiyla to deal with, although she still didn't want to talk about it.

Not until we know if it's spread.

They'd spent the last two days trying not to overthink or over worry, both of which were impossible. But his mother had come through, helping to distract them as much as she could. She and Aiyla had made cupcakes with Phillip on Tuesday, giving Ty a chance to tie up a few loose ends and visit Cole. He'd gone in search of answers, but when he'd seen his brother, he'd lost it and unleashed days of fury that had been simmering inside him. He was so angry at the world, and so sad and hurt, he'd needed to let it all out. Thankfully, Cole had understood that need. He'd dragged Ty's ass down to the gym in their building and let Ty duke it out with a heavy bag—and then *cry it out* on his brother's strong, stable shoulder.

Yesterday Ty and Aiyla had taken a canoe out to a private wooded area by the river where Cole had taken Ty before Cole had gone away to college. Ty and Aiyla had stayed on the peaceful oasis overlooking the river until nearly sundown before canoeing back and then heading over to Tap It, Nate's restaurant, for dinner.

He brushed his lips over her forehead again and whispered, "I love you."

They were in his childhood bedroom, someplace he'd never been with another woman, and it felt like Aiyla had always been there. Like this was *their* room, *their* mattress on the floor.

She made a sleepy sound. "Is it Friday?"

He kissed her again, knowing she was really asking, *Can we skip Thursday and pretend everything is okay?*

"Almost," he answered.

"I dreamed we were on a road trip but we had no destination. We just kept driving, and I was so *happy*."

He wished they could get in the car right now and leave the disease behind.

"We'll go on a road trip, babe." He pulled her warm, naked body over his and ran his hands over her hips, palming her beautiful butt. "We'll go on a plane trip. We'll go on boats and hikes and ski everywhere there's snow." He believed that with all of his heart and wouldn't allow himself to entertain anything short of having Aiyla by his side. *Always.*

She touched her lips to his, and he swept her beneath him, earning that melodic laugh he loved so much. He laced his fingers with hers and nudged her legs apart with his knees. Her eyes darkened, and his emotions came rushing out.

"How did I get lucky enough to have found you?" he asked.

Her eyes teared up. That had been happening a lot lately and he knew better than to ask if she was okay—*she wasn't*—or why she was tearing up—*he knew*. "I *am* lucky, baby, and don't you ever doubt that. For better or worse, sickness or health, I am yours and you are mine."

She laughed, and a tear slid down her cheek. "We're not married yet."

"We're in the Bradonian world, remember?" He nibbled on her neck and said, "There's no escaping us. I have a cousin who's ordained, and if he lived here, I'd drag you to his house right now and marry you."

"We don't even have a marriage license."

Aw, hell. "I forgot about that. First stop after your appointment, Circuit Court Clerk's Office."

She laughed, and he said, "You think I'm kidding?"

As he lowered his lips to hers, she touched his chest, holding the kiss at bay. "Ty, I've been thinking about where to have the treatments done."

The steadiness of her voice surprised him, especially since she hadn't wanted to talk about the impending scan or what they were going through. "You know I'll be there wherever you choose to have them done."

"I know you will. I don't know any of the right doctors back home, and I'm afraid to put that kind of pressure on my sister and her family. I also think you'll need support as much as I will, so it's probably best if we do them here. Unless you think it's too much for your family to deal with?"

His chest constricted. He was glad she wanted to stay here, where they would have the support of his family. "I think my family will be glad we're here."

"Okay." She slid her hand around his neck and tugged him closer. "Now, please love me until you're all I can think about."

The first touch of their lips was electric, flooding him with desire. He released her hands, determined to obliterate her sad thoughts and needing to *feel* more of her as their bodies rocked greedily against each other. He ran his hands through her hair, along her shoulders, and down her torso. Her skin was warm and soft, and so damn sexy. His mouth burned a path to each of her pleasure points, from the tips of her taut nipples to the sensitive skin around her belly button, making her squirm and moan as he kissed and sucked and lavished her with attention. She smelled like the break of dawn, fresh and inviting. Her hips rose off the mattress as he slicked his tongue along the warm skin between her sex and her inner thigh. He loved teasing her, making her body tremble, and her breathing hitch.

She fisted her hands in his hair, writhing against his mouth. "Love me," she pleaded.

"Always." He lowered his mouth to the sweetness between her legs.

She clung to his hair as he loved her with his hands and mouth, her hips pulsing with every thrust of his tongue. He brought her right up to the edge of release, her thighs flexed, her body shaking. He teased her with his fingers as he moved swiftly up and sealed his mouth over her breast. Her body jolted, and a long, low moan escaped her lips. She grabbed his arms, her fingernails carving into his skin as her body clenched tight and hot around his fingers. Her sinful sounds surrounded them, soaking into his skin and whirling inside him until he was holding on to his sanity by a shred.

"Need you—" He moved over her and captured her mouth at the same time his hips thrust, burying his cock to the root. "Love you," he panted out between steamy kisses as they ate at each other's mouths and their bodies pounded out a frantic rhythm.

"Ty—" she gasped as she shattered around him.

He held her at the peak, slowing their pace, taking them both higher, until they were barely breathing, his body tingling from head to toe. Her fingers burned into his skin, her center clenched around his shaft, and he breathed in soul-drenching drafts, filling his lungs with her love. He pushed his hands beneath her ass, angling her hips, loving her deeper, harder, and slow went out the window. They clawed at each other's skin, kissing and biting. Heat pooled inside him, consuming his every breath, until his orgasm crashed over him with magnum force, sending them both soaring to the clouds.

They collapsed to the mattress and he gathered her against him, his heart full of love and tortured with anguish. He was probably holding her too tight, but he was unable to loosen his grip, needing to be as connected as physically possible.

"Love you, Ty," she whispered in a voice devoid of energy and full of love. "Don't let go, okay? Even if I fall asleep."

He pressed his lips to his brave, strong girl's. The woman who didn't want to talk about what they were going through. Didn't she know those three words—*Don't let go*—told him more than a conversation ever could?

LATER THAT MORNING Ty gazed out the windows of the waiting room while Aiyla had her PET scan. It was strange to see life carrying on outside their little bubble of anxiety, when their lives hung on the results of one test. A pregnant woman sat beside Ty's mother awaiting an ultrasound. He'd heard her say that she was having twins. Would Aiyla have a chance to carry their babies? They'd talked about having children when they were in Saint-Luc, and he'd told her he wanted a big family. Now he wished he hadn't. If she couldn't have children, he was all for adoption, or even not having a family if that was what she wanted when they got beyond this, but he knew Aiyla would feel guilty if they couldn't have babies. There were so many unknowns backing up inside him, he struggled to focus on the things he *could* control.

His mother touched his back, pulling him from his thoughts. It was a gentle touch, a touch that said, *I don't want to startle you* and *I love you* at once. A touch he'd felt a million times, but the worried look in her eyes made it feel different.

Wasn't everything different now?

The very air they breathed felt different. It felt like a blessing, and he'd taken it for granted his whole life.

The things he'd worked for now seemed frivolous. He'd give everything up in exchange for Aiyla's health. Hell, he'd give up his own life to protect hers.

"Sweetheart?" His mother brushed his hair from his eyes, a small smile on her lips. Last night she'd asked Aiyla if it was okay to tell his father about today's test, and of course Aiyla had been fine with that, though she'd appreciated her asking first. "I'm used to you being lost in your own world, and I'm trying not to be overbearing, but you look more lost than ever. Is there anything I can do?"

When they'd left Aiyla to have the procedure, he'd felt like he was leaving her behind. He hadn't been sure how to step out of the room, and his mother had put a gentle hand on his shoulder and shown him how. Just as she'd shown him how to walk as a baby, how to study as a young adult, and how to believe in himself. The same way she'd shown him how to love with his entire being. He had a great life, and it had all started with his parents, who had always been there for him, unconditionally. Aiyla had lost the one parent she had, but now she had *him*—and his parents. And everyone else in their circle whose lives she'd touched.

Two weeks ago he'd thought he had the world at his fingertips. What he'd failed to realize was that the world he'd thought he had wasn't the one that mattered.

Ty blinked away the dampness taking up residence in his eyes and said, "I'm not lost, Mom. I'm scared about what this all means, but I'm not lost. I think I'm seeing life much clearer than I ever have."

Chapter Twenty-Two

FRIDAY MORNING TY and Aiyla sat on the back porch of the house Beau was renovating, watching the sun come up over the horizon. They'd grabbed a few pieces of fruit, bottles of water, and blueberry muffins that she, Maisy, and Leesa had made the night before while Ty, Cole, and Ace had played with Phillip and baby Avery. Leesa hadn't let on if she'd known about Aiyla's medical diagnosis, and Ty had said that Cole had probably not told her, since he'd asked him not to mention it to the family. She wasn't sure if she should be thankful, or feel guilty for having his brother keep a secret from his wife. But she assumed that as a doctor, those types of secrets were okay.

Their legs dangled off the edge of the porch. A cool breeze swept up the hill, tickling Aiyla's bare feet. It was so peaceful listening to the world wake up, sitting next to the man she loved, she was almost able to pretend that the pain in her leg was innocuous. *Almost.* Something had happened when she was lying in the machine yesterday getting her scan. As it pinged and knocked, she'd seen her mother in her mind, healthy and smiling, rushing around the way she used to. She'd had the overwhelming sensation that her mother was there with her, trying to distract her from her worries. She still didn't know what it meant, but she'd come out of the scan feeling more at peace than she had for the last several days.

She put her fingertips over Ty's and said, "Did you ever think you'd find a woman who liked to watch the sunrise as much as you do?"

"Before you, I never thought about finding a woman to spend my life with, *period*. There was no looking, no wondering, no wishing."

She put her head on his shoulder, thinking of the sunrises they'd watched together in Saint-Luc, Colorado, and there in Peaceful Harbor. "I think sunrises are our thing."

"We have so many *things*, baby. We've only just begun to figure out what they are."

Ty jumped off the deck and stood between her legs. The dusky light danced in his eyes, the way it did on the rippling creek below. His rough hands skimmed up the outsides of her legs, from her ankles to her knees and back down again. Cupping her heels with a coy smile, he lifted her left leg and kissed his way up to her thigh. Then he did the same with the right. "I love your legs, Aiyla Bell, and your pretty little pointy feet."

She laughed and said, "That's a good thing, because they're the only ones I have."

He ran his fingers lightly over her thighs, spreading shivers like wildfire. He took her hand in his and pressed a kiss to the back of it. "I love your hands, sweet baby cakes."

She reached for him, and he put his hands behind her and hauled her forward so they were nose to nose.

"I love your face, beautiful girl." He kissed her tenderly and said, "I love your kisses. I love your eyes, your voice, your laugh."

She wanted to cry again. Her emotions were all over the place lately, but these were happy tears. Tears of truth, because she knew he meant every single word.

"I love your sense of adventure," she said honestly. "And the heated look in your eyes when you want to fool around. And that boyish smile you flash when you're testing the waters."

"Go on," he teased, and she laughed.

"I love your humor and your arms." She ran her hands along the smooth ridges of his biceps and across his broad shoulders and framed his handsome face. "And this mouth? It's pretty talented."

He waggled his brows.

"But what I love most is right here." She covered his heart with her hand. "I love that you didn't run when things got scary, and that you're strong enough for both of us"—tears spilled from her eyes, and her words caught in her throat— "because I'm not sure I could do this without you."

"You'll never have to," he promised. "I want every sunrise, every sunset. I want it all, baby." Just as he'd said, they'd applied for their marriage license yesterday. They were one step closer to forever.

But how long was their forever? The thought came without warning, and she hated it, tried to push it away, but the words came anyway. "Me too, even if we only have a few left—"

Sobs stole her voice, and Ty crushed her to him, holding her so tight it was hard to breathe.

"We have a *million* left. Do you hear me?"

"We don't know that," she cried, unable to stop the truth from tumbling out.

He drew back, anger warring with the dampness in his eyes. He cradled her face in his hands, his tears falling on her cheeks.

"No more talk about not having many left, okay? We're not thinking like that."

"I don't want to think like that. Don't let me, Ty. Help me stop." She hated sounding so weak that she couldn't control her own thoughts, but this was Ty, and she trusted him. She wasn't afraid he'd turn tail and run from the pressure, or think she was any weaker for being honest. He was her anchor. Her safe haven. He was her *everything*.

"I won't, baby." He wiped her tears, kissing her softly. "We're in this together, every step of the way."

He embraced her, holding her until she calmed down. Then he tipped her chin up and she felt herself smiling. She was liable to give him whiplash with her roller coaster of emotions. But he returned her smile. He should have told her to pull her shit together, but that wasn't who he was. His smile crawled all the way up to his eyes. It was a magical smile. The kind of smile that made her believe in miracles.

His smile shifted, a little cocky, a little coy, with an ounce of surprise, like she was a gift—the best gift he'd ever been given. Her pulse quickened.

"Want to take a picture?" she teased. "It'll last longer."

He shook his head. "Your beautiful face is etched into my mind. I don't need a picture. I'll wake up to that sassy smile and those sexy eyes every single day for the rest of our lives."

He pulled something from his pocket and took her left hand in his. "I love you, Aiyla Lillian Baby Cakes Bell, and I cannot wait to make you my wife."

He slipped a breathtaking ring on her finger, stunning her into silence. Two diamond bands intersected at the center of the ring, glittering in the morning sun. Intertwined with them were two twisted rose-gold bands, in a simple and elegant design that was perfectly *them*.

"Ty...? When did you have time...?"

"I had it made for you, and picked it up yesterday while you were baking." He lifted her hand. "The diamond bands are our paths crossing—one for Saint-Luc and one for Colorado. The twisted rose-gold bands symbolize eternity, because I know we'll be together forever. And our wedding rings are designed to fit around each side of your engagement ring. Showing we're made for each other."

"Fated to be," she whispered.

"Yes, we are. And my engagement gift to you, my sweet girl, is this house, complete with a sleeping porch, and all the renovations you spoke with Beau about."

She gasped. "The *house*? You said you didn't want a house."

He wrapped her in his arms, smiling so hard it had to hurt. "I said I had never found a reason to buy one. You're my reason, baby. We need a place of our own, and the second you saw this house, you lit up brighter than the sun. Now we'll have a home for whatever comes down the road. Whether you're going through treatments, or we just want to watch the sunrise between travels, in a few short weeks this will be ours."

Too overwhelmed to speak, she went up on her toes and he lifted her into his arms, kissing her the way he always did, like he never wanted to let her go—and she knew in her heart he never would.

TY HAD BEEN thankful for many things in his life, but chasing after a four-year-old had never been one of them—until now. Waiting for the results of Aiyla's scan was excruciatingly stressful, and Phillip's never-ending energy was the perfect distraction. Ty and Aiyla and his parents had taken his curious nephew fishing on the riverbanks. When Tempest had first met Phillip, he'd rarely spoken. He'd changed so much since then. Because of Phillip's incessant questions and zest for all things animal related, they'd spent the last few hours digging up worms, baiting his hook—consoling him about baiting the hook *with* the worms—chasing butterflies, and searching for frogs.

Ty stood by the water holding Phillip's plastic fishing rod while Granny Maisy and Phillip gathered rocks for his newest endeavor—a castle made of mud, rocks, and grass. The boy's imagination was endless. They'd brought Ty's camera, and Aiyla was crouched a few feet from where they were gathering rocks, happily clicking away.

He wondered what her artist's eye saw when she looked through the lens. Where was her mind? Was she plagued by the questions he'd had the other night about having a family? Or was she blessed with a few minutes of freedom from thoughts of the disease inside her?

He hoped for the latter.

When she lowered the camera, allowing it to hang from the neck strap, and he saw the thoughtful smile on her beautiful face, he had a feeling his wish had been granted. Relief swept through him. She glanced over, catching him staring, and her smile changed to one meant just for him. Damn, he loved that.

She walked over, and he ached at her uneven gait. She was favoring her sore leg more than ever, but her smile didn't fade as she came to his side. "Can I borrow your phone? I want to make a video of Phillip for Nash and Tempe, but I don't want to use mine in case Jon calls."

"You can have anything of mine." He handed her his phone, warmed by her thoughtfulness toward his sister.

"That's quite a pole you have there," she teased.

"You know what they say. It's not the size of the rod; it's how you use it that matters." He leaned in for a kiss and felt a tug on the fishing line. "You might want to get this on video," he said quickly, then hollered, "Flip! My man, come over here! You have a fish on the line."

Aiyla stepped back, turning on the video and catching Phillip as he sprinted over.

"I do?" Phillip yelled. "I love fishing! Come on, Granny Maisy! I'm catching a fish!"

"Whoa, buddy, slow down." Ty put a hand out to stop him from running right into the water, and crouched beside him. "Okay, you need to focus, buddy, so you don't scare the fish away."

"I know how to focus. Papa Ace taught me. Watch." His brows knitted and his lips puckered, causing everyone to laugh.

"Good job. Now hold the rod, and when you feel a tug, reel it in a little." Ty glanced at Aiyla, who was smiling ear to ear as she watched them through the phone. She stepped closer and crouched to get a better view of Phillip.

Phillip put his face right up to the screen. "Hello? Hello? Hello?"

"This is a video for your mommy and daddy," Aiyla said.

"Look at me!" he yelled at the phone. "I'm catching a fish!" His line bent and he squealed. "Uncle Ty! Help!"

Ty's arms circled Phillip from behind, and he helped him reel in the fish. "That's it, buddy, slow and steady."

Maisy laughed. "I want a copy of that video."

"You and me both," Aiyla said.

Phillip whipped his head toward the camera, bonking Ty in the cheek, and yelled, "Watch, Mom! Watch, Dad!"

Ty didn't know if he should laugh or redirect the little guy's attention toward the water. He didn't have to decide, because his father stepped up beside them and his presence was enough to redirect Phillip's attention.

"Okay, son. It's time to focus on catching that fish," his father said in the authoritative voice that had carried over from his military days.

"Okay, Papa."

As Phillip followed Ace's directions, lifting the tip of the rod and reeling in the fish, Ty draped an arm around Aiyla and kissed her cheek. "I love you," he said for the millionth time that day. He hadn't been able to *stop* saying it since he'd told her about the house. Knowing they were really going to build a life together gave him hope and brought his love to unexpected heights.

She turned with her lips puckered, and he kissed her at the same second Phillip lifted the fish from the water, and they all cheered.

Phillip took one look at the fish and screamed, "He's hurt! Papa Ace! Save him! He needs stitched up!"

Aiyla turned off the video as Ace and Ty tried to console him. "Hasn't he fished before?" she asked Maisy.

"Many times. But he has a big heart, and every time he sees the hook in the fish's mouth, he cries." She put a hand on Ty's shoulder and said, "At Phillip's age, this one was fine when we caught the fish, but he'd tear up when he saw us cleaning them."

"Aw," Aiyla said. "That's so sad."

"I never saw it that way," Maisy said. "They're big-hearted

boys. That's a good thing. There are enough people in the world who don't give a lick about nature. I bet your mother had a few secrets about you like that, too."

Aiyla blushed and said, "I used to cry when I saw butterflies because I knew it meant the caterpillar was gone."

"See? Big-hearted people always find each other." Maisy winked and reached a hand out to Phillip, who had stopped crying, and said, "Ready to go build that castle, little man?"

Phillip nodded, took her hand, and then reached for Aiyla's. "You come, too?"

"I'd love to."

Ty watched them walk toward the rocks and made a mental note about caterpillars and butterflies. "Is that true?" he asked his father. "What Mom said?"

"Your mother has never told a lie a day in her life," Ace said.

"I don't remember getting upset over cleaning fish."

"You don't need to. That's what mothers are for." He handed Ty the plastic rod. "Let's catch some dinner and see if we can bring rise to a few more tears."

Ty laughed. "You're cruel."

His father arched a brow and said, "I meant *yours*, not Phillip's."

A phone sounded, and Ty's stomach lurched as Aiyla's voice landed in his ears. "Hi, Jon. Yes. Just give me a second, please."

Their eyes locked, and the fear in hers sent Ty across the rocks. He guided her away from his mother and Phillip, feeling the weight of his parents' worried gaze following them. "It's okay, baby. Whatever it is, we'll get through it."

Her eyes were already teary as she lifted the phone to her ear and said, "I'm back, sorry."

Aiyla paused, listening to Jon, the seconds ticking by like

time bombs. She grabbed Ty's arm, trembling from head to toe, a flood of tears pouring down her cheeks. He hugged her to him, silently cursing the universe and trying his damnedest to hold back his own tears as she croaked out, "Yes. I understand. Thank you."

Her hand fell to her side and she collapsed to her knees. He dropped down to his, holding her against him, both of them crying. "It's okay," he reassured her, even as his heart shattered into a million pieces. "We'll get through this."

Aiyla lifted her face, her smile confusing him. "It didn't spread." She sobbed. "It's *only* in my leg, Ty."

It took a few seconds for him to process what she'd said, and when she added, "We caught it early," her sobs were drowned out by a rush of relief.

"Baby!" he said between grateful kisses. "Oh, *baby.*"

They cried and kissed, hugging and laughing and crying harder.

"*You* did this," she said through her tears. "You made me get checked. You saved me."

"No, baby. Fate saved us both."

Chapter Twenty-Three

LATER THAT NIGHT, after sharing their news with Ty's parents and explaining to Phillip that their tears were happy tears, Aiyla called the oncologist Jon recommended, Dr. Whiskey, and scheduled an appointment. Jon had already called ahead, and they fit her into next week's schedule. She was thankful for Jon's connections, because knowing the cancer hadn't spread made every minute until she began treatments feel like Russian roulette. The hours seemed to move by in a cloud of relief, but the darkness never lifted completely. Aiyla still had cancer, and they had a long road ahead of them to figure out how to deal with it, and then, of course, to *actually* deal with it. Aiyla paced Ty's parents' backyard, talking—*and crying*—with her sister as she brought her up to speed. As horrible as it was to share the details with Cherise, after shedding tears to the point of not being able to speak, Aiyla felt oddly better. She'd never been a secret keeper, and now she remembered why. Secrets were harder to deal with than the truth. They dragged her down like quicksand.

Once they pulled themselves back together and Aiyla was able to talk without breaking down, she said, "I'm sorry for not telling you sooner, but there was no reason to until after the biopsy, and then I couldn't do it without knowing the extent of the disease."

"I hate you a little for that," Cherise said with an anxious laugh. "I'm your sister. You should let me suffer through waiting *with* you. I get it, and I love you for protecting me. But if you do anything like that ever again, I'll…"

Aiyla felt herself smiling. She knew her sister would never say she'd *kill* her, and Cherise couldn't pummel her, which she'd probably like to sometimes.

"Withhold your famous coconut cookies?" Aiyla suggested.

"Yes!" Cherise sighed. "I love you, Aiyla, and I should be there with you. I don't know how you're functioning."

"As you can tell from how I just bawled my eyes out, I'm pretty much a mess. But Ty has been wonderful, Cherise. You'll love him. He's been with me every step of the way, and it's because of him that we found it so early."

"I am definitely sending *him* a boatload of cookies—"

Her voice cut off, and Aiyla knew her sister was crying again. She wanted to put her mind at ease, so she focused on moving forward. "I think we made the right decision to have the treatments here. I don't want your boys to worry about me, and you don't need the stress of running back and forth to medical appointments. We've been there. Remember how awful it was? We know the toll it'll take on you and your kids. You need to be in a good mental space for them."

"But you're my *sister*," she said softly. "I also need to be there for you."

"I know, and I appreciate that you want to. But you're *my* sister, too, and you were my rock when Mom was sick and when we lost her. You've been there for me more than I could have ever hoped for. Now it's time for you to be there for your boys. We'll fly you guys out once we know more and we have a plan." She had no idea how she was pulling off speaking so matter-of-factly all of a sudden. Maybe it was because she knew she needed to be strong for Cherise, or because the relief of today's news was still giving her the strength she needed. Whatever the reason, she was glad, because she didn't want to upset Cherise any more than she already had.

"I have an appointment next week with an oncologist, and then my doctor will have a meeting with the oncologist and radiologist to talk about treatment options. After that we'll meet with him again. Once we're past that, it'll be easier. We'll know what we have ahead of us."

Another teary sound came through the phone.

"Cher, I'm going to be okay."

"You *know* we don't know that for sure," Cherise said. "We hope, and pray, and—"

Ty's comforting words sailed through Aiyla's mind and came out for her sister. "We're not going to think like that, okay? We can't. We have to believe that we can beat it. I'm not Mom, sis. They caught it early. It's not anywhere else in my body."

Cherise sighed. "I wish it were me instead of you."

"No, Cherise. Don't *ever* say that. My nephews need you. Caleb needs you."

"And *we* need *you*."

They talked until they had no more tears to spill. Then Aiyla caught up on her nephews, and she told Cherise about Ty's family and the night Ty had proposed at the wedding. They talked about the house Ty was buying, which still felt too surreal to believe, and as she gazed at her beautiful ring, she told her about that, too. After several *I love you*s and promises to share information right when Aiyla learned of it, they ended the call.

Aiyla walked back toward the house, feeling better having cleared the air and sad because she knew Cherise would now share that information with Caleb and cry all over again.

She found Ty and his parents talking on the deck. Phillip had been tuckered out from their adventurous day and had fallen asleep right after his bath. As Aiyla headed up the lawn, she thought about how the last couple of weeks had felt like months. Two weeks ago her biggest worry had been trying to place in the charity event. Now she had a disease that events like that raised money for. She had never asked *why me*, and she wasn't now. She knew from losing her mother that those types of questions were wasted energy. Ty pushed to his feet and opened his arms, and she walked right in knowing the *why*s didn't matter as much as the future did.

"Is Cherise okay?" Ty asked.

"As okay as she can be. She wants to come out, but I told her maybe in a few weeks, once we know what we're dealing with." Ty had offered to fly Cherise and her family out tomorrow, but Aiyla had meant what she'd said to her sister. She had Ty by her side. She didn't need to turn Cherise's life upside down, too.

He sank to a chair and brought her down on his lap. "And how's my girl?"

She glanced at his parents, lying beside each other on the lounge chair, and then she brought her attention back to him. "As okay as she can be," she answered honestly. "I'm so thankful for all of you."

Ty kissed her softly, and Maisy said, "And we're thankful for you, sweetheart."

"I bet you never thought when you were meeting Ty's girlfriend that I had all of this baggage."

Ty gave her a stern look.

"This isn't baggage," Maisy said. "This is *life*. When I married Ace, we thought he'd be in the military forever. We had our whole lives planned out, moving wherever the military sent us and raising kids who knew what it meant to make new friends and travel the world."

Ace kissed Maisy's temple the way Ty did so often to Aiyla, and he said, "When I lost my leg, I didn't know what I'd do, where we'd live. It was a scary time for us. I had a new wife, a baby on the way, and suddenly I was starting over without so much as a backup plan. I thought I was going to be Maisy's hero, but it turned out, she was mine."

Aiyla had forgotten that he had a prosthesis. She couldn't imagine what had gone through his head the moment he'd realized his jump was going treacherously wrong. "You both must have been terrified."

"We learned a lot in those first few months," Ace said. "I had months of grueling rehab, and during that time my wonderful wife was making plans I had no idea about."

Maisy smiled and patted his chest. "You knew what I was up to. You were just too busy to process it. Ace's brother, Clint—you met him at the wedding. Beau and Ty's other cousins' father—had settled down in Pleasant Hill, the next town over, and I knew Ace needed to be near family."

"She also knew I'd go crazy without something to put my mind to," Ace said. "Once we saw Peaceful Harbor, with the ocean and mountains at our fingertips, and family around the corner, we knew this was home for us. It was the perfect situation made even more so by Maisy's innate ability to feel her way into the future."

"What does that mean?" Ty asked.

"It means it was your mother's idea to open the microbrewery," Ace said with pride.

Ty blinked several times and said, "How did I *not* know this?"

"Because your mother isn't the type to toot her own horn. It was the early eighties, and for the first time since prohibition, a brewery was allowed to not only sell its beer at its own bar on premises, but also serve food. Within a year, more than eighty breweries were operating, and the top companies—Anheuser-Busch, Miller, Coors, and the other big players—controlled more than ninety percent of US beer production. The idea of going up against them scared the bejeezus out of me. I had a family to provide for, after all." He sat up a little straighter and cleared his throat. "But just as Maisy had been there and believed in me during my rehabilitation, she had faith in our ability to create a successful, community-oriented business. It was her strength and conviction, and her unrelenting support, that allowed us to make a go of it."

Being surrounded by so much love made Aiyla less focused on what she and Ty were going through and more aware of what they had to look forward to.

Love rose in Maisy's eyes, and she said, "First, you always were, and will always be, my hero. And second, I had ideas, but carrying them out took both of us. And often you had to redirect my overenthusiastic notions. We're a team, Ace, and a damn good one." She looked at Ty and Aiyla and said, "The thing about tragedies is that they can drag you under, or they can make you stronger. I have adored this man since the day we met. And yes, there are days I want to kick his heinie into the ocean, but those days are few and far between, and they make the others even better."

Chapter Twenty-Four

OVER THE NEXT twelve days, Aiyla's emotions were all over the place. Most of the time she held it together, but there were times when sadness or anger consumed her. She and Ty cried a lot, and talked even more. They'd picked up their marriage license, met with the oncologist, who was also a family friend of the Bradens, which made the appointment as comfortable as she could hope for, and they'd broken the news to Ty's family one couple at a time, crying alongside each one. They'd told Shannon over FaceTime, and they decided to wait and tell Tempest and Nash when they returned from their honeymoon. The outpouring of support from Ty's family was endless. Faith, Leesa, Jewel, and Maisy were godsends, inviting her to lunch, going shopping, and treating her like she was no different from them. Ty's brothers were as protective as Ty was over her, but Ty assured her that even if she didn't have cancer, they'd be doing the same things. After spending two weeks with his family, she knew it was the truth. Trixie had texted Aiyla to touch base a few times, and finally Aiyla called and told her what she was going through. They cried rivers, and Aiyla asked Trixie to come up when she began treatments and take Ty out to get his mind off of what they were going through. She knew

Ty wouldn't want to leave her even for a minute, but she also knew he'd need a break. And finally, she'd called Ms. F, which had opened the floodgates once again.

Now she and Ty sat across from Jon as he told them about his meeting with Dr. Whiskey and the radiologist and explained that she had Stage II-A, the cancer was intermediate grade and confined within the cortex of the bone.

"Chondrosarcoma does not respond well to chemotherapy or radiation therapy. The best treatment is surgical," Jon explained. "Limb-sparing surgery is very effective. We remove the tumor while preserving as much of the tendons, nerves, and blood vessels as we can, so you can maintain function of your leg."

"You want to cut out part of my *bone?*" Aiyla's chest constricted. "What if you don't get all the cancer?"

"I'm confident that we can remove the entire tumor. With this surgery, we not only remove the affected area of the bone and replace it with a prosthetic," Jon explained. "We also remove a wide margin around the tumor to get rid of any cancerous cells. Done right, you should be cancer free after the surgery."

"So no chemotherapy? No radiation?" she asked, unsure if she should be relieved or concerned.

"No," Jon said.

Ty squeezed her hand and asked, "And recovery? What is that like?"

As Jon talked about healing time and physical therapy, she mentally dissected what he'd just said. *We also remove a wide margin around the tumor to get rid of any cancerous cells. Done right, you should be cancer free after the surgery.* What if the surgery wasn't done right? What if they missed something?

Would the cancer come back? The term she thought she'd never hear again after her mother passed away slammed into her—*quality of life.* How stable would her leg be? Would she be able to ski? To climb? To run? Should any of that matter as long as she was alive?

"Wait," she blurted out, panic mounting inside her. "I'm sorry, but I have questions."

"Of course," Jon said.

"What if the margins you leave aren't enough? Will it come back? How stable will my leg be? Can I do the things I do now? Ski? Run? Climb? And what about complications? Infections? How do you secure a prosthetic bone inside my leg? And will a prosthetic bone wear out if I continue doing all the activities I do now?" She spat her questions rapid-fire, and didn't stop until Ty's arm came around her.

"Take a breath, baby. Let Jon answer these questions, and then we'll ask the rest, okay?"

"Sorry," she said.

"Aiyla, those are all very good questions, and some are going to be difficult to answer, because every case is different. Assuming you heal well, without complications, your leg should be very stable. As far as your activity level goes, that is very individualized. Daily activities should be fine, and many people who have this surgery go on to have very active lifestyles. You're young, athletic, and in good physical condition. You have a lot going for you, and it'll all help with your recovery."

Anxiety mounted inside her with each of his carefully worded sentences.

"But your concerns are not unfounded," Jon added. "If all goes well, you'll probably be fine for a while doing all of the activities you enjoy. But as with any *hardware,* things can loosen and require a modification, and you can lose bone stock with each adjustment. Or you might be fine. There's no way to tell. And yes, there can be less-than-ideal outcomes depending on the damage to nerves and blood vessels, but that is rare, and I'll take great care to ensure that doesn't happen. With any surgery, there is the chance of infection or complications, but our team will do everything possible to avoid them. That being said, limb-sparing surgery is preferred by many patients to a prosthetic leg, for purely cosmetic reasons."

"I don't care what my leg looks like," she said shakily. "I want this disease *out* of my body, and I want the best chance I have to continue doing the things I love." Fear swelled inside her at the question nagging at the back of her mind. Breathing deeply, she said, "What are the pros and cons of amputating?"

"*Amputating*?" Ty looked at her like she was crazy. "He just said he could save your leg."

"Yes, with a million possible complications and a chance that in the long term I won't be able to climb with you, or ski, or run. I *want* to do those things, Ty." As the words left her lips, she realized how *desperately* she wanted to continue doing them. To continue living the life she'd worked so hard to create. "I'm sorry, but as much as I hate the idea of losing my leg, losing my ability to do the things we love would be worse."

Ty leaned in closer. "I support whatever you want to do. It's your body. But don't think for a second that I'd leave you if you couldn't do those things."

"That didn't even cross my mind. The way I see it, cancer is going to sideline me now either way, and once we get rid of it, I want to know it's as *gone* as gone can be. And I don't want to risk a *less-than-ideal outcome* for cosmetic reasons. When this is all said and done, I want to look forward to our life, to our wedding, to all the things we want to do together. I don't want to have a semi-functional leg because of some unforeseen complication."

"Those are valid concerns for an athletic person such as yourself," Jon said. "Some patients prefer amputation as it allows unrestricted activity and less potential for complications. Others prefer limb construction for improved cosmetics and because it results in a less energy-requiring limb for daily activities. It's a lifestyle choice as much as it is a medical one."

"Less energy-requiring?" Ty asked. "You mean, like not having to take off or put on a prosthetic leg?"

"Exactly, and there are other things to consider. The cost of the prosthesis, physical therapy, learning to walk with a prosthetic limb, possible skin irritation, daily cleaning and maintenance. And you know from your father's prosthesis that he has to remove it to go swimming—"

"Will it give Aiyla less of a chance of the cancer coming back?" Ty asked.

Aiyla held her breath.

"I can't give you the reassurance you're looking for, Ty. There are no guarantees when it comes to cancer. Is there less risk of recurrence if you amputate? You're removing more of the area around the tumor, so logic says yes."

Aiyla's breath rushed from her lungs. "Then that's what I want to do."

"You realize it's not a guarantee," Jon reiterated.

"Yes, but it sounds like that wide margin you spoke of would be even less risky if we do this. And I won't have to worry about modifications or other surgeries in the future to correct something fake inside my body."

"We'd have to amputate above the knee, and given your

athletic lifestyle, a prosthesis makes sense. It will give you the best functionality to continue doing the things you enjoy with the least opportunity for future complications once you're healed from the initial amputation. If this is the way you want to proceed, I'll put you in touch with the prosthetist and the physical therapy and rehab departments so you can begin the preliminary process. But there are also a range of emotions that amputees go through that you might not be considering. I would suggest that if you want to go that route, you speak to a psychologist to make sure you're fully prepared. I'll be happy to refer you to one."

"And to Ace," she said more to herself than to them.

"I'd like to talk to a therapist, too," Ty said. "With or without you, if you want to talk to the psychologist in private. I'd like to see what I can do to best support you."

For the first time since they entered Jon's office, tears slipped from her eyes. "Thank you. As scary as this is, I feel like this is the right decision."

ON THE WAY out of Jon's office, Ty was still wrapping his mind around not only Aiyla's decision, but the strength it had taken for her to deal with actively taking part in that meeting. His stomach had plummeted the minute Jon mentioned surgery, and for her—the woman who was going to *have* the surgery—to have been in the frame of mind to process the things Jon was saying seemed remarkable. She was making a courageous—*fierce*—decision. Then again, this was the woman who refused to fail, refused help most of the time, and had survived losing her mother at fifteen years old. She'd seemed nothing short of extraordinary since the day he'd met her, and his respect for her had only grown since.

"Are you sure you're okay with this?" she asked as they crossed the parking lot toward the car.

"Me?" he asked. "You're asking if *I'm* okay with it?"

"I just realized that while we were in there, I was only thinking about what I wanted or needed. I should have asked you if you were okay with my decision."

Ty gathered her in his arms, his chest full of so much love it hurt to speak. "Babe, I'm okay with anything that will rid you of this disease. We have a long road ahead of us, and I will be there with you every step of the way, and love you through whichever path you take."

She smiled, and he lowered his lips to hers, kissing her until she melted against him—and then he kissed her longer, because he simply needed to.

"I love you," he said as he hugged her. "That's not going to change because you have one less limb."

"It's so much for you to deal with all at once."

"No, babe. It's so much for *us* to deal with. But *so much* doesn't equate to *too much*. We're a team, and that's never going to change." He gazed into her eyes, searching for signs that she was going to break down, but she looked stronger than she had in days. "Do you want to go someplace and talk?"

She slipped her finger into the waist of his shorts and said, "If we go someplace alone, talking is the *last* thing I want to do." She pressed a kiss to the center of his chest and said, "I want alone time with you. But before we get lost in each other, I'd like to talk with your dad about what it was like after his accident. Would you mind?"

"Not at all, but, Aiyla, why aren't you falling apart? You just made a huge, scary decision. Shouldn't you be crying or calling your sister, or something? You're worrying me."

"It's weird, I know. I feel like that, too, but we finally have some answers, and that's a really good feeling, no matter how scary it is. Before today, it was like cancer was this monster all around us. We couldn't escape it because it's inside of me, and we didn't know how to get it out. Now I feel like we have a plan, and we're not alone. Jon has a team of professionals and he seems to be looking after our best interests. I mean, he could have just said okay to the idea of amputation, but he wanted me to talk to a psychologist first. Even if he's just covering his ass, it feels like he wants us to be informed and he wants the best solution for *us*."

"He does, babe. He's not covering his ass. Jon's one of the best in his field."

"Then my instincts were right. I'm sure I'll fall apart again at some point, but right now I feel relieved and I feel good about my decision. And don't take my lack of tears as an indication that this is an easy decision, because I'm not fooling myself about that. That's why I want to talk to your dad. If anyone can tell us the truth about what it would be like, it's him."

"We'll go see him, but afterward, you're *mine*. I want you to put on that pretty dress you wore to my sister's wedding, and I'm taking you out for a fancy dinner, maybe have a little wine…"

"Mr. Braden, are you going to try to seduce me?" she asked flirtatiously.

He hauled her against him and kissed her deeply. "There'll be no *trying* about it."

An hour later they were having lunch with Ty's father on

the patio of Mr. B's, overlooking the marina.

"Our situations are quite different," his father said carefully. His eyes were as serious as ever, his shoulders squared, spine straight. Hallmarks of a military man. Ty saw the same attributes in his brother Nate. "My body had endured horrific trauma, and they'd tried to save my leg with two surgeries, but it never healed properly, and then infection set in, which is what led to the amputation. The recovery I went through, and the one you will go through, will be significantly different. That being said, there are some things that I think all amputees experience." He glanced at Ty with a pained expression. "Are you two sure you want me to be completely honest here? Sometimes anticipating an outcome can magnify it in our heads, making it worse than it actually is."

"I'm sure," Aiyla said quickly. "I'm looking at a life-changing decision, and I want to be as prepared as possible."

Ace took her hand between his, smiling warmly. "You are a strong, capable woman, Aiyla, but that alone won't give you what you need to accept and move forward in a healthy way after losing a limb. There will be times when you feel phantom pain, or you reach down to scratch an itch on a leg that is no longer there. You'll have to figure out how to deal with children staring, because their curious little minds will try to make sense of what they're seeing, and don't be surprised if you *miss* your limb. Since you're making the decision, you might even second- and third-guess it days or months down the line."

"I'm sure I'll be questioning it throughout the healing pro-cess, which Jon described as pretty painful."

Empathy rose in Ace's eyes as quickly as it boiled in Ty's gut.

"Yes, it will be painful, but your doctors will manage the

pain with their medical cocktails. It might be more difficult to manage the emotional trauma." He glanced at Ty, then at Aiyla again. "You will need the support of your medical team after surgery, but what you'll need even more is the understanding and the support of the people who love you. They can't see what you feel, what you fear, or the demons that might come to you at night. You're not just losing a leg and a foot, Aiyla. This surgery will redefine how you see yourself. You're going to have to get used to a new you and a new way of life. Buying shoes, or clothes, that fit into your view of how you like to look can be a problem. And although they have wonderful lifelike prosthetics, you might not like how it looks when you wear shorts or skirts. You'll have to *put on* your leg each morning, and sometimes, if I sit for too long, I have to take mine off because it gets uncomfortable. That doesn't always happen in private. It can happen anywhere at any time. On an airplane, for example, which might embarrass you, and you don't know how others will respond. You might not like making the people around you uncomfortable."

"I didn't think of some of those things, but I can honestly say that since talking with Jon, I'm even more determined to get this out of my body completely, and I think this is the best way to do that. If that means I'll look different, or have a different schedule to maintain, then that's what it takes. I don't want to spend my life worrying that he left something behind. I know he's a good surgeon, but this seems a safer bet. Are you embarrassed to remove your leg in public?" She didn't wait for an answer. "Maybe I can say this because I'm not in that position yet, but I feel like it will be part of who I am. The same way some people are born without a limb, or with other disabilities. If it makes anyone uncomfortable that I have to remove a prosthesis, isn't that *their* issue, not mine?" Her voice escalated, and Ty reached for her hand. "I'm serious, Ty," she said vehemently.

"She's right," Ace said. "But knowing that won't make it easier. I can assure you that you'll be tested—your confidence, your ability to turn the other cheek. It's *hard*, Aiyla. You're losing a piece of yourself that you probably don't realize is tied into what none of us want to admit we have. Your *ego*."

She swallowed hard, her brows knitted together. "You're right. I can't deny that. But still the chance of something being missed is a chance I don't want to take. And I know it will mean asking for help a lot more than I'm used to, and that will put extra pressure on Ty, which might be hard for our relationship. I have been thinking about that—"

"We can handle anything, Aiyla," Ty reassured her. "That's one less thing for you to worry about."

"I think it *is* worth worrying about," she said. "I know I'll get frustrated by not being able to manage things myself, and probably at the pain, too, and wondering if I did the wrong thing for *us*, despite knowing you fully support my decision. There are so many things to consider. What I don't know is how I'll handle it. I might yell at you, or say things I don't mean when I'm upset."

Ty laughed. "Babe, I *expect* that. Do you know that when Leesa was delivering Avery she told Cole she hated him for getting her pregnant?"

"That's different. That's over in a few hours, and they took home a prize. Their baby daughter. This is forever, and we're leaving my leg behind. You heard what Jon said. We're looking at *months* of recovery and physical therapy. Maybe even a year."

"She's right, Ty," Ace said. "It won't be easy, and you can't count on your love being enough. Even love needs a shoulder to lean on sometimes. And rest assured, you'll have our family, and we will be there in droves for both of you. But I have an idea that might help for those times that it's just the two of you, when you're questioning your strength. It's called an I-Really-Do-Love-You box. Your mother made one for me after my accident—or maybe I should say, she made it for *her*, because those months were trying for the two of us."

Ty and Aiyla exchanged a curious glance.

"It's a simple idea, really, and for us, it was a marriage saver. The idea is that you write love letters to each other now, before the surgery. When you're at your wit's end and you're arguing, or as I like to call it, *venting harshly*," he said with a smile, "you each go to a separate room and read what you have written. Remind yourself why you chose each other and what you love about the other person. Fill that box with memories and hope. And, Aiyla, you might want to write a letter to yourself about why you chose this route, for those times you question it."

"That's a great idea," Aiyla said. "But your accident happened out of the blue. Had you already written love letters to Maisy?"

"Some, but my wife knew enough to prepare for both of us. She wrote love letters to me, and then she wrote lists of all the things I'd told her I loved about her. She filled our box with memories of our happiest times. She also put in a bottle of water and a bottle of wine. The water was for during my rehabilitation, when I couldn't drink alcohol. The wine was for after I was healed. We've refilled that box hundreds of times over the years."

"That's so romantic," Aiyla said. "A built-in time-out. I love it."

"It's brilliant, Dad. Do the others know about this?"

"No, son, they don't. Some couples are tested more than others. What you and Aiyla are about to go through requires the big guns. The others do just fine with their own ammunition."

Chapter Twenty-Five

LATER THAT AFTERNOON, Aiyla called Cherise and told her what she'd decided. She'd expected her sister to have a hard time with her decision, and instead Cherise told her she thought she was doing the right thing. Her support had bolstered Aiyla's confidence. And as she dressed for her dinner date with Ty, she took extra time to do the things she rarely did, like wearing makeup and giving her hair a little extra wave. She'd brought only one dress from home, a simple empire-waist lavender minidress. The dress that would now forever be her favorite because she'd been wearing it the day Ty proposed and he must have told her a hundred times how beautiful she looked in it.

She slipped her feet into her sandals, and a pang of sadness washed over her. She sat on his bed and lifted her foot, really looking at it, and her leg, for the first time ever. Ty loved her legs, and she could see why. They were long, and because she was so athletic, they were lean and...*pretty*. It was strange to look at her body in that way and think about whether her legs and feet were attractive, but now that she knew she wouldn't always have them, she felt a sense of peace, acknowledging their beauty. Ace was right. She would miss her leg, and not just its functionality.

She made a mental note to speak with the psychologist about that, and then she promised herself she'd set aside her worries as best she could for the night. Tonight she wanted only to be a girl out on a date with her incredibly hot fiancé.

She heard Ty's voice as she descended the stairs. He was in the foyer, talking to Phillip. His short-sleeved black button-down was open three buttons deep. He'd trimmed his scruff, leaving just enough to look like a five-o'clock shadow. She imagined those whiskers abrading her chest, her neck, her *thighs*. Ty's gaze raked down her body, warming all her best parts as he met her at the bottom of the stairs.

"See this woman, Flip?" His hungry gaze bored into her. "She is your future aunt, and she's my future wife, the prettiest woman on earth."

"Daddy says Mommy is the prettiest."

Aiyla laughed, wondering how Ty would handle that little nugget.

"Then I think they'll have to share that title." Ty held a hand out to Aiyla, and when she placed her hand in his, he swept her against him and said, "Close your eyes, Flip. I'm about to give Aiyla a big messy kiss."

Phillip ran into the kitchen laughing. "Granny Maisy! Ty and Aiyla are kissing again!"

"You're so dramatic," she teased.

"I speak the truth."

He dipped her over his arm and took her in a thought-shattering kiss. She came away breathless, and he flashed a cocky smile. "Come on, beautiful. I have some wining and dining to do."

She wondered if it would be rude to drag him upstairs to his bedroom instead.

He leaned in, speaking in a low, sexy voice. "You keep looking at me like that and you're liable to get yourself in trouble."

"I like trouble," she whispered.

He nipped at her lips and said, "And I *love* you. Let's go see what kind of trouble we can get into without little eyes watching us."

They drove down by the marina. One section of the pier was lit up with pretty yellow lights. There were a handful of people moving around, and music drifted in through their open windows.

"What's happening down there?" Aiyla asked.

"It's the monthly senior dance."

"But school's out."

He chuckled. "Not senior like senior prom, but *senior*, as in people of advanced age. During the summer, volunteers bring the residents from Harbor House, the assisted living center, to the pier to dance and have dinner."

"Oh, how fun! Can we go see? *Please?*"

Ty turned toward the marina and parked by the pier, where about twenty couples were dancing beneath the lights. "I've volunteered for the event a number of times."

"Now I *really* want to see it. Can we go up there?"

"Sure." He parked the car and came around to help her out.

As he drew her to her feet, his scent mingled with the salty sea air. It was starting to smell like *home*.

They walked hand in hand up to the pier, where elderly couples were dancing to big-band music. They held each other the way she'd seen in old movies. The men had one hand on their partner's lower back and the other held their partner's hand, leaving a proper amount of space between them. Ty pointed to a couple on the far side of the pier. The woman couldn't have been more than five feet tall, and the rail-thin man she was dancing with had only a few inches on her. He had a slight hump on his back, and his wispy white hair stood on end in the gentle breeze. The woman wore a paisley dress and a pair of white orthotic shoes. His thin frame was nestled against her ample bosom, with no space between them.

"These are the faces I *live* to photograph. Look how carefully they move, how focused on each other they are. I feel like when you get to be their age, you know how precious nights like this are. I wish I had my camera," Aiyla said as she headed in their direction, dragging Ty along with her. "Can we dance?"

Ty shrugged. "I guess."

Aiyla could feel positive energy radiating from the couples as they joined them. Ty put his arms around her waist, and she repositioned them to the proper positions, putting a few inches between them, like the others.

"Seriously?"

"We don't want to get kicked out for misbehaving." She couldn't suppress her smile at his slightly annoyed expression. "Look around. Don't you wonder if they're real couples? Or just friends? Or maybe they just met tonight."

His hand slid down to her butt. "See that couple over there? The lady with the white hair dancing with Old Man Rosby? Rumor has it that they've been caught going at it plenty of times."

"You're making that up." She lifted his hand to her waist, and it slid right back down to her butt again.

"They've been fooling around for years."

"Really? Why not just get married?" She glanced at the couple. The portly man shuffled rather than danced, his baggy slacks held up too high with a thick belt, and his shirt was buttoned all the way up to the top button.

"Because Old Man Rosby is also messing around with Caroline Keller." He nodded toward a woman whose dress clung to her stockings.

"No!" she whispered. "That's awful. How do you know?"

"Because I used to volunteer at the Harbor House. I swear the man probably eats Viagra like candy."

They danced to a number of songs, and Ty filled her in on all the couplings he'd discovered when he'd volunteered. They laughed and talked, and Ty continued trying to cop a feel. A summer breeze embraced them, and when her stomach growled, she realized they'd probably missed their dinner reservations.

"Oh no, Ty. You made dinner plans and I messed them up."

"This is much more fun than sitting in a restaurant." He nodded to a buffet table. "*Dinner is served.*"

"You're like a professional party crasher." She followed him over, and they each filled a plate. "Maybe we should offer to pay for our food."

"Oh, no need," an elderly woman with grayish-blue eyes and pink cheeks said as she joined them. "Everyone is welcome here." She squinted at Ty, and surprise shone in her eyes. "Why, Ty Braden? I haven't see you since the community Christmas parade."

"Hello, Millicent." He leaned in and kissed her cheek. "This is my fiancée, Aiyla Soon-to-Be-Braden Bell."

Oh, how she loved that! "It's nice to meet you."

"And you as well. You're getting married? Your parents must be over the moon."

"They are," he said. "Sorry to crash your dance."

Millicent waved a hand. "Don't be. But you *must* dance

with me."

He laughed, and his sweet smile warmed Aiyla all the way to her toes.

"It would be my pleasure. Aiyla, will you be okay for a moment?"

"Absolutely." She watched as he offered his arm to Millicent and proceeded to dance with her, giving her his full attention and chatting animatedly, like a perfect gentleman.

"I see you've been dumped for Millie," the promiscuous Old Man Rosby said to her. He had kind eyes and the type of smile that could be seen as friendly or flirtatious.

Or maybe that was subliminal, left over from what Ty had said.

"You need to watch out for Millie," he advised. "She'll steal your man right out from under your nose."

"Thank you for the warning. I trust Ty, but I'll keep my eyes on her."

He waggled his brows and said, "Do you trust me?"

She stifled a laugh. "Should I?"

"Dance with me, and you decide." He held out a hand, and when she took it, he walked toward the others and held her as he'd held the other woman. "My name is Ralph. Yours?"

"Aiyla."

"*Aiyla*, that's an awfully pretty name, and it's rare to hear it around these parts. It's my great-granddaughter's name. Do you know what it means?"

"My mother told me it meant 'moonlight.' I was born at three minutes after midnight."

"Your mother was right, but I happen to know that it also means 'a beautiful girl who is a strong fighter and easy to fall in love with.'"

"Did you just make that up?" she asked.

"No. It's actually a Turkish name, and it really does mean that. I was married for fifty-nine years to the most beautiful woman you could imagine. She was Turkish, and her name was Dilara, which means 'lover.' She was an amazing lover," he said with a hint of longing. "Before I retired, I was a linguist, and I've always had a penchant for names. I can tell you the meaning of most any name."

She glanced at Ty and asked, "What's the definition of Ty?"

"There really isn't one. It's usually an abbreviation for names like Tyler, which means *to tile*, or Tyson, which indicates a person with a fiery temper. Is Ty your beau's full name?"

"Yes, it's his given name. Simply *Ty*."

He ran an assessing eye over Ty just as Ty glanced their way, his gaze landing on Aiyla, as warm and soft as a caress. A loving smile lifted Ty's lips.

"I'm sorry that I don't have a definition to give you, but I'd say there's nothing *simple* about that man."

I think you're right.

When the song ended, Ty made a beeline for Aiyla and put a proprietary arm around her. He offered his hand to Ralph.

Ralph shook it and said, "Ralph Rosby. Thank you for sharing your sweetheart with me."

"Thank you for dancing with her," Ty said with a twinkle of something mischievous in his eyes. "You don't remember me, do you?"

Ralph leaned in closer, taking a long, careful look at him. "Can't say that I do."

"Ty Braden. I volunteered at the Harbor House ten or so years ago."

"So many people come in and out of that place. I do apologize. My eighty-eight-year-old brain isn't what it used to be. Thank you, Miss Aiyla, for the dance. Now..." He rubbed his hands together, looking over the ladies who were mingling by the railing. "Which beauty should I allow to be the recipient of my affections tonight?" With a wink, he left them.

Aiyla and Ty laughed.

They finally ate dinner and then they fell back into each other's arms, dancing alongside the others. At some point Aiyla gave up on remaining an appropriate distance apart. Ty moved sensually against her, brushing kisses along her shoulder and whispering sexy innuendos into her ears. His hands rested on her lower back. So low, his fingers played over the top of her butt, sending shivers of anticipation with every touch. She rested her head on his chest, listening to the beat of his heart, her thoughts floating in happiness.

The music grew quieter, and Aiyla closed her eyes, trying to hold on to every note. She didn't want to stop dancing, or leave Ty's arms. She didn't want this night to end.

"Can I have your attention, please?" Millie called out.

Aiyla pried herself from Ty's embrace, but he pulled her back in, gazing deeply into her eyes.

"I want more of this," he said heatedly. "I want to dance with you on our porch one day, and come here when we're old and wrinkled and have young couples look at us and wonder how long we've been in love."

Her heart swelled, happiness soaring through her. "I want that, too."

He kissed her as Millie's voice sounded again.

"Tonight is Earl and Jane's seventy-fifth wedding anniversary." Millie motioned toward the couple that had been dancing as close as Ty and Aiyla were. Earl cradled Jane's face in his hands the way Ty always did to Aiyla and wordlessly took his wife in a kiss that was far more than passionate. It was a kiss that told of years of friendship and unwavering love, and when he put one hand around her, holding her even closer, everyone cheered.

Aiyla mentally captured the image, imagining Ty kissing her like that at their age.

"One day that'll be us." Ty brought her in closer. "Next time we'll bring a camera."

"You knew my fingers were itching?" They were so in sync. As much as she was enjoying the evening—and she did wish she had her camera—what she wanted even more was to be in his arms, kissing and touching, and loving him.

"I saw it in your eyes."

She stepped in closer, aligning their bodies as she went up on her toes and kissed him again. "What else do you see?"

Her answer came in another press of his lips, a discreet rock of his hips. *Oh yes!* She was vaguely aware of Millie offering cake and talking about marriage, but all Aiyla wanted was right there in her arms.

"Take me someplace," she said. "Someplace *private*."

TY HELPED AIYLA onto his family's boat, kissing her as he set her on her feet. His hands moved over her hips, and he clutched her ass the way he'd craved all night.

"Down below," he said between hungry kisses as they stumbled toward the cabin.

He descended the stairs and, too anxious to wait for her, he lifted her down, claiming her mouth once again as she tore at his shirt, sending the buttons flying to the floor as they rushed into the bedroom. He closed the door behind them and crashed his mouth to hers again as they feverishly toed off their shoes and he lifted her dress over her head and tossed it away. Holy hell, she was finally naked, save for a sexy lace thong. A guttural noise climbed from his throat as he greedily drank her in and shed his remaining clothes.

She hooked her thumbs into the thin strips of lace across her hips, then stepped out of her thong and twirled it on her finger. She flung it across the room with a sultry gaze and crooked her finger, beckoning him closer. He'd never seen anything as sexy as Aiyla right that second. In one swift move she dropped to her knees, wrapped her fingers around his cock, and lowered her gloriously hot, wet mouth around his shaft, stroking slow and tight. His senses reeled as she quickened her pace and cupped his balls so exquisitely, his chin fell to his chest, and he leaned a palm on the door just to remain standing.

"Christ, baby," he panted out.

His other hand tangled in her hair. She sank lower, licking his sac and sliding her tongue along the length of his shaft. Sparks shot up his spine, and he grabbed her roughly and laid her on the bed, desire burning through him from his cock to his mouth and every fucking inch in between. He tugged her legs apart, and her wicked grin told him she was on the same page.

"Love me like there's no tomorrow," she demanded, and curled her fingers around his biceps as he slammed into her.

Fireworks exploded in his mind, and heat seared through his core. He kissed her possessively, their bodies pounding out a frantic rhythm. She moaned and rocked, meeting every thrust with one of her own and driving him out of his frigging mind. He lowered his mouth to her breast, slowing their pace so just the head of his cock moved in and out of her slick heat. He grazed his teeth over her taut nipple and she cried out, her hips bucking wildly as she came. Her sex pulsed tight, and he drove into her again, hard and deep, and sealed his mouth over her neck. Her fingernails cut into his skin. He grabbed her wrists, trapping them above her head.

"Put your legs around me, baby."

She did, and *oh fuck*, he sank even deeper into her. She was heaven on earth, and he never wanted to leave. He used one hand to hold her wrists, lowering the other beneath her, between her cheeks, to the dark place that had enraptured her before. He teased around the rim, wetting his finger with her arousal.

"Do it, Ty. Take all of me," she pleaded.

He covered her mouth with his, their tongues thrusting roughly as his finger invaded her, and her whole body clenched, taking him right up to the edge of madness. She whimpered into the kiss, and when he began withdrawing, she tore her wrist from his grip and pushed his hand back into place. Holy fucking hell, he *lost* it, slamming into her, and catapulted them both into oblivion.

Their bodies thrust and jerked with shocks long after their mutual release. Ty collapsed to the mattress and gathered her in his arms, kissing her face, shoulders, and lips, and panting out *I love you*s like a mantra. He couldn't say it enough, couldn't figure out a way to show her how immensely and completely he adored her.

"Baby?"

She gazed up with a sleepy, sated smile. "Hm?"

"Do you want to get married before your surgery? I want you to know that I'm not going anywhere and that you can always count on me. Nothing will ever change that."

"That's why I *don't* want to get married first. I trust our love, and the wedding will give me motivation to push even harder through the physical therapy."

"God, I love you, baby. I love you so much I want to give you the world."

"You do, with every touch, every kiss, every word that leaves your lips." Heat glittered in her beautiful eyes as she moved over him. Her breasts brushed against his chest, her sex slid along his shaft, and her hair fell around them like a veil as she whispered, "Now, future husband, let's set our world on fire again."

Chapter Twenty-Six

AFTER SEVERAL WEEKS of what felt like endless medical appointments, each one bringing new light to her diagnosis and upcoming surgery, recuperation, and rehabilitation, Aiyla felt as prepared as she could be. Ty had gone to every appointment with her, including the psychologist. They had also made time to help Beau with the renovations on their house. Working there had given them both something to focus on other than her life-changing surgery. But more than that, working with Ty on the renovations made the house feel like a home—*their* home. They had closed on the house yesterday, and she couldn't wait to live there. It was the evening before her surgery, and if all went well, in two weeks her wish would be granted. Ty's family was going to help him move in during her hospital stay. Aiyla had arranged for Cherise to pack up all of her belongings from her apartment in Colorado and ship them to Ty.

Tonight everyone had come together at Ty's parents' house to wish her well. Not only had Ty's entire family shown up, but Beau and all of his siblings except Zev, who was still traveling, were there, as well as Cherise and her family, Jon, and Trixie. Trixie had insisted on coming, and Aiyla was glad. She'd missed her new friend's sassiness.

Aiyla sat on a blanket near the bonfire with Shannon, Trixie, Cherise, and Tempe. Tempe was playing her guitar and gazing out at the beach, where Maisy, Ace, Jon, and Ty stood by the shore with Nash and Caleb, Cherise's husband, watching over Aiyla's nephews, Danny and David. The kids were dipping their toes in the waves with Phillip, then running in fits of giggles up the beach.

"I can see why you wanted to have the surgery here." Cherise tucked a strand of her dark hair behind her ear. "Ty's family has really rallied around you. I'm not sure how to repay them."

"Don't be silly." Shannon bumped Cherise's shoulder with her own. "You came all the way from Oregon to be with Aiyla. You of all people know that this is what families do."

"Aiyla and I have never had extended family like this." Cherise had sea-blue eyes like their mother's, which Aiyla had always envied. Her skin was pale, also like their mother's, and when she tilted her head with a thoughtful expression, it was their mother's eyes Aiyla saw gazing at Shannon. "Thank you for loving my sister as much as I do."

"We aren't crying tonight, remember?" Shannon reminded them.

A lump rose in Aiyla's throat. She and Shannon had cried enough tears since she and Steve had arrived a few days ago. They'd gotten so close, Aiyla had confided in her about worries she'd kept to herself. *What if Ty no longer finds me sexy with a stump instead of a leg?* The worry had surprised her, because she had never given her body much thought in that regard. *What if sex is different afterward?* She would no longer be able to move the way she did now, and then there would be other things to slow them down, like removing her prosthesis. Shannon had whipped out her phone and immediately Googled each of her concerns, starting with pictures of women with missing limbs in all stages of undress. They looked even more beautiful than similar pictures of women with all their limbs. Aiyla had always found beauty in the hardships of people's lives. She couldn't imagine why she hadn't realized the same would be true of herself. Shannon had moved on to articles about sexual intercourse with amputees. There was nothing Shannon wouldn't talk about, and she did it in such thoughtful, funny ways that by the time they were done Googling, they were hugging and laughing. Later that night, Aiyla had confided in Ty, and he'd surprised her by *not* reassuring her with an off-the-cuff comment, but by talking out her concerns and admitting that yes, things in all aspects of their lives would likely be different—and that he looked forward to discovering those differences together.

Aiyla looked around now. Jillian sat a few feet away chatting with Faith, Jewel, and Leesa, who was nursing her sweet baby girl. Down the beach, Beau and his very large brothers, Nick, Jax, and Graham, were playing football against Cole, Nate, Sam, and Steve. Aiyla's gaze was drawn to Ty again, standing with his parents. He glanced over and smiled.

Maisy headed her way. She knelt on the blanket beside Aiyla and put a hand on her shoulder. "How's it going, honey? Can I do anything for you?"

This is what families do. Aiyla already felt like part of theirs.

"You've done so much already, and you promised to take care of Ty while I'm in surgery. That means the world to me." She would be out cold during the surgery, but she worried about Ty. Last night they'd gone to their house and sat on the porch and then had gone down to the creek and taken pictures of their legs and feet. As he'd done in Colorado, he'd massaged her unhealthy leg and her foot, kissing every inch, and they'd both broken down in tears. How could they not mourn the loss of her leg? She was sure there would be many more tears to come, but they'd also spent the last few weeks filling up a beautiful wooden I-Really-Do-Love-You box that Nash had built for them. Aiyla had taken Ace's advice and written not one, but *several* letters reminding herself why she'd chosen amputation over limb-sparing surgery. She didn't know what the future would be like, but she knew she'd made the right decision. She didn't want to worry about lingering cancer cells, or a leg that no longer worked properly. And as Ty came to her side, carrying her nephew David on his shoulders, she knew he'd love her no matter what the future held.

Ty lifted David from his shoulders and her nephew toddled over to Cherise and curled up in her lap. "Can I borrow you for a minute, babe?"

"Borrow?" Trixie rolled her eyes. "Who are you kidding? You put a ring on that girl's finger to be sure you had her for keeps."

"I sure did, and I'd do it all over again." He took Aiyla's hand and lifted her to her feet. "Can you manage a walk?"

"Definitely." The pain in her leg was constant, but there was no way she'd give up what was probably her last walk with Ty along the beach with *both* of her natural legs.

They walked down the beach arm in arm, the din of their friends and family fading in the distance. They didn't talk, and it was nice just being together, with the sand between her toes and the ocean breeze on her face. Ty held her against his side, serenaded by the waves lapping at the shore.

"We should call it a night soon," he finally said. "We have

to be up early."

"I know. I really wanted to sleep outside since I won't be able to do that for a while, but I don't want to kick everyone out."

"Hm. I had forgotten that you wanted to sleep outside." He stopped walking and sat on the sand, bringing her down beside him. The breeze swept his hair away from his face, and he looked so handsome, he took her breath away.

"We can sleep in your room," she said. "We'll just open the windows."

With an arm around her shoulders, he pulled her closer. "That's not the same, but soon we'll have our own sleeping porch. Babe, do you want to talk about tomorrow?"

She didn't really. "Do you?"

"Are you scared?"

"Terrified," she admitted. "You?"

"I'm not afraid of the amputation or what it means. But I just spent half an hour begging Jon to let me be in the operating room with you."

"You did *not*." She laughed, but he turned a serious, sheepish look her way, and she realized he was telling her the truth. "Ty. You *know* you can't be in there."

"I thought I could pull some strings." A cocky smile lifted his lips, and just as quickly, it faded. "I should be by your side."

"You will be by my side. I'll carry you here." She patted her chest over her heart. "You're my strength. Without you, all of this would have been a hundred times harder." She moved onto his lap and rested her head on his shoulder.

"I don't want much," he said. "I just want to wrap you up in a protective shield and never let anything hurt you again."

She laughed softly. "You do that every minute of every day."

He lifted her hand to his lips and kissed it. Her ring sparkled in the moonlight, reminding her that she wasn't allowed to wear it during her surgery. The thought of taking it off was heartrending, but it would be even harder tomorrow.

"Ty, I can't wear jewelry in surgery. Will you hold my ring for me?"

He nodded, sadness rising in his eyes. "Of course."

She moved to take it off, and her fingers curled into a fist against her will. "I hate taking it off."

"I know." He embraced her and whispered, "I'll be waiting to put it back on your finger the minute you're out of surgery. It's only a symbol. It doesn't negate our love or commitment by taking it off."

"How do you always know what to say?" She drew back, but she missed him and cuddled in close again.

"Because we belong together. When the powers that be were doling out answers, I stood in the Aiyla-only line."

She held out a shaky hand, and he slipped the ring off her finger and put it on his pinky.

They sat together for a long time, and when they finally made their way back down the beach, the bonfire had been doused and the yard was pitch-dark, save for a sprinkling of moonlight.

"Where is everyone?"

Ty took her hand as they walked up the steps and into his parents' backyard. "Do you believe in fate?"

"You know I do."

He turned toward her and said, "Do you believe in me?"

"More than I believe in fate."

"Then you know I'd never forget a single word you said."

He drew her into a warm and wonderful kiss, and when

their lips parted, he took her hand and began walking toward the woods. She saw something white flapping in the breeze. As they neared, an arbor came into focus, with gauzy white sheets hanging along the frame like curtains. Aiyla could barely see through her tears as he drew back the curtains, revealing a low wooden platform with a king-size mattress and fluffy blankets and pillows. Dozens of red roses surrounded the bed.

He wrapped her in his arms and she said, "How did you arrange this without me knowing?"

"Baby, don't you know yet? For you, anything is possible."

THE NEXT MORNING moved by in a blur of anxiety. Ty and Aiyla drove to the hospital with his parents and Cherise and found their friends and family waiting there to greet them. Caleb and Nash had stayed home with the boys, but everyone else was there to give Aiyla one last round of tearful hugs and well wishes. When Ty was forced to leave her so she could go down to pre-op, he felt like he'd left his heart in that room.

The wait was painful. Time passed with everyone trying to console him. But the only thing that could make him feel any better was seeing Aiyla again and knowing she was okay. He looked around the room, taking in the worried faces of the people he loved, the hands being held, the sweet embraces, and the whispered prayers. There was so much love and support in that waiting room, and it was all for the woman he adored. He didn't know what to do with the emotions bowling him over.

He twisted Aiyla's engagement ring on his pinky, *please let her be okay* playing in his mind like a broken record. When he heard his name and saw Jon closing in on him, his heart leapt.

He pushed to his feet, hands fisted at his sides. "Is she okay?" rushed from his lungs.

"She did great," Jon assured him. "The surgery went well, and we got *all* of the cancer. Nice, wide negative margins."

Tears sprang from his eyes as he threw his arms around Jon. "Thank you. Thank you so much." Behind him collective sounds of relief and gratitude filled the room. "Can I see her?"

"Yes. She's sleeping, and she's going to be out of it for quite a while, but you can go back. But she can't have more than one person with her right now."

Ty looked at Cherise, silently offering her the chance to go in, but Cherise shook her head. He hugged her tight. "Thank you. I'll tell her you're here."

Jon put a hand on Ty's arm, guiding him away from the others and talking quietly. "Ty, it can be a shock seeing someone you love in a hospital bed, especially after major surgery."

"Thank you for the warning, but I'll be fine. I *need* to see her."

"I know, buddy. I just want you to be prepared. People react differently when seeing their loved one without a limb for the first time. Would you like me to go in with you?"

Ty swallowed hard. "No. I'm good." *Just get me in there. Please.*

A few minutes later he stepped into the recovery room, taking in the monitors, the IV running from Aiyla's arm, and the device on her finger. She looked so vulnerable in the sterile hospital bed. The pit of his stomach plummeted, while his heart filled up at finally seeing her. The conflicting emotions rivaled inside him as he moved toward the bed where she lay sleeping. His gaze drifted down her body, dozens of emotions speeding through him as he took in her thin frame tucked warmly beneath blankets, her narrow hips, and finally, the lifeless area where her leg would have been. More tears fell down his cheeks. All the weeks of worrying came rushing forward. Seeing her there, without her leg, brought it all home. Made it *real*. If it were possible to love a person more than he already loved her, then he soared past that level, because all he felt was the desire to crawl into bed with her and hold her tight.

He carefully bent to kiss her forehead and cheeks. Beneath the pungent, antiseptic hospital smell was the familiar scent of *his* sweet, strong Aiyla. His *heart*. His whole world.

"I love you, baby. I'm right here." He pressed his face into the crook of her neck, carefully holding her, and he stayed there, feeling her heart beating beneath his arm, listening to her steady breathing, until the nurse came in to check on her. He moved to a chair and covered Aiyla's hand with his.

"She's doing just fine, honey," the nurse reassured him.

Ty nodded. He was sure she was telling him the truth, but he'd feel better when Aiyla woke up.

After the nurse left, he put his forehead on Aiyla's hand, softly telling her how much he adored her and how everyone was in the waiting room and that they'd been there the whole time. Her fingers twitched against his palm, and he lifted his head.

Aiyla's eyes fluttered open, and he rose so she could see him. Her gaze drifted sleepily up his chest, and then her beautiful hazel eyes focused on his face.

He caressed her cheek. "Hi, baby cakes."

She smiled, and it drew more tears. He wiped them away, not wanting to upset her, but he was so damn happy it was hard to keep them at bay.

"Did they get it all?" she asked groggily.

"Yes, baby. They got all of it. The surgery went well. You're going to be fine."

Tears slipped from the corners of her eyes, and he kissed them away. He leaned in and hugged her. "Oh, my brave girl. I love you so much."

"Can we plan our wedding now?" she asked sleepily.

A half laugh, half cry fell from his lips. "Yes, we'll plan our wedding."

She lifted her left hand, and he slid her ring onto her finger.

"Sleep, baby. Get some rest," he said, and kissed her softly.

"I can't sleep without you."

He wasn't sure he should, but he went around the bed to her other side so he wouldn't accidentally bump her stitches and carefully climbed onto the bed, lying sideways next to her. She rested her head against his chest and whispered, "Don't leave me."

"I never will. Close your eyes, baby. I've got you. I'll *always* have you." He ran his fingers through her hair, and a while later, when the nurse came in to check on Aiyla again, he said, "Please don't ask me to move, or we're going to have trouble."

The kind nurse smiled and said, "Honey, you are right where you're supposed to be."

Epilogue

FALL AND WINTER were difficult for Aiyla and Ty as they bullied their way through Aiyla's rehabilitation, physical therapy, and learning to live with a prosthetic limb. Between the pain and adjusting to needing help every single day, mood swings came too frequently—for both of them. Tears of frustration and tears of sadness were mixed with reprieves of laughter and closeness. It was not an easy road. Aiyla mourned the loss of her leg more than she'd anticipated, but Ty was always there for her, and Ace was a godsend for both of them. They'd made it through the worst of it together, with the endless support of family and friends and constant reminders from their I-Really-Do-Love-You box. Spring arrived with beautiful bluebells and wildflowers, restoring beauty to their land, and by late spring, with the worst behind them, their emotions settled and their love was stronger than ever.

Aiyla stood before the mirror in their bedroom admiring her wedding gown. Jillian and Jax had created the perfect dress, with soft macramé detail around the neckline, leaving her shoulders bare. The gauzy silk bodice had a sheer crocheted lace waist and fell to a maxi skirt with two high side slits, stopping a few inches from the ground, allowing for easy movement. It was elegant and simple, and perfect for her and Ty's wedding day. She opened the doors to their sleeping porch and walked into what she and Ty thought of as the most peaceful room in their house. She needn't have worried about feeling sexy, or about how their lovemaking would change. Ty was just as loving and as sensual as ever. He never hesitated to kiss her stump, or touch her like he used to, and because of that, those worries had disappeared.

The air was crisp and fresh, and voices floated up from the creek where Ty and their family and friends waited for the ceremony to begin. She couldn't believe their wedding day was finally there. She'd dreamed of the day their lives would no longer revolve around her recuperation and her leg. Things had normalized so much lately, and her leg had become as much a part of her daily routine as brushing her teeth. Sometimes she worried about getting a sore spot and not being able to wear her prosthesis, and before they went out, she always did a mental accessibility check, but those things were part of their lives now—as would be quarterly CT scans for the next twelve months.

"Is Auntie Aiyla wearing her *show* leg today?" Danny's voice drifted into the bedroom.

My *show* leg. They'd begun calling it that for her nephews and Phillip's sake, and the name had stuck. She had several prostheses, and yes, today she was wearing her *show* leg, which was the one that looked most like a natural leg. Most of the time she didn't bother with her show leg, but wore the one that showed the hardware because it felt less cumbersome. The boys called that one her *bionic* leg. Ty had found a goat-inspired prosthesis for mountain climbing, and they were hoping to be able to try that out sometime in the next year. She also had a prosthetic called a Cheetah, made just for running. She hadn't tried that one out yet, but one day…

"Yes, my little man," she said to Danny as she came into the room. Danny, David, and Phillip wore khaki shorts and button-down shirts. They looked adorable. "Today I'm wearing my show leg."

He peeked between the slits in her dress and touched it. She was used to that. Children *were* curious. They stared and asked questions, and sometimes strangers—adults and children—shied away from her. But in those times, she reminded herself of how other people were scared of what they didn't understand and how lucky she was to be cancer free. How lucky she was to have caught her cancer early, and to be alive.

Danny wrapped his arms around her legs and smiled up at her with the same big baby blues as his mama. "I love you, Auntie. Happy wedding day!"

She bent down and kissed his mop of dark hair. "I love you, too, honey. Thank you."

"It's time," Shannon said as she came into the bedroom carrying Aiyla's headpiece in one hand and Charlotte Sterling's latest erotic romance in the other. "By the way, this book? There are no words for how awesome it is. I might need to borrow it for some…*research.*"

Aiyla laughed. She'd been shocked when Charlotte had called Ty and asked for her address. When she'd received an autographed copy of the book, she and Ty had scoured it for the office scene. Sure enough, the whole thing was on the page, including the mad make-out session they'd carried on while they'd thought she was typing.

Danny darted out the door and Cherise called after him, "Slow down!" Her sister was stunning in her royal-blue above-the-knee dress.

Shannon put a hand on her hip and whistled. "Damn, girls, you two are *gorgeous*." She set the headpiece, a wreath of pretty flowers and greenery, on Aiyla's hair and said, "My brother is one lucky man."

Aiyla teared up, as she'd been doing all day. "I'm the lucky one. I not only have an amazing sister and the most incredible, loving, sexy, soon-to-be husband, but I have his—your—wonderful family, too."

The three of them hugged, sniffing back tears. Cherise broke away, glassy eyed and fanning her face. "Stop. No tears! We've cried enough these last few months for a lifetime." Cherise had come to stay with them for a week one month after Aiyla had left the hospital, and she'd come out again over New Year's and a few weeks later to see Aiyla try on her wedding dress for the first time. Their visits had been wonderful, even if tearful.

They all fanned their faces, breathing deeply.

"Everyone is ready," Shannon said excitedly. Her peach dress gave her a vibrant appearance. "You should see our men. They *all* look nervous, and Nate has Skype all set up so Ms. F can watch the whole ceremony."

She'd finally told Aiyla why Steve called her *butterfly*. *Because he said I flit about from one happy thought to the next.* It was the perfect endearment for her.

"Okay, time for the rundown," Cherise said. "Something borrowed?"

"Check." Shannon pointed to Aiyla's bracelet. "The bracelet my dad gave my mom on their wedding day."

Aiyla's heart fluttered wildly, remembering when Maisy had offered it to her. *May you and Ty have a marriage as long and happy as we've had. We love you, honey.*

"Something blue?" Cherise waggled her brows.

Aiyla lifted her dress, revealing a pair of sky-blue lace panties.

"So hot," Shannon said. "Something old?"

Cherise and Aiyla exchanged a thoughtful glance. Aiyla touched her necklace. It was a locket her mother had given Cherise when her sister was a little girl. Inside was a picture of the two of them with their mother.

"And something new," Aiyla said, and lifted her dress, revealing her prosthesis. "I think I'm ready!"

They all squealed, and after another group hug, Aiyla closed her eyes, sending a silent message of love up to her mother. She'd felt her mother's spirit around them since the moment she'd gone in for her surgery. She didn't feel her presence as strongly these days, but she sensed that was because her mother knew she was going to be okay. Aiyla knew she was going to be okay, too. The amputation had taken her leg, but it had also given her a sense of invincibility. Was there anything she and Ty couldn't get through? Was there anything she couldn't handle?

As she headed outside and stood at the top of the walkway Beau and Ty had built for their nightly walks down to the water, she knew *they* were going to be okay, too. *Better* than okay. Ty was right. She was fierce in her own right, but together they were unstoppable.

TY HAD CLIMBED the highest mountains, he'd traveled all over the world, and he'd never been happier, felt more complete, or more in love than he did as he watched his beautiful bride walk down the aisle on her sister's arm. She was beyond stunning in her bridal gown, but she could have worn rags and she'd still outshine every other woman on earth. She was walking slowly and steadily, *stable*, and pride showed through her glassy eyes. She had done just what she'd said she would and had used their wedding as motivation to push through her healing process. She was confident, funny, sexy as sin, and even after all they'd gone through, she was still as adventurous as ever—and looking at him like she wanted to run into his arms—the way he wanted to run into hers.

She hugged Cherise and they both wiped their teary eyes, and then she turned toward Ty, and his insides turned to mush. He was sure everyone could tell, as tears rose in his eyes for all they'd gone through and all they had to look forward to.

As they said their vows, his hands itched to hold her, and his lips burned to touch hers. When they were *finally* pronounced husband and wife, he captured her luscious mouth in a soul-reaching kiss as everyone cheered and clapped. He pushed his hands into her hair, taking the kiss deeper and loving her until the claps quieted, and then he kissed her longer—until Sam put a hand on his shoulder and tore them apart.

"Dude, you've got little eyes on you." Sam motioned toward the three boys, who were scrunching their adorable faces.

Ty's gaze swept over their friends and family, and up to the house, where the walls were filled with photographs from Saint-Luc, Colorado, and their journey from the race to becoming Mr. and Mrs. Ty Braden. He gazed deeply into the eyes of his beautiful, loving, strong *wife*, and said, "The kids better get used to it, because I plan on kissing you a lot. Here's to the rest of our lives, baby cakes."

He lowered his lips to hers, not caring how many eyes were on them and knowing nothing could ever tear them apart.

Ready for more Bradens?

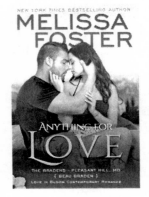

Fall in love with Beau Braden and Charlotte Sterling in ANYTHING FOR LOVE, the first book in the Bradens at Pleasant Hill.

Have you read STORY OF LOVE?

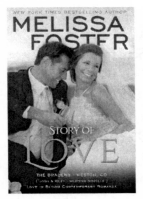

If you haven't read the Braden novella, STORY OF LOVE, now is the perfect time! Readers were first introduced to Charlotte Sterling in this hilarious and sexy wedding novella. It's also a great introduction to The Bradens at Weston!

New to the Love in Bloom series and the Bradens?

I hope you have enjoyed getting to know the Bradens at Peaceful Harbor as much as I've loved writing about them. If this is your first Braden book, you have many more love stories featuring loyal, sassy, and sexy heroes and heroines waiting for you. Each of Ty's siblings has their own book. Search for The Bradens at Peaceful Harbor on your favorite retailer and start with **HEALED BY LOVE**, Nate and Jewel's love story.

The Bradens are just one of the series in the Love in Bloom big-family romance collection. Each Love in Bloom book is written to be enjoyed as a stand-alone novel or as part of the larger series. There are no cliffhangers and no unresolved issues. Characters from each series make appearances in future books, so you never miss an engagement, wedding, or birth. You might enjoy my other series within the Love in Bloom big-family romance collection. You can start at the very beginning of the Love in Bloom series absolutely FREE with **SISTERS IN LOVE** or begin with another fun and deeply emotions series like the Remingtons, which begins with GAME OF LOVE, also free.

Below is a link where you can download FIVE first-in-series novels absolutely FREE.

www.MelissaFoster.com/LIBFree

More Books By Melissa

LOVE IN BLOOM SERIES

SNOW SISTERS
Sisters in Love
Sisters in Bloom
Sisters in White

THE BRADENS at Weston
Lovers at Heart
Destined for Love
Friendship on Fire
Sea of Love
Bursting with Love
Hearts at Play

THE BRADENS at Trusty
Taken by Love
Fated for Love
Romancing My Love
Flirting with Love
Dreaming of Love
Crashing into Love

THE BRADENS at Peaceful Harbor
Healed by Love
Surrender My Love
River of Love
Crushing on Love
Whisper of Love
Thrill of Love

THE BRADENS at Pleasant Hill
Anything For Love

THE BRADEN NOVELLAS

Promise My Love
Our New Love
Daring Her Love
Story of Love

THE REMINGTONS

Game of Love
Stroke of Love
Flames of Love
Slope of Love
Read, Write, Love
Touched by Love

SEASIDE SUMMERS

Seaside Dreams
Seaside Hearts
Seaside Sunsets
Seaside Secrets
Seaside Nights
Seaside Embrace
Seaside Lovers
Seaside Whispers

BAYSIDE SUMMERS

Bayside Desires
Bayside Passions

THE RYDERS

Seized by Love
Claimed by Love
Chased by Love
Rescued by Love

SEXY STANDALONE ROMANCE

Tru Blue
Truly, Madly, Whiskey

THE MONTGOMERYS
Embracing Her Heart
Our Wicked Hearts
Wild, Crazy, Heart
Sweet, Sexy, Heart

BILLIONAIRES AFTER DARK SERIES

WILD BOYS AFTER DARK
Logan
Heath
Jackson
Cooper

BAD BOYS AFTER DARK
Mick
Dylan
Carson
Brett

HARBORSIDE NIGHTS SERIES
Includes characters from the Love in Bloom series
Catching Cassidy
Discovering Delilah
Tempting Tristan

More Books by Melissa
Chasing Amanda (mystery/suspense)
Come Back to Me (mystery/suspense)
Have No Shame (historical fiction/romance)
Love, Lies & Mystery (3-book bundle)
Megan's Way (literary fiction)
Traces of Kara (psychological thriller)
Where Petals Fall (suspense)

Acknowledgments

I know Aiyla's story is not a typical one for the romance genre, and despite many people trying to talk me out of writing her amputation into the book, I felt her story needed to be told in the way it had come to me. I hope you have enjoyed reading about the strength of Ty and Aiyla's love, the commitment of family, and the determination of one woman to make the right choice for herself and for her relationship. In researching Aiyla's story, I learned a great deal about cancer, treatment options, and the strength it takes for those who are faced with the disease—from the moment they are diagnosed, and ever after. I chose not to show Aiyla's months of healing because this is not a women's fiction novel, and Aiyla's story was about more than the healing process. It was about love and romance and making it to her happily ever after. Here's a secret fun fact about Aiyla and Cherise—part of the reason I chose their names was for the meanings:

Aiyla: (EYE-LUH) (www.babynamewizard.com)
A beautiful girl who is strong, a fighter, and is so easy to fall in love with. Her smile will light up the world and her eyes looking into yours is like heaven. She can be stubborn at times but very sweet and huggable. She loves kisses and will do anything for her friends and family. She sticks up for what she believes and won't ever back down. She is the most lovable girl and she will change the world. "Aiyla"— Like a soft tiger.

Cherise: (www.sheknows.com)

People with this name tend to be orderly and dedicated to building their lives on a solid foundation of order and service. They value truth, justice, and discipline, and may be quick-tempered with those who do not. Their practical nature makes them good at managing and saving money, and at building things in the material world. Because of their focus on order and practicality, they may seem overly cautious and conservative at times.

I'd like to thank Susan Stottlemyer, RN, BSN, OCN, from the John R. Marsh Cancer Center in Hagerstown, Maryland, for her patience and willingness to answer my endless questions. Any and all errors are my own and are not a reflection of Susan's input. I'd also like to thank the many other medical professionals who took the time to speak with me but chose not to be mentioned. And heaps of gratitude go to Kristen Weber and Lisa Bardonski for standing by me while I wrote this story in the face of many suggesting that I save Aiyla's leg "because it's a romance." Having written more than sixty books, I enjoyed pushing the limits of the typical genre-appropriate stories and taking my readers on a more intense and emotional journey.

Cancer is never to be taken lightly, and I hope I did Aiyla's story justice. There are many wonderful cancer resources available, and a good starting place for those who want to read about chondrosarcoma is www.cancer.org.

I hope you enjoyed Ty and Aiyla's story and are looking forward to reading about Beau Braden and Charlotte Sterling in *Anything for Love*, the next Braden novel and the first of the Bradens at Pleasant Hill. I can't wait to bring them to you!

If you haven't yet joined my fan club on Facebook, please do. We have a great time chatting about our hunky heroes and sassy heroines. You never know when you'll inspire a story or character and end up in one of my books, as several fan club members have already discovered.
facebook.com/groups/MelissaFosterFans

Remember to like and follow my Facebook fan page to stay abreast of what's going on in our fictional boyfriends' worlds.
facebook.com/MelissaFosterAuthor

Sign up for my newsletter to keep up to date with new releases and special promotions and events and to receive an exclusive short story featuring Jack Remington and Savannah Braden.
www.MelissaFoster.com/Newsletter

And don't forget your free reader goodies! For free family trees, publication schedules, series checklists, and more, please visit the special Reader Goodies page that I've set up for you!
www.MelissaFoster.com/Reader-Goodies

As always, loads of gratitude to my amazing team of editors and proofreaders: Kristen Weber, Penina Lopez, Elaini Caruso, Juliette Hill, Marlene Engel, Lynn Mullan, and Justinn Harrison. And, of course, I am forever grateful to my husband, Les, who not only supported my desire to get this story right with research and endless hours of medical explanations put in layman's terms so I could understand every detail, but also encouraged me to be brave enough to tell this difficult and important story.

~Meet Melissa~

www.MelissaFoster.com

Melissa Foster is a *New York Times* and *USA Today* bestselling and award-winning author. Her books have been recommended by *USA Today's* book blog, *Hagerstown* magazine, *The Patriot*, and several other print venues. Melissa has painted and donated several murals to the Hospital for Sick Children in Washington, DC.

Visit Melissa on her website or chat with her on social media. Melissa enjoys discussing her books with book clubs and reader groups and welcomes an invitation to your event. Melissa's books are available through most online retailers in paperback, digital, and audio formats.

CPSIA information can be obtained
at www.ICGtesting.com
Printed in the USA
LVOW11s0731121017
552045LV00001B/87/P